I0763548

*A new Path must be forged in the blood of heroes*

TAYLOR CROOK &
RYAN KIRK

# A PATH REFORGED

THE SENTINELS SAGA
BOOK III

Cover designed by MiblArt

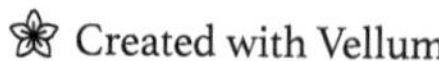

*For Cole.*

*Sorry we couldn't finish it quicker. I think you would have loved it.*

# PROLOGUE

*We're home.*

Emperor Kordano frowned as Samas came into view. He'd seen it in plenty of visions and through the eyes of his summoners, but this was the first time he'd seen it in person. Somehow, it didn't seem the same.

In his visions, the island nation had been a vibrant place, full of both power and possibility. Even in the sight granted to him through his summoners, he'd seen little but the strength of their enemies.

But in person, it looked like no more than another rock. A place to conquer like so many others that had already fallen to his sword and his will.

He'd expected more.

"General Kordak, ready my warship. I want my feet on Iru as soon as possible," Kordano commanded.

"Right away, Emperor." Kordak turned to one of his subordinates, barking out a long stream of specific orders. The officer nodded, then scurried off to complete his tasks. Kordano thought he looked eager to be as far away from the emperor as possible. Kordak cleared his throat. "What about the reports from our summoners, about the northern island being completely overrun with ferals? They claim the rift has been wide open for months. Even for you, it may be too much."

*Kill the fool.*

Kordano ignored the voice and stepped toward Kordak, forcing his general to look up. Even among the Maramans, Kordano stood a head taller than average. Competent as his general was, he'd started to ask too many questions on this journey. "I can handle the ferals. Do you doubt me?"

Kordak wilted under Kordano's attention. "No, sir."

"My Unnamed will be with me. They'll provide enough protection to ease your concerns." He gestured to his personal guard standing close by. Kordak flinched.

Every Maraman was trained to fight from a young age, and generations of breeding for size and strength made the Maramans taller and stronger than any other nation of people. They were warriors unlike any the world had ever seen. And even they cowered before Kordano's personally selected guard.

The Unnamed were something else entirely.

Their creation began before birth. Only the strongest, largest, and most skilled of warriors were invited to couple on behalf of the empire. The children created from those unions were taken at birth. From then on, their lives were dedicated to one purpose, dying for the emperor.

While other Maramans received tattoos based on the weapons they were most skilled with, the Unnamed's skin remained untouched until the day their training ended. Their final test was to endure the pitch black, full body tattooing without so much as flinching.

Most who survived the training did fine until it came time to dye their eyes.

Kordano observed the Unnamed flanking him and felt a surge of pride as he looked into those pitch-black eyes. He wondered how many warriors across the world had suffered that gaze as the last thing they'd ever seen?

Kordak looked as though someone had made him swallow a bitter brew, but he held his tongue.

"Out with it, Kordak."

"I'd feel better if I sent at least a few summoners with you."

*Kill him.*

This time, Kordano was tempted. He'd already told Kordak his desire. Though Kordak's objection no doubt came from his sense of loyalty, it reflected poorly on his obedience. Innocent this may be, but a single crack in a man's obedience could cause trouble later.

Still, Kordak was crucial to the invasion's success. "I've made my wishes clear."

His general swallowed hard and bowed. "Of course."

Before long, Kordano's personal warship was ready, and he prepared to leave. The skilled juggernaut captains had slowly brought their vessels to a stop. He looked back at the two juggernauts flanking his own, and cautioned himself not to feel too confident. The Samasians had twice thwarted plans that had brought other nations, nations of far greater size, under the yoke of the Maramans. There was a strength here.

A strength that he intended to break personally.

Kordano reached the deck of his ship and supervised the preparations. The captain was one of his most trusted, and there was little for Kordano to do. He watched his warriors move about with an easy efficiency. No one came too close to him or his Unnamed, but the sailors on this warship were used to working around the disruption.

The warship was winched down to the ocean below, pushed off from the juggernaut and put under sail. Favorable winds made the last leg of the trip to Samas pass quickly. He stood near the bow, watching the island grow. The captain steered them toward the port of Bulas. His generals hadn't understood why he insisted on attacking Iru first, instead of Versun, where the resistance gathered.

Part of it was simple logistics. The juggernauts were marvels of engineering, but they still weren't suitable as bases to launch this invasion. They needed food, and they needed space. Iru had plenty, and the Samasians had been so kind in abandoning it for him.

But the other part was symbolic. It was a desire he'd felt deep in his heart for years now. Bulas was the heart of Samas, and he would rule from there, no matter the obstacles in his way.

Besides, his generals still overestimated the threat from the feral demons. There was the knowing of the mind and the knowing of the heart, and their hearts had forgotten his power. Seizing Iru alone served one more purpose. It would remind his people that they fought for a power this world had never seen.

Before long, the warship came to a stop in the harbor, and the emperor and his Unnamed boarded a long ship speeding to the shallows.

The demons waited for them, the piers of the harbor packed tightly with the creatures. It was probably the closest humans had come to the island in months. He commanded the longship to alter course, heading instead for an open beachhead. The piers would be too difficult a landing, even for the Unnamed. As soon as the demons realized they weren't going to land at the piers, they started streaming out through the ruins of the city, no doubt hoping to meet their prey on the beach.

It wouldn't matter.

The Unnamed hopped out of the boat before they hit the beach, striding through the water toward the first of the demons that waited for them. They fanned out in front of Kordano and drew their two-handed great swords. They moved up the beach and within moments, the first demons met bared steel. Others might fear the Unnamed, but as they strode fearlessly into the demons, Kordano believed they were beautiful.

The Unnamed sliced off demon heads with every cut, and the emperor sent the demons back to their rift with a casual flick of his wrist. It was as easy as taking a deep breath.

He had made his sacrifice long ago.

Soon, the beach was filled with demons charging and breaking against the wall of Unnamed that protected him. The emperor gathered his will, preparing a feat humanity had never even attempted.

A demon that had taken on the form of one of the sin, or maybe it was a sentinel, leaped over his Unnamed and charged Kordano with its sword arm raised. Kordano waited until the creature was about to land the blow and reached out, placing a finger on its forehead. He focused his terrible will.

"Stop." The word was barely above a whisper. He pushed out his will, working in concert with the demon that gave him such strength.

The entire hoard of feral demons, as one, froze in place.

"Kneel."

As one, the hoard of demons kneeled, or sat depending on the creature it had inhabited, and waited. With a thought, the emperor sealed the rift. There were tantalizing possibilities to leaving it open, but if he did, he would spend his entire life turning the ferals into loyal subjects. Besides, he had more than enough here to conquer the rest of Samas.

Soon, Samas would be his.

*Soon Samas will be ours.*

He gritted his teeth, remembering the one sacrifice he'd made.

# 1

Shin took another sip of her mead and closed her eyes, enjoying the drink on her tongue. The din of the tavern soothed away the worries of the day. Rowdy laughter reminded her that at the end of the day, happiness wasn't too hard to find. All one needed was a mug of ale and a friend across the table. Lacking a friend, an even taller mug would do just fine.

Fortunately for her, she had her best friend sitting beside her at the bar.

"I'm telling you, a second weapon is far more effective than the extra reach you get with Harmony," Corin said, his speech only slightly slurred.

"If that's true, then why do I beat your ass every time we spar?" Shin asked.

"Because your weapon is fucking magic!" Corin shouted in mock outrage.

"I almost never use Harmony's abilities when we spar."

"That's not how I remember it."

"Seems like you're remembering wrong."

Corin tried to fix her with a stern glare, but they both broke out laughing.

The Corin who sat beside her now was a completely different man from the boy she had once known. A solid year of training had turned him from skinny to lean and muscular. That same training, combined with a late growth spurt, had broadened his shoulders. He'd even sprouted a passable beard in the last two months.

"Petra!" Corin called out to the bartender. "Another round."

"Captain?" Shin heard the voice behind her, but it took her alcohol-infused thoughts a few seconds to realize the young woman was addressing her.

She turned around, recognizing the young sentinel as a new transfer to her unit. "Yes, Nina?" New or not, she knew every name and every story in her unit.

The sentinel damn near blushed at being recognized by her commander. The reaction caused Shin's stomach to twist. She and Yuki had jointly agreed to keep the truth of Shin's actions on Iru quiet. A few people knew, but not many. All most people in Versun knew was that she was one of the sin's strongest and most capable adepts.

Thus, behavior like this.

Nina bowed. "I just wanted to say how excited I am to be serving under you. It's a great honor, ma'am." Nina's cheeks turned redder than Corin's after his third drink.

Shin's sense of duty overcame her inebriation. "I appreciate that. It's good to know my new sentinels are just as dedicated as the ones I've had from the beginning. I watched you in training today, and I've been impressed by how well you've fit into the new tactics of our unit. Keep it up and you'll have a command of your own one day."

Nina mumbled something that sounded like a thanks before bowing even deeper, turning on her heel, and fleeing back into the crowd.

"Can't help but notice you didn't bother giving your second in command any credit," Corin said. "He's the one who spends most of his time teaching the sentinels how to adapt to the demons."

"Well, you let me know when he does something above and beyond the very task I ordered him to complete, and I'll shout it from the rooftops."

Corin answered by throwing a nut at Shin's forehead.

"Very mature," Shin said. Then she realized Corin might be masking a legitimate complaint with his sarcastic humor. She found it annoying that he wasn't strong enough to simply speak what he felt, but she knew better than to act on that impulse. Instead, she said, "You know I couldn't do any of this without you, though, right?"

Corin smiled. "I know, Shin. We're in this together."

"Damn straight."

Corin could have had command of his own unit long ago, but he didn't want to leave Shin's side. In his mind, not only was he her second in command, but he was also the one who was responsible for helping her uncover her old self. It was because of him she led her unit as well as she did.

He had told her stories of Mateo so many times that the memories started to feel like her own. At first, listening to the stories had been hard. Though Corin didn't mean it as such, it felt like he was guilting her every time he spoke of their time together. Mateo had only been in her life for a short time, but he'd done more in those months to shape her into who she was today than even the years of sin training had accomplished. How could she have forgotten him so casually?

But when she felt Harmony, thrumming in her hand, she knew. That was the whole point of sacrifice: to give up what mattered most to change the world in ways that mattered.

Now, she only occasionally felt guilty when Corin spoke of their friend. More often, she was grateful that Corin worked so hard to bring Mateo's memory back to life.

The memories of her father were another story. Corin did his best to tell Shin all the things that she had told him, but there just wasn't all that much to share. She knew, from what Corin said, that he had been a wonderful man, but aside from that, there wasn't much to learn. She did her best to extrapolate what she could from the memories she had of her mother, but the blank spaces in her mind were often jarring. From what she could tell, they had been happy.

She told herself knowing that was enough. Maybe if she repeated it enough times, she'd even start to believe it.

Corin had suggested they return to Dahl and speak to some of the neighboring farmers about him, but Shin wasn't sure she was ready for that. Besides, Ilos was no longer the island she grew up on. After the fall of Iru, the refugees in Versun and Dahl had almost overwhelmed the cities.

Sato, with his brutal efficiency, had insisted they build farm communities on Ilos. Now, instead of peasant families living on small plots of land and sending what they farmed to the sentinels for distribution, large communities had been built in the center of large tracts of farmland. People lived together and worked together to produce more than the small families ever could have.

The communities were also easier to protect than the scattered farmsteads. Most had at least a few sentinels stationed there permanently. For protection, of course, and to make sure all of Samas was pulled, kicking and screaming, onto the Path. Sato had a remarkable ability to give one order that met several of his goals at once. It was hard to fall off the Path when a zealous sentinel stood behind you, watching your every step.

Despite that, Shin had to admit Sato's system worked far better than the old system ever had. There'd been rumors he was to be the next Firstborn for many years, long before the demons and the Maramans had upended life for everyone. Now it was practically a certainty. Shin feared what that day would bring. As it was, the Firstborn, Yuki, and Sato formed a small council that checked the worst impulses of the zealots. And, to Sato's credit, he'd changed, too.

But people didn't change that easily.

"I think we've almost got the wall defense drills down. A few more weeks and we'll be better than any other unit," Corin said, dragging her from her reverie.

"Please, Corin. I don't want to talk about drills. We've got a leave day tomorrow and I intend to do nothing but lie in the sun."

"And nurse your hangover?"

"Only if you stop talking and let me drink!"

Corin was right about their progress, though. Their unit was far better suited to combat on the ground, but Shin believed that to be true of everyone. The tactics used to defend the walls, mostly involving long polearms that could remove demon heads from a greater distance, were an adjustment for everyone.

One adjustment among many. A whole year of adjustments.

In those early days, since they were among the few with

experience in a blended unit of sin and sentinels, they'd been a key part of training the new forces. But now the entire military of Samas was blended. Sentinels worked side by side with sin adepts, and the sin learned the advantages of the disciplined formations that the sentinels had drilled in for generations.

Shin still smiled at the memory of Sato's face when the Firstborn had told him of the plans. Shin wasn't terribly familiar with the Path, but she doubted it included anything about working with the sun-cursed sin. It still drove Sato mad, especially when the first sin adept joined the Sun Stalkers. Shin laughed as she remembered the loud curses that Sato had shouted all the way down the hall when he'd learned.

"Hey!" a voice cried out over the crowd. "Hanz is taking bets again."

The crowded tavern rushed to settle tabs and head for the door. Shin looked at Corin and shook her head. She hadn't known the twins all that well, not like Beast had, but a light had gone out in the giant's eyes since his brother had died. "I wish they wouldn't encourage him."

"I know, but he's a legend. Beating him in a duel could make someone's career. Also, it doesn't hurt that he pays out ten to one," Corin said.

Shin sighed and slid some coin across the bar. She knew it was destructive, but maybe getting drunk and taking on all comers was what Hanz needed? All she knew was that the man put on quite a show.

"I wonder if he'll let people team up tonight. Those are the best to watch," Corin said before ducking out the door.

Shin nodded and drank the rest of her ale in a few smooth gulps. Then she chased Corin out into the night.

Life in Versun wasn't anything like she'd imagined her future to be, but as she looked around at the emptying tavern, at her friends and fellow warriors excited by an evening of entertainment, she grinned. This was enough for her, and it was good.

# 2

Beast wiped tears of laughter from his eyes before quaffing what was left of his ale. “Then he smirked at me because he knew what I had to say. He knew it!”

Colas got her own laughter under control and looked at him expectantly. “So?”

“So, I said it! ‘At breakneck speeds.’ I think Raya thought we’d both taken too many blows to the head.”

Gorou shook his head and smiled, which was about as demonstrative as the man got, but Vala was wiping tears from her eyes. Beast had initially been reticent to have a sin adept join them when they defected from Yuki, but Gorou had vouched for her. Evidently, the young woman had never been too keen on sacrificing life and limb for the sin cause. When Beast had thrown the sentinels off his juggernaut and set sail, she’d been happy to stay.

And she laughed at his jokes, which was more than he could say for any other sin. He was glad to have her along.

“Raya must have thought you a bumbling fool,” Vala said when she regained her composure, “How long did it take before she realized even that was being generous?”

Beast roared his approval. The girl probably weighed less than his right arm, but she didn't back down. He like that about her.

After the laughter died out, Colas stepped in, and her tone was far too serious. "I called this meeting for a reason, Beast, and it wasn't to watch you drink and remind us of how stupid you can be."

"I recognize that tone," Beast groaned.

"You should. It's the tone I use whenever I want to explain to you the problems with this so-called island paradise you love so much."

"We all love it! It's the freedom we always wanted! No sentinels, no sin—"

"Hey!" Vala said, with mock indignation.

"—and nothing but miles of open space. What's not to love?"

"For the record, I wanted the freedom of open waters," Colas said.

"And I go where she goes," Vala said, resting her hand on the pirate captain's arm.

"Exactly. We all got what we wanted. Speaking of which, I'd like some more ale!"

"Afraid you're out," Gorou said.

"Beast, listen. We've got some problems that need to be addressed soon," Colas insisted.

"Fine, walk with me while you bore me. We'll get some ale at the fire. I hope they roast a pig tonight. Seems like it's been fish every day this week."

"That's because there aren't any pigs left on the island," Colas said.

"That can't be true," Beast replied.

"If they're here we can't find them," Colas said, following Beast out the door of his tiny, leaning shanty.

"Our attempts at farming haven't yielded anything but tiny onions, either."

"Onions are good."

"When I say yielded, I mean we have five."

"Five bushels?"

"Five onions, Beast, because none of us are farmers. When we went to harvest, we didn't know what was a weed and what was food. So we pulled it all, and most of it was weeds."

Beast chuckled as he walked out into the small village that his crew had made into a home. Despite the fact that the buildings leaned at odd angles, Beast was proud of the work they'd done. "I don't like vegetables, anyway."

"That's fine, but our crew is getting sick. We need a greater variety of food, and soon. We'll have teeth falling out before long."

"Nothing wrong with a few missing teeth," Beast said and grinned to show off some of the holes in his smile.

"To be fair, not everyone considers losing a few teeth to be an enjoyable way to pass an evening," Gorou said quietly, "and I think Colas is referring to the crew losing teeth without them getting knocked out."

Beast stopped walking and looked at his three captains. "What does that have to do with vegetables?"

"Fruits and vegetables keep you healthy, Beast. That's why when we head out to sea, we stock up. Fish are easy enough to catch, but if that's all we eat, then we get sick. Same is true here," Colas said. "I'm realizing that a small island has all the same problems as a ship, you just can't turn it around."

Beast could tell she was losing her patience but struggled to understand her concerns. This was one of the first islands they'd landed on after they'd left Samas, and

Beast had fallen in love immediately. He also realized that as big as the juggernaut was, he really wasn't built for the constraints of a ship. They'd had a meeting, and all agreed to create a settlement here from which they could sail out on expeditions. Since then, it had been nothing but building a village and celebrating in the evenings with food, ale, and, if Beast was lucky, a good fistfight.

"It's fine, Colas. Our next attempt at farming will go better."

"No, it won't. We don't have any seeds left to plant. We also aren't getting any better at building homes, Beast. Do you know why? Because we're pirates, not carpenters. All the roofs leak, and that's on the houses that remain standing!"

Beast considered his captain for a moment. "Tell you what, we'll go down to the fire, drink some ale, and I'll think it over. We can talk about it tomorrow."

"Beast—" Colas began, but Gorou cut her off with a raised hand.

"I think Beast is correct. We've done a lot of work on our little settlement. We would be rash to desert it so quickly."

Colas looked like she was about to spit fire, but kept her mouth shut and nodded.

"Good!" Beast said, "I'm thirsty." He turned on his heel and led them toward the fire. Everything would make more sense once he had a few more drinks in him.

"Beast! Care to spar tonight?" asked Edgar, one of the Colas's original crew and largest man on the island next to Beast.

"Thought you'd never ask!" Beast shouted back to the man as he passed by.

It wouldn't be much of a fight, though. Back when they'd landed, Edgar had been a challenge. He wasn't usually strong enough to fight Beast off, but the duels had been worthy of some songs, at least. Edgar was still willing, but he didn't have the strength he'd once had. The giant needed some more meat. Maybe tomorrow Beast would organize a bit of an expedition to hunt down some game.

Fish was fine, but real muscle required something bigger. Like a cow.

Unfortunately, there were no cows on the island. There were some wild pigs, though. Beast would have to hunt some of those down. It would be good to get out and stretch his legs, anyhow.

Beast sat down at the fire and before long a flagon of ale was in his hand. He sat back and enjoyed the revelry of his crew.

"Gorou, fetch us another, would you?"

"I'm afraid I can't."

"Too good to serve me, are you? Well, no matter, I'll get it myself."

"No, what I mean is that the ale is gone," Gorou said, and Beast thought he saw him flick a quick glance at Colas.

"Gone?"

"Well, yes, we don't know how to make more and there was only so much on the ship."

"But I had the stores of the juggernaut filled! I think I put three taverns out of business when we left!"

"You did, but ale is a finite thing, Beast. Unless we learn to make some, there's none left."

"None?"

"Not a drop."

Beast stared into his flagon, wishing for it to produce some more ale for him, but it remained stubbornly dry. He turned his stare to Gorou. "We can't live on an island without ale."

Gorou shrugged. "We tried making our own, but the batches went bad. We're bandits. We steal ale, we don't make it."

Beast considered his long-time friend and advisor for a moment. He thought about his shack, which was always leaking, and his crew, who were all weaker than they had been.

*Well, shit.*

He turned to Colas. "Dust off those Maraman maps. I think it's time we left."

She stared at him, as though she couldn't believe the words he was saying. "*Because we're out of ale?*"

He tried to look offended. "Of course not. Because of the crew and the homes. All the things you've been telling me about."

Colas's jaw went up and down, but no words came out. Finally, she found her voice. "You are the greatest fool the world has ever known."

Beast grinned from ear to ear. "It's called leadership, Colas, and you best get used to it."

# 3

Sato, looking three moves ahead, saw the weakness in his opponent's strategy and took advantage. He blocked a series of blows but refused to give ground like the man opposite him expected. Instead, he lowered his shoulder and checked the man, knocking him off balance. Then he pressed his own attack. Too late, he realized that was what his opponent expected.

Well, too late for most sentinels.

But Sato wasn't most sentinels.

With a speed and accuracy that few possessed, Sato brought his blade up and blocked what would have been a killing blow. The two wooden blades cracked loudly and, despite being off balance, Sato followed the block with a kick to the midsection. By the time the Firstborn recovered, Sato's practice blade was at his mentor's throat.

"I yield," the Firstborn said, chuckling through ragged breaths. "That was the last trick in my bag."

"It almost worked. If I'd been just a bit slower, you would have gotten me."

"One day, you'll find that your speed is the first thing to

go. Then all you'll be able to do is lay traps for faster opponents."

"To be fair, I still think you'd defeat most sentinels." Sato, never one for false praise, wasn't just being kind to his ruler. Although he rarely lost to the Firstborn, the older man was one of the few opponents that pushed Sato to his limits.

The Firstborn gestured to the pillows on the floor. "Let's sit. I'll pour."

Sato acquiesced gratefully. It was late for a training session, his second of the day, and his body was already protesting from all the work he'd done in between. The moment his meeting with the Firstborn was done he planned on running to the hot springs.

Sato was only mildly surprised when the Firstborn ignored convention and jumped straight to the point of their meeting. "In your opinion, how is the integration fairing?"

Despite the fact that very subject had consumed most of his time for nearly a year, Sato still bristled at the idea of the sin and sentinels fighting side by side. "Better than I expected, sir."

"Now," the Firstborn added.

Sato sighed. "Yes, now. You know it pains me to admit it, but Crispin and Alonzo were, as usual, indispensable in their roles." Sato gripped his teacup tighter as he imagined the smug looks on his lieutenants' faces if they ever discovered he had admitted as much to the Firstborn.

But they deserved the praise. Combining not just two militaries, but two very different ways of life, required an imagination and a willingness to try new things that Sato didn't possess. If not for the two of them, Sato didn't think they'd be anywhere as close to successful as they were today.

The Firstborn nodded. "I know I've asked much from

you since I put you in charge of hunting down the mugon, but you've risen to every challenge. You credit your lieutenants, but you deserve some praise as well. Seeing the great General Sato adapt to the new ways so quickly set a precedent for our younger sentinels that couldn't be ignored."

Sato smiled and bowed graciously. Inside, his stomach roiled. Volunteering the Sun Stalkers to be the first unit to integrate had, of course, been Crispin's idea. Sato had reluctantly agreed, but only after he and his lieutenants had worked out ways to free themselves of the sin among them when the need arose.

They might be allies now, but Sato expected that to be a temporary problem.

He thought he'd kept any expressions that betrayed his true feelings off his face, but as usual, the Firstborn seemed to see right through him. "I see you still feel working with the sin to be a great compromise."

For a moment Sato was concerned that the Firstborn understood just how deep Sato's hatred of the sin, as well as his preparations to remove them from the sentinels someday, reached. But Crispin, again, had been his guide. Sato had publicly supported the integration, but he was mostly honest with his feelings behind closed doors. The Firstborn knew how Sato felt, even if he didn't know the extent of Sato's preparations.

It meant that it moments like this, Sato didn't have to bother with an outright lie. Sato wondered if all the deception he engaged in to preserve his place on the Path would someday push him off of it.

But that was a problem for another day. "I've learned that the Path requires interpretation, especially during times like these. I don't like working with the sin, but I acknowledge we have little choice."

"A ringing endorsement, as usual," Yuki said from the doorway. "May I join you?"

"Please," the Firstborn said with a slight bow. Sato clenched his fists. Though the doorway was behind him, he would have heard anyone else approach. But the damned sin leader moved as quietly as a shadow. And then, when she stood in the presence of the Firstborn, didn't so much as bow her head in deference.

Besides, he'd hoped to speak to the Firstborn about some issues in private. "Sir, perhaps she should wait until we have finished our meeting?"

"It was my idea to call this meeting, Sato." Yuki said.

Sato swallowed hard. Yuki was, if anything, a guest among the sentinels and the citizens of Versun. Yes, she led the sin, but Sato didn't recognize any authority beyond that. The idea that she might have summoned him, especially through the Firstborn, made him want to draw steel and settle their differences for good. He settled for attacking her verbally. "Where's Shin?"

It was hard to see, but Yuki's face darkened a little at the mention of her supposed disciple. It was no secret that Shin had resisted any training in sacrifice beyond that of an adept. Yuki was so weak she couldn't even lead her strongest fighters. "Enough of that. I called this meeting because I am certain the Maramans are within weeks of hitting Samas, if not days. I've spoken with my adepts about their progress, but I wanted to hear how the sentinels fare."

Sato looked from Yuki's emotionless face and back to the warm, friendly expression on the Firstborn's. He calmed himself. For now, he had to be the dutiful sentinel. "We are as ready as can be expected. Against warriors and siege engines, I am confident the walls of Versun will hold.

Against demons? I am only confident that we've prepared as well as possible. The rest is up to the adepts."

"My adepts are ready. We'll send them back as fast as you can get them out of their corporeal form. The burden remains on the warriors to remove their heads quickly enough," Yuki said.

"We're drilling daily on the walls with every polearm imaginable. The problem remains that the conventional methods of defending walls does not involve removing the heads from your enemies," Sato said through gritted teeth.

"Innovate," Yuki replied in her insufferable calm.

"We have. Our smiths have created spears with longer blades and handles, and our warriors are doing their best to learn how to use them. Perhaps your adepts could innovate as well?"

"That isn't how sacrifice works. I would suggest you stick to your area of expertise," Yuki replied.

"Gladly, when you stick to yours."

"I assure you, General Sato, I am more than accomplished at removing heads from bodies."

"And I am no stranger to your sun-cursed realm of sacrifice," Sato snapped, holding up his ethereal pinky.

"Accidentally stumbling your way into one of our simplest spells does not make you an expert."

The Firstborn took a long sip of his tea, a grin on his face. "Perhaps you two should spar."

"What?" Sato and Yuki asked in unison.

"Obviously you two hate each other. Which is fine. But we need to fight together against the Maramans, so it's best if you two work out your differences now. Just don't do any lasting damage, please. I need you both."

Yuki looked at Sato. "I could use a workout."

Rather than answer, Sato stood up and picked out the

practice sword he'd put down only a few minutes ago. He gestured Yuki forward with his free hand.

The sin leader walked smoothly to the weapon wall and picked out her own sword.

And then he was on his knees.

The force of sacrifice was like nothing he'd experienced before. His first reaction was to glare at Yuki, assuming she'd resorted to her petty tricks to beat him. Then he noticed that she, too, was on her knees and breathing heavily.

"What is it?" The Firstborn asked.

"The Maramans are here," Yuki said, "And I think they just summoned an army of demons."

# 4

"How do you know it's him?" Corin asked as he matched her brisk pace.

"Power like that? It couldn't be anyone else," Shin replied.

"Yuki?"

"Yuki isn't using sacrifice, and even if she did, I'm not sure she could wield power like that. Besides, it came from Iru."

Shin could sense that Corin had more questions but was holding his tongue. Shin wasn't sure if it was because he could tell she didn't want to talk or because he didn't want the answers.

Shin understood. She'd prefer not to know how strong their enemy was, either.

She'd been driven to her knees when the emperor had accessed the realm. Every adept watching Hanz fight had been as well. The moment would be etched in her memory forever, not just because of what she'd sensed, but because of how the other adepts had responded. Their concerned faces had swiveled, as one, to look to her for answers.

Answers she didn't have.

She'd tried to reassure them. But it was hard, because anything she might say in response to the emperor's display of power was nothing but empty comfort. Still, she'd told them not to fear. In any case, they had all looked relieved when she'd taken off towards the palace district. So long as someone of rank was reporting to Yuki, they could rest easily.

As they passed through the gates of the palace district, a sin messenger greeted them. "Yuki wishes to see you. They are in the Firstborn's training room."

Shin nodded. "Who else?"

"Just Sato when I left."

"Thank you," Shin said.

"Should I come?" Corin asked.

"Yes."

"But they didn't send for me."

"I don't care."

"But—"

"I said I don't care. I need someone there I can trust. I haven't spoken to Yuki in weeks, and Sato is Sato. You're coming."

Corin took in her expression and put up his hands in mock surrender. "Yes, ma'am!"

Shin couldn't bring herself to tell Corin the whole truth. It wasn't Yuki or Sato that concerned her most. She wasn't looking forward to seeing Yuki, but there was nothing new between them. Sato, while still cold to her, was always professional. He recognized what she'd done with her unit and respected it in the same way she respected what he'd done with the farmers of Dahl. They would never like one another, but their relationship was clearly defined.

It was the Firstborn that made her uncomfortable.

She'd had a few occasions to spend time with the man as they began the integration of sin and sentinel. Each time, she was struck by the kind of leader he was. Each time, she found it hard to hold on to her disdain for the sentinel order that kept so many Samasians firmly under its thumb. The Firstborn was far from perfect, but he would be the first to acknowledge it, and the first to seek ways to improve.

Watching him made her think the sentinels weren't all that bad. And she couldn't bear to lose that hatred. Samas couldn't afford to let her lose it. Likeable as he might be, it was still his sentinels that had killed her family. And so many more besides.

When Shin entered the Firstborn's chambers, she was greeted by a crisp nod from Sato, a featureless expression from Yuki, and a bow from the Firstborn.

"I assume we don't need to brief you on what happened?" Yuki said.

"No, he closed the rift on Iru and did... something else," Shin responded.

"And Yuki won't tell us what," Sato snapped.

"I preferred to wait until we were all present."

Shin rolled her eyes at Yuki's penchant for politicking. Telling the details earlier would have changed nothing. "He took control of all the feral demons on Iru," she said.

The Firstborn raised an eyebrow and looked at Yuki for confirmation.

Sato cursed under his breath. "Is that what you think?"

"I do. You felt it too, did you not?" Yuki asked Sato.

"As you said, I'm not an expert."

Shin sensed tension between the two, but that was normal. For all the bridges that had been built between the two orders, the chasm between Sato and Yuki was as wide as ever. Thankfully, the Firstborn was adept at working with both. Here, he ignored their spat and focused on Yuki. "Do we know how many demons he controls, or what their abilities are?"

Yuki shook her head. "Unfortunately, I could only understand the form of the sacrifice. In terms of useful information, there's little I have to share."

The Firstborn nodded. "Do you have any information on what force he might command besides the demons?"

Again, Yuki shook her head.

"We need more information," said Sato. "My Sun Stalkers can be ready within the hour. We can scout the coast of Iru and be back before anyone knows we were there."

The Firstborn shot Sato a hard look, one that Shin didn't fully understand. She wasn't privy to the full relationship between the men, but there was something there. "I'm not sending my highest ranking general on a scouting mission. Especially not one to an island crawling with demons and Maramans. It's nearly a suicide mission, even if it is vital."

"I think Shin should go," Yuki said.

Shin glared at Yuki. Hadn't the woman heard the Firstborn say it was a suicide mission?

"I agree," the Firstborn said.

Shin was still hung up on the fact this was a mission they weren't expecting everyone to come back from. "Why me?"

Yuki answered, and Shin saw Sato clench his fists. "Because you're an adept strong enough to keep your unit alive. Otherwise, we're just sending scouts to die. Despite your lack of desire to learn more about sacrifice, you're still one of the most sensitive adepts we have. And, given your lack of desire to progress, if we lose you, we won't be losing a vital warrior like Sato here. You are the perfect choice."

Corin stepped in and saved Shin from attacking everyone in the room. “We can be ready to go tomorrow morning, ma’am.”

“Very well,” the Firstborn said. “We’ll have a ferry ready for you at first light.”

Shin grimaced at the thought of telling her soldiers they’d have to be up so early. For many of them, the night was just getting started. They wouldn’t like having their break cut so short.

“Wait,” Sato said, “I don’t believe this discussion is closed.”

“The Firstborn gave an order,” Yuki said.

“No, he agreed with a suggestion. I want a stronger sentinel presence in that scouting party.”

“My unit is more than half sentinels,” Shin said.

“But you are the commander, and your little friend is your second. I fear the first loyalty of your soldiers is to you and not Samas.”

“By the sun, Sato! We’re all on the same team,” Corin said before realizing who he was talking to.

Sato turned to him and glared. To Corin’s credit, Shin noticed, he didn’t back down from the look.

“That kind of disrespect is exactly the lack of discipline I’m concerned about,” Sato said. “I would feel better if a higher-ranking sentinel accompanied them.”

“Did you have someone in mind?” the Firstborn asked.

Sato thought for a moment. “Lieutenant Alonzo, sir.”

The Firstborn agreed, and Shin wondered if it was more to keep the peace than for any actual reason. “Very well. Alonzo will meet you at the port at dawn. Are we satisfied?”

No one looked like they were, which Shin figured was probably the mark of a good compromise. No one argued further, at least.

Sato faced the Firstborn. "If there's nothing else, I'd like to report back to my Sun Stalkers. I'm not sure what's going to happen next, but I would guess we'd best be as prepared as possible to repel a demon siege."

"I fear you're correct, my friend. Yuki, if there is any thing that can be done through sacrifice, I would like you to look into it."

Yuki nodded. "I have some ideas. Perhaps once Shin is back with more information, I can discuss it with her."

Shin recognized the words for the olive branch that they were. Yuki still hoped that Shin might serve their defense against the emperor and his summoners. That she would continue her training and do what Yuki couldn't.

But Shin knew it didn't matter. No matter what they found on Iru, her path was already decided.Shin would fight, but she'd never let herself fall so deep into the clutches of the realm again. If they were going to defeat the Maraman emperor, Yuki would need to find a different way.

# 5

"We need to head back to Samas if we're planning a long expedition," Colas said. "At best, our supplies would last a month on the water."

Beast shook his head. "We stole a juggernaut, one of her adepts, and robbed her of my immense talent. Yuki will turn my dick into sawdust the moment she sees me."

Colas waved the concern away. "She couldn't find it even if she squints. Besides, we'll park the juggernaut out of sight and take a ship in. I can be in and out of Dahl with supplies before word reaches anyone. It's what I did before you came into my life and upended everything."

Beast was comforted by the sturdy feeling of the wheel in his hands as he considered Colas's argument. Manning the helm was not Beast's job, but he found that steering his monstrous ship through the open ocean helped him to think. He liked the way the well-worn wheel felt, liked imagining what far off places the wheel had taken the juggernaut. "We'd burn through our remaining supplies getting back, right?"

"Just about."

"So what happens if we return and every port on Samas is overrun with demons?"

"Do you really think that could happen?"

"We helped them evacuate Bulas. *Bulas*, Colas. If the jewel of Samas can fall in the time it takes me to capture one juggernaut, who knows? There are several islands within a week of each other marked on those Maraman maps. I think our odds are better with them."

Colas thought for a moment before putting up a final argument. "None of us can read Maraman. And yes, there are obviously islands, but you've seen the notations. The Maramans have already visited those islands, and we don't know what they've left behind. For all we know, the symbols say, 'We planted a demon family here!'"

"True, but there are multiple islands. Islands where we don't know for sure the authorities would kill us on sight. Surely, we can find someplace."

"There's no guarantee that there's ale on any of these islands," Colas said, but Beast could tell by her tone that she'd exhausted her arguments.

Beast laughed. "True, but Gorou informed me that Peter used to make his own mead. It's not ale, but it'll do."

"Peter, our best navigator, Peter?"

"No, Peter, our mead maker. That's his job now."

"But—"

"That's his job now," Beast repeated.

"With what supplies?" Colas demanded.

"Captain! Land in sight!" A call relayed back from the forward crows' nest interrupted their conversation and saved Beast from having to answer the question.

"Let's take *Cutter* in. Get Vala as well. Whatever we come across, I don't want to have to call a meeting to discuss it," Beast ordered.

Colas nodded and shouted orders of her own. She was tough as nails and more than occasionally a pain in his ass, but he was lucky to have her. A lifetime of piracy had made her a natural captain, and she had a head for logistics and details that reminded him of Benji. Beast hated the minutia of command but was, to any who laid eyes on him, a beacon of inspiration. They were a perfect match.

By the time Beast made his way to *Cutter,* the crew was ready and waiting, along with Vala and Colas at the helm. Over the months at sea, Beast and Colas had integrated their forces. Those that served on Cutter were among their best, befitting the command vessel of the juggernaut. Beast would confidently take them into battle against any foe on sea or land.

"Let's go," Beast said, and Colas nodded to a crew member aboard the juggernaut. They began to descend to the ocean below.

"You look pleased," Colas said, sounding anything but.

"I was just thinking there might be something for me to kill on that island. If we're lucky, it'll be something big, too. It's been a while. Honestly, Colas, how did I let you convince me to try to start my own island village?"

Colas ignore Beast and instead turned to Vala. "Do you feel any summoners? Demons?"

"No, nothing on the island," Vala said and a strange expression crossed her face.

"What is it?" Beast asked.

"I'm not sure. I felt something a few nights ago, the last night we were on the island. It was distant but powerful. I was worried it might be from here."

"Anything we should be concerned about?" Colas asked.

"I don't think so. Sacrifice of that scale leaves a scar, but I don't sense anything nearby."

Beast nodded. Sacrifice was the last thing he wanted anything to do with. If Vala wanted to keep it to herself, all the better.

As they closed in on the island, any hopes of finding ale faded. He saw no evidence of cities or ports and the island itself was too small to be hiding much. The Maramans had marked it, however, so perhaps there was something.

"Doesn't look like much," Colas echoed his thoughts.

"No, but let's be ready, all the same. Big as they are, those Maramans can be sneaky bastards," Beast said.

Once they dropped anchor, Beast ordered the crew into the longboats. They rowed steadily through the surf, and before long the longboats were being dragged onto the beach. Once they were secure, Beast's crew fanned out, weapons drawn.

"Still nothing, Vala?" Beast asked the adept, who shook her head. "Ok, we'll take point. The rest fall in behind. That trail looks like more than a mere animal run."

Beast moved forward and heard the crew fall in behind him. Weapons drawn, they moved through the woods that lined the beach a short distance before coming upon a small village.

Or what was left of it.

Beast took in the razed village and was reminded of the farm on Ilos that he'd come across what seemed like ages ago. Charred corpses were scattered amongst the burned remains of buildings. From what Beast could tell, the villagers hadn't put up much of a fight. There wasn't a single Maraman corpse to be found.

"You think the notation for this island meant 'destroyed?'" Colas asked.

Beast closed his eyes and tried to remember the map. "How many more islands had the same notation?"

"Five, I think."

"If that's what it means, then they're like a plague," Beast muttered.

"They also aren't our problem. Let's see what we can find here and then we can work on getting as far away from them as possible," Colas replied.

Beast nodded, and the crew moved through the village, looking for anything of value. Beast couldn't help but wonder if this would be the fate of Samas.

Then he scoffed at the thought. Yuki and Shin were as strong as anyone he'd ever met, and if they were working with Sato and the Firstborn, they could put up a formidable defense. He didn't have to worry about Samas. It was in good hands, even if he wasn't there to save the day.

"Captain!" a sailor called out, interrupting Beast's thoughts.

Beast and Colas moved through the village and through another copse of trees. When they emerged, they found a large, clearing.

"It's badly overgrown, but it looks like there are some vegetables we can salvage here. Potatoes, carrots, and the like," mused Beast.

"Good, take what you can. Those other islands are close enough that we can check them quickly. Another find like this, and we'll be good to set out," Colas said.

"Set out where?" Beast asked. "Where do we go?"

"Away from the monsters that did this."

"Fine. We'll see what else we can gather, but I'd like to check all the islands. If there are survivors, perhaps we can help them."

"That's just more mouths to feed. More supplies to take," Colas argued.

Beast shrugged. "I still want to know, and besides, they're

close. We might find something more useful than potatoes. Like a cask of ale."

"What if all you find are Maramans?" Vala asked.

Beast grinned at the possibility. "Then we get to kill them."

# 6

Sato handed Nightmane's reins to the stablehand, then gave the horse an apple. "Good work, girl. You, at least, I can an always rely on."

The number of humans that fit that category seemed to be shrinking daily. Crispin, Alonzo, and the rest of the Sun Stalkers were as dependable as ever. Roko remained his most trusted confidant and, increasingly, closest friend.

After that, the list was close to empty.

His governance of Versun seemed satisfactory to the Firstborn, but the man still flexed his influence where he could. In theory, Sato didn't mind. The Firstborn remained the supreme representative of the eternal sun's will upon Samas. Sato was his subordinate and therefore subject to his decisions.

Unfortunately, Sato was growing more concerned about Yuki's influence on those decisions.

Sato took a calming breath and made his way to the magistrate's tower. Checking the walls and informing his Sun Stalkers of the events on Iru had been procrastination and nothing more. The walls were as solid as they could be, and anyone could have briefed his unit. Sato was avoiding the ongoing task of punishing the corrupt sentinels that aided Izuki during her tenure.

On its face, it was a job Sato should have had no problem with. He didn't relish punishing fellow sentinels, but the Path demanded discipline. The issue was, once again, the Firstborn. With increasing frequency, Sato's punishments were being amended by the old man.

An execution was changed to a magistrate being stripped of their title and sent to work on Ilos.

A public flogging was made private, and the number of lashings reduced.

An order to pay back stolen funds was cut in half.

Thus far, the Firstborn's amendments had been carried out without discussion, as was the Firstborn's right, so Sato had no choice but to let it go. Soon, though, he would need to discuss his master's leniency. What good was discipline if it was never enforced?

"Sir, the Firstborn is waiting for you," Crispin reported as Sato entered the waiting room of the Magistrate's tower.

Sato raised an eyebrow at his lieutenant. Perhaps he would be having that discussion sooner than later.

"Thank you, Crispin. Ensure that we aren't interrupted. By anyone."

Crispin nodded and Sato was certain that he understood who Sato was talking about.

He wanted Yuki nowhere near this meeting. If they weren't careful, soon sin would be fulfilling the roles of magistrates.

"Sato, how do our defenses look?" The Firstborn asked with his customary warmth.

"Strong as ever, sir. It's amazing what can be done with

the funds allocated for repairs and maintenance when they are used for repairs and maintenance."

"Straight to business, then."

"There's no time for anything else. How can I help you today, sir?"

The Firstborn smiled despite Sato's steely tone. "I take it you are aware that I've listened to some appeals regarding your orders?"

"I am."

"And I assume you aren't happy about it."

"I am not."

"Well, then, you aren't going to enjoy this meeting very much. What are your plans for magistrate Caldwell?"

"Former magistrate Caldwell, and you know exactly what they are. They were in the report I sent you last week."

"I think you should reconsider."

"No, thank you. Will there be anything else?"

The Firstborn's smile faded. "Then I'm ordering you to reconsider. Stripping him of his rank, status, and all his land is excessive."

"He stole more funds from honest citizens of Samas than anyone aside from Izuki herself. He should be put to death, but you don't seem to like that much, so I'm sending him to toil in the farm communes on Ilos instead, as you've done already with others I've sentenced to death. Seems fitting that he should spend the rest of his days working to feed the very people he stole from his whole life, wouldn't you say?"

"It certainly is poetic, but Caldwell is a well-connected man. He has family within all three guilds—"

"And has been known to visit the Firstborn for tea regularly," Sato interrupted.

"Yes, but we both know I was unaware of the extent of his crimes. Much as you were, before all of this started. My point is that our control is tenuous at best. These people you're dealing with are all connected, and if we lose too much support, we won't be able to rule. Hate it if you will, but the Firstborn's role isn't absolute. Especially now, when so much has already been lost. Surely you understand that."

Sato took deep, measured breaths to remain calm. For a time, he had thought that perhaps the Firstborn was willing to go as far as was needed to put Samas back on to the Path. The cowardice he saw before him was proof that he was wrong.

And that Sato was the only person left who could truly cleanse the sentinel order.

"I do," Sato said tightly. "What would you suggest instead?"

"Strip him of half his fortune and put it into the farming system. You're right that he should contribute to the people he stole from. He will then be placed on house arrest for a month."

Sato saw no point in arguing. "Consider it done, sir."

"You think me too lenient?"

"No, sir, a month in his estate, eating and drinking the finest Samas has to offer should send exactly the kind of message you're looking for."

"Careful, Sato. You presume much in the way you speak to me. I would have thought by now you would understand that the world operates in shades of grey. Your lieutenants certainly seem to," the Firstborn said.

"With all due respect, Crispin and Alonzo were integral in using abhorrent means to remove abhorrent people from power. We were in a war, and we did what was needed because the infection of the sentinel order had been allowed to fester for so long. I will also add that along the way those two sentinels were brought back onto to the Path. But that war is over now, and if we can't put away the shameful tools that were needed to win, what did we even fight for?"

"Your idealism, as always, honors you, Sato, but one day you're going to have to wake up. Can I trust you to follow my orders regarding Caldwell?"

Sato bowed deeply and kept his voice measured. "Of course."

The Firstborn looked like he wanted to give Sato his customary embrace, but thought better of it and left. After the door closed, Sato sat behind his desk and began to make the changes to the sentencing file for Caldwell. He heard Crispin enter but finished his work before he looked up at the sentinel.

"I trust you heard everything?"

"Yes sir," Crispin responded.

"You're still working on contingencies to remove the sin from the Sun Stalkers if needed?"

"Almost done."

"Good. Perhaps it's time to add Yuki into the plans as well."

"That's a little more complicated, but I think we can get it done," Crispin said.

"Good."

"Anyone else?"

Sato locked eyes with Crispin for a long moment before speaking again. "I'll leave that to your discretion."

Crispin nodded and left the room.

# 7

Shin's mouth felt like cotton and her body ached everywhere with the effort of remaining perfectly still. The moment they'd gotten within view of Iru, it became clear that her entire unit couldn't hope to scout the island without being seen. The place wasn't exactly crawling with enemies, but it was close. She elected to send a smaller group instead.

So she, Corin, and two of their most experienced scouts had slipped into the water and swum silently to the easternmost shore of Iru. They came ashore near a small cliff that they were able to scale with relative ease without being seen by anyone on the island.

Or anything.

Now the four of them crouched atop the small, rocky rise and looked out over a nightmare. One she couldn't believe was real.

And one that she had helped create. That thought was never far from her mind, twisting her insides and turning them to water.

They weren't far from Hankala, and the area was filled

with demonic animals and people. Deer, bears, wolves, sin, and sentinels were everywhere, and there were more of them than Shin expected.

But it wasn't their numbers that frightened her the most. It was their behavior. Shin was used to the rage-fueled movements of the demons. Seeing them gnash their teeth and sprint towards anything with emotions was a terrible reality she had learned to accept.

The stillness before her was so much worse.

"How are they doing that?" Corin asked.

Shin shook her head. The demons were all lined up in perfect formations. It was disconcerting enough to see the strangely elongated limbs and rictus grins of the sin and sentinels standing at attention, but far worse were the animals standing on their hind legs beside them. "I don't know, but I imagine the power we felt from the emperor has something to do with it."

"So, we've seen enough? We can head back now?" Corin asked.

"I don't think so. There's no telling how many more chances we'll get to scout the island, so we need to learn all that we can. Arvo, what did you see?"

The sentinel scout took a moment to pry his eyes away from the demons on the beach. "You can see there, between two of the formations, the tracks of something big being dragged through the sand. Possibly many large objects. I would guess that means siege engines, but if I know General Sato, then he'll want specifics."

"Do we have to head all the way to Bulas?"

Arvo thought for a moment and shared a look with Neisa, who shook her head. "I doubt it. More likely, they would bring them straight to port. It's a little closer. The main road takes us there, but I wouldn't suggest we use it."

Shin nodded. She might be a little quieter than the sentinel scouts, but they knew this land better than she ever would. With one last look at the demons, Shin turned and gestured for the scouts to lead the way.

"Can you sense anything about the emperor?" Corin asked. "Now that you're closer?"

"I haven't tried. I don't want to draw the attention of the emperor or any of his summoners."

Corin gulped at the thought. "Smart."

Shin was glad he didn't feel like arguing the point. Corin had been, for the most part, supportive of her decision to stop her training in sacrifice. Since the emperor's arrival, however, it was clear to Shin that he felt she should be doing something more.

But she'd already done more than enough. Hell, Iru was evidence of that. If Corin thought she should be messing with sacrifice, even while walking through the nightmare she had started, then he was a fool and more.

The route they took paralleled the main road between Hankala and Bulas to the south. Their trip was uneventful, but every once in a while they would hear hoof beats in the distance and would stop until they passed. Though she couldn't see the road, Shin knew she was getting closer and closer to the former site of the rift on Iru.

The place where her failure crescendoed into a disaster.

"Shin?"

She heard Corin's voice, but it seemed distant. Like her head was underwater, and he was speaking to her from above. The world seemed to narrow into a single point of light, and Shin's breathing became rapid. She could feel the rift. It was so close, and she was certain it was opening again, tearing into this world like claws rending flesh.

She had to close it.

She had to do what she couldn't before, and so she reached out to the realm.

The other rifts had closed at her command. This one would be no different.

A sharp pain across her face brought the world back into focus. She looked around and finally saw Corin standing in front of her with his hand raised, as if to slap her again.

She blinked away the last of her confusion and shook her head. "I'm fine, I'm fine. I'm sorry I just..." Shin could feel the point where the rift used to be, but there was nothing there now. "I thought... never mind."

"You good to keep going?" Corin asked.

"Yes, fine. Are we almost there?"

Neisa nodded and gestured for them to continue.

"I'm fine," Shin said to Corin before he could ask her again.

She wasn't so sure. She could have sworn she felt the rift opening again. Felt that terrible place seeping through. She'd been so ready to stop it she'd almost touched the realm. Was she going mad? Or was it another trick of the realm?

By the time they made it to the port, Shin felt more connected to reality. They'd stuck to the woods and, as a result, were still a fair distance from the port itself. The tree line ended at the top of a hill that looked down onto the port. Despite the distance, Shin shivered at what she saw.

If the demons lining up in formation were unsettling, what she saw in the port was an abomination.

Shin immediately recognized the large, Maraman demons that had nearly torn Dahl apart. They were still chained to their summoners, but rather than destroying, they were helping to erect giant catapults, larger than any weapon Shin had ever seen. Those that weren't on the beach were down in the water building giant floating platforms. The demons weren't handling any of the tools, but they could lift and position the giant pieces of the siege engines with ease.

"They're going to float those things across to Egzuki," Corin said.

"That enough for Sato?" Shin asked Arvo.

Before the sentinel could answer, he held up a hand and cocked his ear as if listening. He put his finger to his lips and disappeared back into the woods behind them. Corin went to draw his swords, but Neisa held up a hand, stopping him. For a few minutes, there was nothing but silence and then Arvo appeared again.

"They know we're here. I saw a few of them moving this way through the trees. I think there's a—"

Shin flinched backwards as a spurt of blood from Arvo's mouth decorated her face. Eyes wide, his mouth continued to move as if he were trying to finish his final scouting report, even as a glowing blade was jutting from his chest.

The blade retracted and Arvo fell to the ground. Standing in his place was a crimson robed Maraman summoner, whose wicked grin frightened Shin almost as much as the siege engines below.

# 8

For the next week, Beast's crew visited every island between them and the one with the unique markings on the map. It was a tour of destruction the Maramans left wherever their over-sized feet touched land. They found burned villages, broken bodies, and shattered pottery. What food they found was little more than the scraps left behind by the raiders.

The only thing they never came across was a Maraman body. But everything Beast saw made him want to add a few to the landscape.

When they arrived at the island with the unique markings, Beast allowed himself a moment of cautious hope. Using their looking glasses from the deck of the juggernaut, they were able to make out more signs of civilization than they'd seen since leaving Samas.

"Doesn't look like they've destroyed this island," Colas said. "At least, not yet."

"Seems that way. I don't see any Maraman vessels, though. Why would they leave this place alone?"

"Couldn't say. Only way to know will be to land. But it

looks safe enough. All I'm seeing are fishing skiffs and a small pier. Makes me think there's a village a little farther in."

Beast brought the looking glass down from his eye. The Maramans knew about this island, but hadn't completely burned it to the ground. It made him wary. "We'll send two of the ships. That gives us enough strength that we can handle a Maraman presence if we find one, but we leave you and your crew here to defend the juggernaut."

"Makes sense. Or we could sail away from this place and remove any chance of having to fight Maramans."

Beast smiled at his second in command. "Where's the fun in that?"

Colas rolled her eyes but issued the commands.

He wouldn't risk pushing her too far. She was too valuable to him to lose and, if he was being honest, he liked having her around.

So they wouldn't stay here for long, but he wanted to know what was happening on this island. From everything he'd seen, the Maramans were a scourge, but one driven by some higher purpose. He wanted to know what that purpose was before they explored too much more of this world. And if seeking that answer allowed him to crush a few Maraman skulls, so much the better.

It didn't take long for them to crew the ships and detach from the juggernaut. They'd gone through the routine often enough Beast would have gladly raced his own mixed crew against the juggernaut's original inhabitants. He stood at the helm of his ship as they approached, scanning both sea and land for any sign of the Maramans.

When there was none, Beast ordered them to sail for the piers. They stopped short of the actual landing, as the piers were shoddy and in shallow water. Beast ordered the anchors dropped and they climbed into the longboats.

Soon, Beast was the first to set foot on the island. He walked up the beach and past the various fishing lines and rigging, his heart leaped as he saw movement in the trees. He unlimbered his great axe and grinned viciously.

His smile soon faltered. The figure running towards him was far too small to be a Maraman, and once it got closer Beast could make out a very tanned man dressed only in a loincloth. Beast held up his hand to his crew and waited for the man to approach.

"Local?" Gorou asked.

"I'd guess. Nice that someone's alive on this island," Beast responded.

"You're disappointed it's not a Maraman, aren't you?"

"It's been so long since I've killed something worthy of my skill."

Their conversation was interrupted as the man ran up to Beast and threw himself prostrate onto the ground. After a few moments like that, he stood up spoke rapidly in a language Beast couldn't understand.

"Sounds familiar, don't you think?" Beast asked Gorou, who nodded.

The man looked from Beast to the crew, clearly confused, but gestured back the way he had come.

"Let's see what he wants to show us," Beast said.

They followed the local up the beach and onto a well-used path through the forest. The design of the buildings and the boats left Beast feeling uneasy, and it took him a moment to figure out why. It wasn't until they passed a small hut that Beast figured it out. He'd been confused because the hut hadn't been burned down. But these people used the same building design as on the other islands.

The observation led Beast to ask a dozen more questions. Were the villages on the islands related? If so, did they have contact or trade between the communities?

Did these people know that their neighbors had all been slaughtered?

Gorou interrupted his wondering. "Why did he bow to you like that?"

Beast smirked. "The better question is: why don't more people bow? Seemed like an appropriate reaction to me."

Soon they reached the village proper, and Beast was impressed. This was the largest of the villages they'd seen yet. The buildings shared the same basic design as on the other islands, and were also made of wood and thatch, but the scale was different. Homes here were larger, and the layout of the village was more orderly, with long straight streets running between clusters of buildings. It reminded Beast of the sin village on the hidden island.

Most of the buildings were clearly homes. Children played out front while grandparents sat in chairs under the shade of porches. Life here seemed pleasant enough, at least until they caught sight of Beast.

As a Maraman who had grown up on Samas, Beast was used to strong reactions to his presence. He tended to inspire awe no matter where he went. But even so, he wasn't prepared for reactions the islanders had as he strode through the village.

As soon as they saw him, the children stopped their games and ran into their homes. Some grandparents joined them, but those that remained on the front porches all bowed deeply to him as he passed. They showed him more respect than his own crew did. Hell, even the mugon who had served under him since the beginning of his rise to power weren't nearly so obsequious.

Made him a bit uneasy.

They were led deeper into the village, up a small rise toward what looked to be the largest building around. Beast assumed that was their destination.

“There's a lot more trade here than in the other villages we've come across,” Gorou observed.

“Perhaps the other islands were little colonies?” Beast guessed. "Their first attempts to expand beyond this island?"

“Perhaps.” Gorou didn't seem convinced.

They reached the large building and were led inside. Beast expected to meet an elder or leader of some sort, but the receiving chamber was empty. The man that had greeted him gestured towards a large chair in the middle of the room. It took Beast a moment to understand.

“I think—” Gorou began.

“They want me to be their leader.”

“I was actually going to say—”

Beast interrupted him again. “You saw the way he bowed to me. The way these people have been looking at me with awe in their eyes.”

Gorou grunted. “I think that was fear.”

“Yes! A healthy dose of awe and fear. They recognize me as the leader I am.”

As they were speaking, Beast watched more locals follow them in. The group argued among themselves, and Beast got the feeling he was the cause of the argument. The man who had guided them this far spoke loudest and fastest.

The argument ended abruptly as everyone suddenly left. Beast watched them through the open windows as they ran deeper inland. He masked his concern with a boast, mostly because he knew it would annoy Gorou. “Look, they’re off to make accommodations for their new king! The language barrier will be tough, but I think we can make it work.”

“I think I should go get Colas,” Gorou said.

“Yes! Tell her the good news.”

“No, I think we need all our forces here. Or we should retreat to the juggernaut.”

Beast tapped his fingers on the arm of his new throne. "This is a mighty comfortable chair. Far better than anything I have on the juggernaut."

"It seems to me," Gorou said, doing his best to ignore Beast's comments, "that this island is most likely still occupied. They clearly fear Maramans and must have thought you were an occupier when you arrived by juggernaut. Alas, I fear the language barrier you aren't worried about gives us away."

It was as much as Beast had suspected, but coming from Gorou's lips, it all sounded so depressing.

What should he do about it? Had the decision been up to Colas, she would have turned the juggernaut around and sailed happily away.

But Beast couldn't get the destroyed villages out of his mind. The Maramans deserved to pay dearly for the blood they had shed. And who better to do that than their lost son?

"Shall I send for Colas?” Gorou asked.

Beast considered for another few moments. A wiser man would have left the island. The ships weren't far away, and they could quickly be gone before any Maramans arrived. Beast would have a fun story to tell about the time a village had mistaken him for a ruler.

But why should it just be a story? If they had forges here, they almost certainly had ale. And this was a really comfortable throne.

"Yes," Beast said. "And tell her to come ready for a fight."

# 9

"So it's just luck?" Sato asked, bemused by Crispin's enthusiasm.

"Well, yes. Assuming you play by the rules." Crispin picked up his dice and tossed them around in his hand.

"But that's not how you play?"

"Not when I want to win, sir."

"Why did you think I'd enjoy being taught this game?"

Crispin shrugged. "Not sure. It seemed like a good idea when I suggested it. I forgot you can strip the fun out of anything, though."

Sato shook his head and reminded himself how far the younger man had come. Crispin would never live up to the expectations a younger Sato would have had for his sentinels, but there was no one else Sato would trust to have by his side. Now, if he ever doubted his lieutenant, he needed to look no further than his friend's missing hand.

Even so, there was something deep in Crispin's bones that would always resist the Path. Loyal and useful as Crispin was, Sato couldn't help but think of how much more Crispin could achieve with some more discipline.

Another sentinel burst into the room. "Crispin, I — Oh, sorry, General Sato, I didn't realize you were here." The sentinel dropped to one knee.

"It's no problem, Oren. Make your report," Sato said.

"Janson's unit has been dispatched to the eastern coast, sirs. Scouts have reported demon activity."

"Thanks, Oren," Crispin said. He turned to Sato. "Is this it?"

"Don't know when we'll get another chance."

"How many stalkers do you want?"

"Just you and Roko. If one of our units can't handle a demon incursion, then we've wasted this past year."

Crispin looked as though a heavy weight had settled on his shoulders. "You'll be stirring up a hell of a hornet's nest, sir."

Sato looked at the leather glove he'd taken to wearing on his hand since his experience with the rift. "If you've taught me anything, Crispin, it's that however abhorrent I might personally find something, it would be foolish not to use it to its full advantage."

"I'm hurt, sir. I don't think I've ever been called abhorrent."

"Go get Roko and meet me at the gates. And get the details from Oren on exactly where Janson's heading."

Crispin bowed and left. Sato's lieutenant was by no means abhorrent, but the sin and their sun-cursed sacrifice certainly was. Unfortunately, the demons were even worse, and sacrifice was required for Samas to be rid of them. Which meant the sin were required.

For now.

As Sato made his way down to the stables, his mind reeled at the variety of enemies aligned against him. Maramans. Demons. Sin. Maybe even the Firstborn? He'd set out to bring the sentinels back to the sun, and now his enemies grew as his allies were whittled away. He flexed his hand.

Now, more than ever, he needed to understand every tool at his disposal.

"I heard Crispin taught you how to play dice," Roko said as Sato approached on Nightmane.

"Unfortunately. Were you aware it's all luck?"

"Not the way Crispin plays," Roko responded.

"Even worse. Once we're done here, I'd like to play some chess, if you're amenable."

"Of course. I made the mistake of challenging Crispin to a game of dice last week, and now my coin purse is far lighter than it should be. Watched his every move like a hawk, too."

"I offered to let you stop," Crispin said as he rode up beside him.

"You also let me think I had a chance to win my money back," Roko said.

"Know your enemy, captain. A strategic retreat would have been advisable."

In spite of himself, Sato laughed at Crispin's quoting of the Path to Roko. "That's enough, you two. We have to catch up to that patrol or there won't be anything to observe."

Sato kicked Nightmane into motion, and the two sentinels fell in behind him. As they rode, Crispin called out directions, but Egzuki was a small island, and it didn't take long for the sounds of battle to guide Sato to his destination.

The fight took place within the dense woods, and while it wasn't ideal terrain, the combined unit of sentinels and sin performed well. All the knowledge the sin had on how to fight demons combined with the centuries of military experience held by the sentinels was deadly. The sentinels acted primarily as a shield for the unit. They formed a line with spears and pole arms that kept the demonic menagerie at bay. The sin formed the cutting edge of the unit, darting in like snakes to remove demon heads whenever the sentinels created an opening. The adepts remained in the rear and sent back the mist the demons became after they were beheaded.

Even with all their training, the conflict's resolution balanced on a knife's edge. Their strategy had changed, and the fight was nothing like their first encounters with the demons. The improvement was impressive, and Sato wondered what they might have achieved had they simply been prepared a year ago. Perhaps the crown of Samas wouldn't have been overwhelmed in less than a day.

But there was no time for idle thoughts. He could embrace his regrets later. He was here to observe, and, if possible, to help. So he studied the battle, looking for new knowledge in the chaos.

The sentinels held the line, even if only by the slimmest of margins. For all their training, many sentinels hadn't fought a demon yet. They had trained in theory, and now it was finally being tested.

Sato was proud of what he saw. When a demon broke through in one place, the line shifted to respond to the threat. Even when multiple holes appeared in the line, they were nothing but temporary setbacks.

The sin, too, impressed him. Their cuts against the demons were works of art, and though the adepts looked like they were having a hard time, they never let the mist forms take shape again.

"How did the demons get here?" Roko asked.

"That's a question for one of the sin, I think."

"No, I mean how did they get on the island? The ocean has always acted as a barrier. Why would they cross it now?"

"Because they have help?" Crispin suggested.

"That's a good question. I want you two to find me an answer," Sato said. His command sent the two sentinels wheeling their mounts wide around the battle and farther east, toward the shore.

Any information they gleaned would be useful, but in truth Sato was happy to be left alone. His cheeks flushed with shame as he thought about what he was about to do.

When the next demon had its head removed, Sato allowed himself to feel the realm. The source of the sin's unnatural powers. Though he tried not to think about it, it was always there, tugging gently at his awareness.

Today, he finally turned his attention that way.

He was surprised at how easy it was to sense the realm and the sacrifice the adepts wielded. He wasn't sure if that was because the spell he sensed was one that was woven into his very being, or if sacrifice was something that came naturally to him. The latter thought sent a shiver down his spine that he ignored. For now, the cause didn't matter. All that did was that he knew what had to be done.

When another demon's head was removed, Sato opened himself up the realm and wove the sacrifice he had just witnessed a moment before. He laid the weaving out and took hold of the misty form. Once it was secured, he sent it back to the rift.

It almost immediately slipped out of his grip.

Sato panicked and flailed out with his mind, trying to find the sacrifice that had just come to him so easily. Before the misty form could return, though, one of the adepts secured it and sent it back. Once it was gone, the adept looked over at Sato and gave him a nod, which Sato returned politely.

"General!" Crispin's voice boomed through the woods as the sentinels advanced on the last of the demons.

With the battle in front of him nearly finished, Sato rode in a straight line towards his lieutenant. One of the few remaining demons swiped at him as he passed, but it was the creature's final mistake. A sin took advantage of the demon's distraction and took its head.

Sato emerged from the trees and rode onto a small beach to find Roko and Crispin looking out across the water. A ferry ship tugging a large raft was heading back towards Iru. Standing on the raft was the largest Maraman Sato had ever seen. His skin was ink black from head to toe.

"Looks like you were right about them getting help," Sato told Crispin.

"I wish I wasn't," his lieutenant answered.

As Sato continued to stare at the boat floating away, the Maraman on the raft raised his hand and waved.

# 10

Niesa dashed forward with her sword drawn before Shin could register exactly what had happened to Arvo. Her blade was a blur as she drove the summoner backwards. The crimson-clad Maraman gave ground, though he appeared to find Niesa's efforts more amusing than frightening. Shin fought through her initial shock, then drew Harmony and joined the fray, Corin right behind her.

A handful of Maramans and two demons emerged from the forest and stopped them in their tracks.

"Go!" Niesa shouted. She danced away from the summoner long enough to produce one of the sin pouches from a hidden pocket and throw it to the ground. It struck with a loud, sharp explosion, and dark smoke billowed out. It swallowed Niesa and the demons but did nothing to silence the clashes of steel and grunts of effort.

Shin swore. How many times would someone sacrifice their life just so that she could escape?

*As many times as it takes for you to grow up and embrace the gifts that have been given to you.*

The voice in her head was not her own. It was that of a young man. Shin couldn't place it, but there was something about it that was achingly familiar.

This was not the time to carefully consider it, though. She wouldn't let Niesa's sacrifice be meaningless. "This way," she said to Corin and led him across the main road that led to the port and into the woods that lined the opposite side.

"Back to the boat?" Corin asked.

"Not yet. Those demons are faster than us."

"So what do we do?"

"For now? Let's leave them a trail."

Corin didn't fight her or argue. After every mistake he'd seen her make, he still trusted her. They rushed through the wood heading north, breaking every branch and stomping every twig along the way.

A primal scream rang out behind them, and Shin gave a silent thanks to Niesa for the time she had bought them.

*If you used your strength, she wouldn't have had to die.*

Shin ignored the voice. There, up ahead, was a place that fit her needs. "Up into the trees," she said.

Corin nodded, still holding any questions he had close to his chest.

They climbed into the canopy of the thick forest. Once they were high enough, Shin and Corin started clambering from branch to branch, slowly working their way back toward the beach they had landed on. The trees were old and their branches thick, and they made a passable route for the two sin.

Soon, the sounds of demons crashing through the trees below came close.

"That didn't take long," Corin whispered.

With the demons so close, Shin wanted nothing more

than to run. But there was no outrunning the demons below. She focused instead on moving as silently as possible. It took all her training, and all her patience, to find ways through the canopy without rustling more leaves than the evening's gentle breeze.

In time, the sound of the demons faded behind them. Shin grew optimistic that they had lost the Maramans. They moved steadily toward the beach where they'd left their boat.

The sound of a demon crashing through the underbrush directly beneath her made her freeze.

She and Corin hugged the trunks of their respective trees. Shin couldn't believe the summoner had tracked them. They'd been careful and quiet, and Shin hadn't used any sacrifice. She risked a look down.

The elongated and distorted Maraman features were terrifying. Though more controlled than the feral demons, Shin could see in its movements that the monster was casting about on instinct alone. It was used to seeing its prey and moving in for the kill.

Relief swelled inside her.

The demon hadn't tracked them. It was just getting desperate. The summoner had most likely sent the demons out to look for them, probably in all directions. She caught Corin's eye and gestured for him to stay calm and quiet. He rolled his eyes at the obvious instructions. After a few minutes that felt like hours, the demon heard some other movement in the woods and took off after it.

Shin waited another minute before relaxing. "If we keep moving quietly, we should be fine. I think."

"That's very reassuring."

Shin shot Corin a withering glare that softened when

her friend grinned at her. She took a deep breath and resumed their escape.

Unfortunately, it wasn't the last time the demons came close. Any time a demon neared, she and Corin would freeze and wait for the demon to pass them by. As they got closer to the beach, they encountered more demons and Shin began to worry that they would be lying in wait.

Shin decided that hurrying to the beach was worth sacrificing some of their silence. They drew closer to the main path, which would force her to make another unpalatable decision.

"We're going to need to cross the main road," Shin whispered to Corin.

"Which means we need to get out of the trees," Corin whispered back.

Shin nodded. "We can't afford to wait too long. Our luck can't hold out forever."

Shin's statement was interrupted by a sickening crack of wood as the tree they were standing on pitched at an extreme angle. They both leaped from the branch they were on to the branches of the tree beside them. Below them, a demon was moving onto the tree they'd jumped too.

Corin took the decision out of her hands. He scrambled down the tree before the demon could push it over as well. Shin followed, and a moment later they were on the ground again.

The demon moved to give chase, but Shin whipped Harmony away, and the flying blade cut through one of the demon's legs. It roared and scrambled toward them, hopping after them on its one good leg. Shin was about to throw Harmony again when Corin grabbed her arm. "No time, Shin. We've got to get out of here before another one of those things finds us."

Shin fought the urge to deliver a killing blow for a moment before allowing herself to be pulled away. Corin took off through the woods. Shin followed, but soon found herself struggling to keep up. At full speed, at night, any misstep would trip them. Any poor angle could run them into a waiting tree. But every movement Corin made was the right one. He bounded through the trees like a deer, and Shin couldn't quite keep up.

Thankfully, the trees began to thin. Somehow, Corin ran even faster as the spaces between the trees widened. Shin's ears strained to hear any sound of pursuit and she allowed herself a glimmer of hope as nothing but silence followed them.

Then Corin stopped, and Shin didn't understand why. Before she could ask, he was pulling her to the ground. A streak of crimson flared in the space where Shin had just been standing.

Corin reached his feet first, in plenty of time to meet the summoner as he strode from the woods. The crimson great sword returned to his hand, and he and Corin dueled. Shin got to her own feet as Corin expertly blocked the summoner's clumsy attempts with the great sword. Of the two fighters, Corin was by far the better trained.

The summoner wasn't concerned, and when he struck again, Shin understood. The crimson sword shattered Corin's blades and threw him backward.

Shin stepped in to protect Corin while he recovered, deflecting a blow with Harmony. Shin attacked, carving complex patterns in the air that forced the summoner to give ground. She'd make him taste her steel and get revenge for her fallen soldiers.

"He's buying time!" Corin called out.

With a start, she realized Corin was right. The

summoner wasn't just giving ground because he feared her weapon. He wasn't even attempting to counter her. She halted her own advance and realized the summoner was flaring his sacrifice, calling for aid.

"Go!" Shin called out and turned to run.

As she did, she saw the summoner strike at her. She ducked, and the great sword went flying over her head. It stopped in mid-air and hung there, blocking her path to the boat.

Panic pounded in Shin's chest as she imagined the hoard of demons descending upon them. She turned back to the summoner and was forced to dodge as the great sword returned to his hand. For the first time, she knew what it was like to have to fight against her own skill with Harmony.

It was damned annoying, was what it was.

*He's no match for what you really are.*

The voice spoke true. Shin readied a sacrifice.

Then Corin was beside her. The broken swords in his hands might as well have been daggers, but his attack against the summoner was fearless.

Corin beautifully blocked a blow and stepped into what would have been the perfect distance for a killing cut if his swords hadn't been broken. Without hesitating, he took the extra step needed. The summoner brought his sword back around. Corin raised one broken sword to stop it, but the great sword still cut into his shoulder.

Screaming, Corin drove his other broken blade into the summoner's face. The crimson blade winked out, and the summoner twitched once before falling to the ground. Corin let go of his ruined swords and clutched his wounded shoulder.

"Let's get out of here," Shin said.

Corin grimaced in pain, but nodded and followed after her. Shin heard the demons' reckless pursuit through the trees behind them but wouldn't let herself turn to look lest it slow her down. With every step, she imagined a demon's claws tearing through the flesh on her back. All they could do was run, as fast as their tired legs would carry them.

They reached the coastline, the demons not far behind.

Corin pulled ahead of her. Shin had imagined they would climb down the cliff face, but forgot that Corin's wounded shoulder wouldn't allow for a controlled climb down. Corin, though, already had a solution. When he reached the edge of the cliff, he jumped.

With absolute trust in her friend, she squeezed the last bit of strength into her legs and leaped. She was falling into the darkness, and then her feet smacked into the water. She sank like a stone, and though she kicked with all her strength, she didn't know if she was rising or not.

She broke the surface and gasped for air. On the cliff side above them were two Maraman demons, casting about in frustrated rage.

Corin bobbed beside her, and when their eyes met, they started swimming toward the boat. Shin risked another glance up. More demon forms were silhouetted against the night sky, but nobody pursued them. For now, they were safe, and her thoughts already turned toward the concise scouting report she'd deliver to Sato.

They were fucked.

# 11

Beast crouched low in one of the huts that circled the middle of town. Beside him, Colas ground her teeth and tried to look everywhere at once. The family of locals that Beast had dragged into the hut with him huddled fearfully in the corner.

"I still don't like it," Colas said. "They know we're here and as soon as they see the village empty, they'll know it's an ambush."

"It won't matter to them. As near as I've been able to tell, most Maramans are arrogant fucks. These aren't the sick and starving sailors we stole the juggernaut from. I doubt this batch has lost a fight in a long time."

"You aren't making me feel any better."

"My point is, they're going to charge in because they think they don't have anything to worry about. They're going to be complacent."

Colas didn't look convinced but let the issue drop. Not like there was much she could do about it, anyway. Beast had already corralled all the villagers in their homes, and they were ready for a fight. Colas had left enough sailors behind to crew the juggernaut in case any Maraman ships showed up. They couldn't repel an attack, but they should be able to retreat long enough for Beast and the rest to come to their aid.

If they survived this fight.

Beast was confident, but that meant little. He woke up every morning convinced he was the strongest warrior that had ever been born.

Not only did they have his skills at their disposal, but they were also set up in a defensible position and had some element of surprise on their side. Their fighting force had split up and occupied the small homes closest to the to the village center. Archers lay prone on the roofs, hidden amongst the thatch. If the Maramans entered the village, as Beast expected they would, they'd be walking into an ambush more dangerous than they'd probably ever seen on these islands.

"Are Vala and her unit in position?" Beast asked.

"They are, but I don't love that either. Just because she's been training our crew doesn't make them as strong as the sin."

"We probably won't even need them," Beast assured Colas. "But it's good to have support, just in case."

Then they came, just as Beast had predicted. They came in a column, running toward the village with a confident pace. He watched them approach, and his focus was drawn toward a particularly large Maraman in the lead. He stood a head taller than anyone else and his skin was painted entirely black.

"That one's mine," Beast growled.

"Obviously," Colas answered.

Beast waited, the anticipation almost too much to bear. Just as the Maramans were about to enter the center of the village, their leader's ink-black eyes snapped up towards one of the roofs. He barked a series of orders. The Maramans halted.

"Fuck," Beast said. He burst out of the hut. "Fire!" he shouted.

His crew reacted at a moment's notice. The short bows, designed to repel boarders, were devastating at the close ranges found within the village.

Unfortunately, they'd lost the key element of surprise, and the archers were easy targets for the Maramans' giant spears. Beast had told them to break off the ambush as soon as their positions were compromised, and that moment happened after only a single volley. They scrambled down from the roof tops as spears punched into the thatch.

"That didn't go well," Colas said.

"More for me to kill." The sentiment was true, but Beast had anticipated more dead Maramans before the fighting started in earnest.

He'd just have to double his efforts.

Beast raised his fist and a horn sounded. His crew poured out of the huts and attacked the Maramans. Unfortunately, because they had halted their march and the archers had attacked early, too few of the Maramans were surrounded by the huts. And even fewer were surprised.

What should have been a heavily reduced force of Maramans was far more intact than Beast had anticipated.

He gripped his giant axe and joined the fray.

The world faded away into a haze of blood and violence. Beast's weapon became one with his body, moving with his arms. The world slowed down so that Beast could do the work that he did best.

Deal out death.

Every strike led him towards the giant Maraman who

commanded their forces. The universe seemed to be weaving a tapestry that brought Beast closer to his target with each stitch. He grinned ferociously as he buried his axe in the skull of a Maraman that stood between him the giant.

"Beast!" A hand on his arm pulled him out of his trance.

"We're pushing them back, but they've got more forces in the trees. Give the order for Vala's unit," Colas said.

Beast looked around and realized he hadn't been paying any attention to the larger battle. There was a path of destruction in his wake, but outside of that, the battle had been a stalemate.

He raised his fist and made a sign. This time, two peals of the horn rang out. His crew, well-drilled on formations by Colas, shifted tactics and retreated towards the village. The Maramans pressed their advantage, but their commander gave orders of his own. The battle became a more cautious, balanced affair.

Beast fought to hold their line. As cautious as the Maramans were being now, once they realized there was no additional ambush waiting in the village, they would use the momentum that they'd gained to crush Beast's crew.

Red once again seeped into the corners of his vision, and Beast turned towards the commander.

Once again, Colas stopped him with a hand on his arm.

"You can't, Beast. You're what's holding this line. If you break formation, we'll fall apart."

Beast growled as he watched the Maraman commander give orders. The man stood with impunity, just beyond the range that Beast trusted himself to throw his axe. "Fine."

Beast's patience was rewarded as the Maramans turned to face an unseen enemy. Vala and her unit had moved through the trees, killing unsuspecting Maramans as they went. Now, they moved through the Maramans' rear guard like murderous shadows.

As the Maraman formation sagged under the pressure of a seemingly invisible enemy, the villagers that had been hiding in the huts burst forward armed with whatever they could find. For a moment, Beast was worried that they were going to aid the Maramans, but instead they swarmed their former masters.

That hadn't been part of the plan. But it lit a fire in his chest no amount of water would put out.

Beast roared and ordered his forces forward. He tried to fight his way to the commander, but before he could get there, he watched the painted man grimace and fall to a blade that appeared out of the crowd and disappeared just as quickly.

Beast raged, scouring the battlefield with his gaze, searching for another worthwhile enemy. That was when he realized that the last of the Maramans were falling. The battle wasn't quite over, but against all odds, they'd won the day. He stood up straight and forcefully slowed his breathing.

"Could have been worse," Colas said.

"I wanted to kill the big one," Beast grunted.

"The important thing is he got killed. You, however, need to pay more attention to the battlefield if you're going to be the one issuing the orders. You can't just wade in and kill everything that moves by yourself."

Beast considered Colas for a moment and then grinned. "But that's what I'm best at."

Colas rolled her eyes.

"For what it's worth, I vote Beast stays on the front lines," Gorou said. He approached from another part of the battlefield, covered from head to toe in the blood of his enemies. "What do we do about them?"

Beast turned and looked at the villagers. They were grinning and chatting to each other as they kicked at and danced on the dead Maramans. When they noticed him looking, they suddenly quieted down. One of them ran to the Maraman commander and picked up, as best he could, the man's giant weapon. He half carried, half dragged it over to Beast and presented it to him, dropping to one knee. The rest of the villagers followed suit.

Beast took the great axe in his hand and admired the craftsmanship. He spun it once and then looked at the villagers, all kneeling before him.

"Let's see if they can get that throne onto the juggernaut."

# 12

"Is everything all right, Sato?" Yuki asked.

Sato looked up and realized his jaw was clenched shut. The memory of the Maraman waving casually to him was stuck in his mind. "I'm fine. You said Shin would be along presently?"

"Yes. They've returned to Versun but wanted to change into some dry clothes before they delivered their report."

*They*, of course meant Shin and Corin. The two were inseparable. Sato respected Shin's choice in a second, though. Despite the insolence he'd shown in their last meeting, in another life the lad would have made an excellent sentinel. Sato would still take him on as a Sun Stalker if given the chance. The boy reminded him of Crispin. Rough around the edges, but willing to learn and change. Though, if he did become a Sun Stalker, Sato would have to show him the error of trying to master a two-sword style.

As if summoned by his thoughts, Shin and Corin entered the room, still looking like drowned rats despite their dry clothes. Shin gave a quick nod to Yuki and fixed

Sato with her customary glare, reserved, it seemed, for him alone.

Corin looked from Shin to Sato expectantly, then shook his head and sighed. "Niesa and Arvo were killed on our scouting expedition. I wanted to let you know personally before you read it in a report."

See, he was trainable. And unlike Shin, Corin still aspired to basic decency. "Thank you, Corin. Their skill as scouts was well known. I'll be sure to write their families personally."

Corin gave Sato a small bow.

"What else do you have to report?" Sato asked.

"We're fucked," Shin said.

Sato raised an eyebrow. "Care to elaborate?"

Shin rolled her eyes and Sato found he was clenching his jaw once more. Despite her attitude she gave a concise report. Few among his Sun Stalkers would have done better. He had only a few clarifying questions, and those were answered with short, but complete, answers.

The two survivors painted a grim scene.

"Did you see any Maramans that were larger the than the others? Or anyone covered in black ink?" Sato asked.

Shin said, "No. The summoners were commanding the demons. Otherwise we saw nothing more than your average Maraman."

"What are you thinking?" Yuki asked.

"The Maraman that brought the demons to the shores of Egzuki was no summoner. I didn't catch even a whiff of sacrifice about him. They're frightening bastards, I'll give them that much. I'm wondering what, exactly, they are, and how many of them there might be."

"Good questions. And ones we don't know the answers

to." Yuki's gaze was fierce. "There's still too much we don't know."

"We can guess at their strategy, though," Sato said.

"How could you possibly do that?" Corin asked.

Sato grimaced. So much potential, hidden behind such a rough upbringing. Still, the disrespect coming from Corin was more annoying than angering. He answered slowly, as though Corin was a child. "I'm almost certain their plan is to soften us up with the feral demons they've taken control of. We can expect wave after wave of them. It's the natural conclusion of their plan to tear open the rifts after their failed attack last year."

"How can you be certain?" Shin asked.

"Because it's exactly what I would do. Why waste your forces when you can send expendable demons to wear us down?"

"But we're ready for the demons now," Corin interjected. "We trained all year for them."

Sato continued his patient explanation. "We're more prepared than we were, but you're no fool. They'll wear us down just like they planned, and there's not much we can do to fight back. We don't have the forces to take Iru back, even if we used every sin and sentinel on all the islands."

"See, we're fucked," Shin stated.

Sato forced himself to remain calm. As much as he wanted to straighten the young woman out, there was nothing he could do. He'd have better luck trying to conquer Iru single-handedly.

"Not yet," Yuki said. "And watch your tongue. Your crude language has no place here."

The sin leader turned to Sato. "You agree, then, that the feral demons represent the greatest threat?"

Sato considered for a moment, then nodded. "If we kill a

Maraman, they're dead for good. If we kill a demon, it can just return."

Shin surprised him with a contribution. “What if we cut the emperor off from the realm? What if we could prevent him from calling more demons?”

Yuki’s face was hard to read at the best of times, but Sato swore he saw the trace of a smile on her face as Shin finally engaged in a conversation about sacrifice.

Better late than never, Sato supposed. Shin was supposed to be the one who could stand against the emperor.

“A dangerous proposition, child,” Yuki said.

“But not impossible. When I was constructing the sacrifice needed to close the rifts I saw the scaffolding they were built on. There’s a way to cut this world off from the realm, isn’t there?”

“There is, but the risk is incredible,” Yuki said.

“Why?”

"Because to cut the worlds apart requires a trip into the realm, and even if that impossible task is completed, no one can know what will happen. That sacrifice has never been attempted. For all we know, it might destroy both worlds."

That threat was sufficient to silence the discussion for more than a minute.

Yuki spoke again. "I do not think we will need to take such drastic measures. At least not yet. I have been considering the problem of the demons since the emperor took control of them, and I believe I may be able to remove them from Iru. Maybe.”

“All of them?" Sato couldn't keep this disbelief out of his voice. "Why didn't you tell us earlier?"

Yuki shook her head. “Not all of them. Just the ones that the emperor took control of. And I didn't tell you because I only recently stumbled upon the solution. It's by no means certain, and it will require Shin to complete her training."

Every eye in the room turned to Shin, who looked like she wanted to run away, the same as she always did.

Sato detested this about the girl. There was only one correct decision. And yet she dared to stand among the leaders of this land, looking like an animal caught in a snare. Sato could guess well enough the guilt that tore at her. He knew what she had tried to do with the rifts and how it had played a role in the loss of Iru.

Now Yuki offered her a chance at redemption. A chance to make good on all the promises she'd made.

Anyone else would have spoken without a moment's hesitation.

But she stood there, no answer forthcoming.

She was a coward.

Sato stepped toward her. It was time to end this charade once and for all. Samas demanded an answer. "What will it be, Shin? Will you help us or not?"

# 13

The question felt as though Sato had taken a pile of dead bodies and piled them on Shin's chest. She fought for air, but her lungs refused to expand.

This was the moment she had dreaded since she had first realized what destruction her sacrifice had wrought on Iru. The moment when there was no place left to hide from her abilities.

She had hated Sato from the first time she had laid eyes on him in the magistrate's cells underneath Dahl. That hate had ebbed and flowed, but it had never been stronger than it was right now. Childish as the reaction was, all she wanted was to reach out and choke the life from his stiff neck.

She settled for fixing him with a glare that she imagined could strip the stain off a plank of wood.

Rather than let him stoke her anger, she focused her attention on Yuki. "You act as though I didn't doom us all the last time I used sacrifice."

Sato looked as though he was about to snap an angry comment her way, but Yuki held up a hand. "There's nowhere left to run, Shin. I gave you the time I did because I can guess at the guilt that consumes you. And if I had a choice, I would lift this burden from you. But all I can do is offer you a chance to atone. To save the lives of those who remain."

"Lives that wouldn't be in danger if I hadn't used sacrifice in the first place."

Sato interrupted before Yuki could respond. His voice was a snarl. "You talk so much about helping the people of Samas. Ever since I've met you, you've done nothing but remind me how the sentinels have failed in that duty. But now, when asked to protect the people you claim to represent, you wallow in indecision. It's sickening."

Oh, what she'd do to get her hands around his throat. "You want me to just ignore the mistakes I've made? To pretend like my hands aren't covered in blood? That's a very sentinel way of thinking, Sato."

"No, you foolish girl! You take responsibility for your mistake and then move on. You do your duty. Like an adult."

Shin stepped toward Sato, ready to end this disagreement between them once and for all.

Corin's voice was barely louder than a whisper, but it froze her in place. "Shin. Please stop."

His simple request broke down all the walls she'd built around her heart. She swallowed the lump that suddenly formed in her throat. Then she tore her attention from Sato to look at Yuki. "Why? Why do you need *me*? If you know the sacrifice to remove the feral demons from Samas, why don't you just do it?"

Her voice sounded childish, even to her ears. But she couldn't stop herself. Yuki and Sato looked to her as though she was the answer to all her problems. But she was just a farmer who'd once had delusions of becoming something more. Why didn't they see that?

"I'm going to," Yuki said quietly.

Shin blinked rapidly, certain that she'd misheard. "What?"

"I am going to be the one who makes the sacrifice to remove the feral demons. Honestly, I think I might be the only one who can," Yuki said.

"What about all those times you told me that you can't use sacrifice anymore?" Shin couldn't follow Yuki's thoughts.

Yuki looked like she had expected the objection. "I spoke true. This will be my last sacrifice. Once it's complete, you'll have to cut me off from the realm completely. You will become the leader of the sin"

"Excuse me?" Sato said, his jaw hanging open. "What?"

For once, Shin found herself in complete agreement with the sentinel general.

Yuki looked between the two of them, then leaned back in her chair. The older woman's posture made Shin realize how tense the argument had made her, and she forced herself to relax and lean back, too. At the very least, Yuki's wild statements had pulled all the fight out of the room. Everyone's attention was on the mysterious sin leader.

Sato still sat on the edge of his seat, and he didn't seem pleased that Yuki hadn't answered his question. He rephrased them. "Why would you let take her your place? Sacrifice or not, you're still a leader. Shin is a soldier, at best."

The way he emphasized their roles made it clear which of the two of them he valued more highly.

Not that the information came as any surprise to Shin. By the sun, even she valued Yuki's strength more than her own. She'd be a fool not to.

Yuki considered the two of them for a moment, then nodded. "I suppose it's worth an explanation."

She turned to Shin. "You remember my concern about your giving up memories to power sacrifice?"

Shin did, although she didn't understand where Yuki's question led. "Of course. I was losing myself and didn't even realize it."

The older woman's question dug up parts of Shin's recent past that she'd prefer would remain buried. At the time, giving up important memories of her past had seemed a small price to pay for the power she gained. But giving up those memories had changed her in ways she was still struggling to understand.

She looked over to Corin, whose expression was unreadable. Her first sacrifice had been to give up the memories of Mateo, a young man who had meant the world to both of them. It was a wound that had scabbed over, and Shin feared Yuki was picking at that scab, threatening to reopen the rift between Shin and her closest friend.

But Yuki took a different path. "When faced with a similar option, I did not. I created a deal with the realm. A one-time sacrifice that allowed me to wield sacrifice with seeming impunity. At the time I thought I was very clever."

"What deal did you make?" Shin asked.

"I crafted a sacrifice wherein I suggested to the realm that instead of requiring a new sacrifice each time I wanted to use the realm for my purposes, that it could take a small piece of my emotions. Happiness, sadness, anger, joy, all the things, I realized too late, that make you human. My demeanor is not some practiced mask that I present to the world. It is what is left of my humanity. Every day I have to remind myself how to be a human being. I suppose others might find it tragic, but..."

"But you can't," Shin finished.

The weight of it hit her like a blow to the body.

To think she'd once thought the older woman ignorant of her problems. If anyone understood what Shin endured thanks to her sacrifices, it was Yuki. The realization jolted her out of the patterns of thinking she'd settled into over the last few months. She looked at Yuki with new eyes. "You should have told me earlier."

Sato interrupted before Yuki could respond. "So what?"

Both women shot him glares that bounced off his ignorance.

"You had to give up some emotions for incredible power! Who cares? Are you worried that if you cleanse the world of feral demons, you'll give up your one last shred of emotion?" Sato looked like he was close to tearing out his hair in frustration.

Now Shin wasn't the only one who appeared ready to choke the life out of the sentinel commander. But Yuki remained relaxed in her chair. "You don't understand, Sato, and I hope that you'll never have to. I've studied sacrifice for longer than anyone else has been alive, but I still feel that my understanding is incomplete. For elites like me and Shin, it's an agreement, a compromise between us and the realm. But no matter how clever we think we are when we strike our bargains, the realm always gets what it wants. It shapes us, even as we think we control it. Shin knows this well. She believed memories a small price to pay, but the loss of those memories changed the way she thought. They led her to making the choice that ripped the rift wide open on Iru. As always, the realm came out the victor in the exchange. The same, I'm sure, is true of me." Yuki's eyes drifted to the window, and Shin wondered what it was her mentor was thinking about.

Yuki returned her attention to the others. "I can't say for sure what will happen when I give up the last shred of my humanity,but I would not be surprised to see myself turned into some sort of puppet for the realm. That can't be allowed to happen. Thus, Shin must cut off my connection before I can become a danger to Samas."

"Isn't there someone else? Someone better suited to lead?" Shin asked

Yuki shook her head. "You can do this, Shin. You alone have the same capacity for sacrifice that I do, but you need to learn the rest of what I have to teach you because after this, my power will be gone, and you'll be the only one left to stand against the Maraman emperor."

Shin gulped, and the weight of her fears pressed once again against her chest, as though they'd just been waiting for her to forget about them for a moment. Didn't Yuki understand? She *couldn't* take Yuki's place. She wasn't strong enough. Or clever enough. She'd thought she was, and it had destroyed *Bulas*, the strongest city in Samas. The Firstborn had been forced to flee from his palace, because of her!

"I...I'm sorry, but I can't." Shin said. She stared down at her feet.

"There is no other choice, Shin," Yuki said. "I've spent the last year thinking about almost nothing else. If you can't wield sacrifice, we lose."

"I think if I use any more sacrifice, we'll lose anyway," she answered. She remembered the demons crawling over the walls of Bulas, hungry for the pain and suffering of those still trapped inside.

Because of her.

Corin rescued her from drowning in her memories. His voice was as strong as his swords, and it was pointed at Yuki. "Can you promise Shin that she'll be able to avoid the same mistakes?"

Yuki glared at the young swordsman. “No. I can only promise her to teach her everything I know. It will be up to her to use that knowledge well.”

Corin considered the answer for a moment, then stood up. His sudden motion drew every eye, and he walked deliberately around the table until he was standing beside Shin. Shin turned her chair so she could see him. He stood over her like this, and it made her realize once again just how strong he’d become.

He kneeled before her, then bowed, his forehead pressed all the way to the cold stone of the floor. “I know you’re scared, Shin. But please, do this for all of us. Do it for the luan, and for the farmers you know on Ilos. Do it for me.”

Corin raised himself up and took her right hand in his own hands, their callouses scraping against one another. His hands were unbelievably warm, but most of her attention was on his gaze. He stared at her with an intensity that made her want to hide. “I trust you, Shin.”

By the sun, she trusted him, too, but the words didn’t reach her lips. For over a year now, he had been her guide, even if he didn’t know it. His words unearthed other memories. Of the luan laughing on the beach of the sin island. Of farmers, wiping the sweat from their brows as they tilled their fields.

Those thoughts clashed with those of the demon hordes waiting on Iru.

Iru had terrified her. Not just because of the demons, but because of the knowledge she’d had some role in what happened there.

But Corin had been by her side the whole time, and he still trusted her.

She thought of their final sprint on Iru. Their jump from the cliff.

She swallowed hard and turned to Yuki. This leap was even more terrifying. But Corin's hand was in her own, just like before. She nodded. "I'll resume my training."

"Good," Yuki said.

Corin looked like he was about to tear up, but Sato was less impressed. He'd been watching the exchange with a critical eye. "You all are forgetting another option, which seems far superior," he said.

"What's that?" Yuki asked.

Sato jabbed his thumb at Shin. "Now that she's willing to train, teach her how to send the demons back. Then we still have your powers in reserve. Maybe we'll even have both of you."

Yuki shook her head. "I don't think it will work. I'm the only one who can complete this particular sacrifice."

Sato wasn't buying it. "Why?"

Yuki fixed him with an icy stare. "Because I'm the one who created the demons in the first place."

# 14

"Another!" Beast shouted as he held up his tankard.

A cheer rose from the throats of his crew, and Beast revelled in the adulation. Colas sat at his side, doing her best to look dour despite the celebration. Gorou, five cups deep, was off in the crowd, and Vala studied the islanders with a curious expression on her face. Beast sighed. Even Benji had been more fun.

"Have you two ever enjoyed yourselves?" Beast asked as a particularly attentive young man from the island filled his cup once more. He would have been much more annoyed at the behavior of his closest friends if it weren't for the two women dancing to a complex drumbeat in the corner of his vision. The celebration wasn't just for Beast and his crew, but for those who called this island home, too. Beast considered trying to introduce himself, but the language barrier made boasting difficult.

"I just think we haven't given enough thought to what comes next. We took over a Maraman stronghold. There are bound to be consequences," Colas said.

"Liberated a Maraman stronghold, Colas. Look around. We're in the business of freeing people. Not ruling them."

"Aren't you sitting on a throne being served drinks by these newly free people?" Vala asked.

"The chair I'm keeping. Spoils of battle. As for the service, we never demanded it. Who am I to say no to hospitality? This young man, in particular, is exemplary. Maybe I'll offer to take him with me and show him the world." Beast smiled and gestured at the islander who had just filled his cup, but the man only smiled back uncomprehendingly.

"As a servant?" Vala pressed.

"No! As a... well, maybe an apprentice? He could learn the ropes of battle and leadership from a master."

Colas wouldn't let go of her concern. "I know you're having fun, but we need to think about what's next—"

Beast held up his hands for silence. "Please. We killed Maramans. We found ale. Even better, Peter says he found the ingredients for both ale and mead, so he can finally be of some use."

"You mean aside from navigating?" Colas asked.

"He's our brewmaster, Colas. We shouldn't be wasting his talents on trivial things."

Colas rolled her eyes so hard Beast was worried she was going to hurt herself. He tried a different tack. "Come on, Colas. Can't you just enjoy the win, for one night?"

She surrendered, as Beast knew she would. "Fine, but tomorrow we have a real discussion about our next moves."

Beast was a magnanimous victor. "As you wish."

He was right, of course. Celebrating amongst his warriors at the conclusion of a great victory was the best life could get. The only experience greater than battle was the rush that came after surviving it.

Yet, if he spent a moment to consider his feelings, something *was* off. At first, he'd attributed the feeling to the lack of his compatriot's enthusiasm. But that wasn't it. Not quite. Beast finished his ale as an odd silence came over him. His thoughts faded as he let the experience carry him away.

It lacked something vital, like ale that hadn't been spiced with hops.

He blinked and shook his head. He turned to talk to Vala, but found that she was still staring at the islanders. "What's your problem?"

"Nothing worth talking about. We can discuss it tomorrow."

This night was not turning out the way Beast thought it should. "You can't just leave me curious. Now you have to tell me."

"I'm concerned you're not paying enough attention to the people you just fought for. Have you seen any of the weapons they've made?"

"I didn't do an inspection, no."

"The craftsmanship is good. As good as most of what's produced in Samas. It's a different culture here, but they're capable of incredible designs. I can see why the Maramans wanted to control this land instead of simply destroying it like they did the other islands."

A spark of anger flared in Beast's chest. "So you're saying we can use them somehow? I'm not like Yuki, Vala. People aren't tools for us to use at our convenience. I didn't fight to free them just to enslave them again."

Vala shot him an angry glare. "Come on, Beast. You have to know that wasn't what I meant. I'm saying that perhaps they could be valuable allies. They could be a lot more than just 'the people we freed that one day.'"

Beast considered Vala's proposal and found it immediately appealing. Truthfully, his thoughts had been so focused on the Maramans, he hadn't thought much about the islanders. He wished them well, but they weren't weighing much on his mind. Beast assumed they'd been fine before the Maramans had shown up and they'd be fine after Beast and his crew left.

But Vala was right. They had lost more than a few mugon in their attack on the Maramans. Shoring up their numbers would be a good idea. It wouldn't be that much different than recruiting various bandit groups into his mugon back on Samas. "How do you propose we suggest that to them? We don't even speak the same language."

Vala was about to answer, but was interrupted by an unexpected visitor.

"If I may, Admiral Beast, perhaps I could be of use in that area?"

Beast's jaw hung open for a moment as he stared at the young villager that had appeared out of nowhere in front of him. He was dressed in one of the loincloths that the islanders favored and held a jug of ale in one hand. Though likely no more than twenty, there was something about his eyes that made Beast think of a far more experienced man.

"You speak our tongue?" Beast growled.

"Fluently. The Maramans taught it to me, and a few others inclined towards language. Translation is a valuable skill."

Beast blinked. "How did the Maramans teach you our language?"

"They aren't all warriors. Most in positions of high authority speak at least a little Samasian. Most of the summoners are fluent, as well."

"And why would they teach *you*?"

"As I mentioned before, the need for translation is great. I can't speak to their grand intent, though. They didn't see fit to share that with us."

This changed everything, and this young man was about to become one of Beast's new best friends. "What's your name, son?"

"Keff."

"Well, Keff, it seems you have a nose for gathering information. Judging by the fact that you figured out the best way to linger around me and my captains and listen in on our conversations, I'm willing to bet you were able to gather all kinds of interesting facts about the Maramans. So, I don't believe for a moment you don't even have a guess as to why you speak our language."

Keff smiled appraisingly at Beast. "You're not quite as much a fool as you look. I spoke true, though. I do not know exactly why they taught us your language. If you forced me to guess, it is because their summoners and administrators are obsessed with the acquisition of knowledge. Translators are as valuable in that endeavor as smiths are in equipping their warriors with axes and swords."

Beast considered that piece of information, but there was little for him to do with it at the moment. He had more pressing problems, and he could just imagine Colas smirking as he was forced to think about their next steps here. "Do you think your people would be willing to help us resupply our ship?"

"I can bring it to the elders. I believe they will want to show their gratitude for your help in liberating us from the Maramans."

"Good. Please take the request to them. And please, make sure your people know that my crew does not expect to be waited on. We've appreciated your kindness, but it isn't necessary. We wish to celebrate with you, more than anything else."

Keff bowed slightly and vanished among the crowd.

Beast took another long sip of his ale, and it tasted better than it ever had before.

# 15

Sato sat in his office and tried to focus on Crispin's report. But every few sentences his attention drifted down to the sturdy feeling of the chair against his spine and the back of his legs. He worried that if he didn't keep his mind tethered to the physical reality of sitting at his desk, he, and everything else in the room, might float away and disappear into nothing. Never before had his grasp on reality seemed so tenuous.

"Sir?" Crispin asked.

It took Sato another full moment to realize his lieutenants must have been staring at him for a while, waiting for his response. Sato cast back in his memories to piece together the last question Crispin had put forward. Though the moment had only been a few seconds ago, he felt as though he was searching for something small in a dark room.

Then he remembered. Crispin had wanted to tighten up the patrol schedule since the ferals had landed. That decision was easy enough, and one Crispin probably could have made on his own. "Very good. Make it happen."

He tried to sound as though he'd been deep in thought, but the skeptical looks from his lieutenants told him he hadn't been successful.

Sato tamped down a flicker of anger. "Please continue. What's next?"

"Alonzo's report, sir." Crispin handed him a sheet of paper.

Sato skimmed the document, grateful for Alonzo's brevity. The report confirmed most of what Shin had told him at last night's meeting, but he noticed that it ended when the party went ashore and picked up again when they returned. "You remained on the ship?"

Alonzo nodded.

"Why?" Sato pressed.

Alonzo shrugged again and made gestures that Sato recognized as orders and commanding officer.

Sato scoffed. "Since when do you listen to orders?"

Alonzo grinned and made a series of more complex gestures that Sato couldn't follow as well.

"He says he always listens to sensible ones, sir," Crispin said, barely keeping his amusement out of his voice.

Anger threatened to flair again, but Sato knew it was misplaced. Alonzo was a uniquely talented sentinel, but he wasn't a scout. If the decision had been to send a smaller party, a decision Sato would have made himself, there was no reason for Alonzo to set foot on the island. That his report matched with Shin's up to the point they separated was heartening. As for what happened on Iru, well, he'd just have to trust the sin.

A proposition that stoked the kindling of his anger to a low smolder.

"Good work Alonzo. Crispin, continue." Sato leaned back in his chair and took a calming breath.

Crispin sighed, as though injured. "We followed your orders and launched a quiet investigation into sentinel misbehavior. Among the units most loyal to you, gambling remains minimal. Dice and cards are frequently played amongst units during down time. Not sure if it's your orders, or more reflective of how busy everyone is preparing for the invasion, but I'm sad to say discipline is better than I've ever seen it. There was a small problem where Desmond was trying to get a larger operation off the ground, but we shut it down."

Sato tried to focus on Crispin's report, but his mind kept returning to Yuki admitting to creating those abominations that had overrun the seat of power in Samas. She had claimed it was to stop the Maraman threat back when Samas was a fledgling nation and the sentinels were just formed. The implications of which, frankly, made Sato's mind reel.

Just how old was Yuki? The sentinels traced their history back almost two hundred years. And by the sun, he believed her when she said she was there, by the side of the founding Firstborn.

He focused again on his chair. It was solid, as was he.

The tactical part of Sato's mind snapped back into action, and he forced himself to deal with the problem at hand. If Yuki could create the demons, what else was she capable of? And how much did he dare trust a woman who would create demons?

If he had another option, he would have jumped at it. But the only other adept was Shin, and she was a mess of incredible proportions. At least he trusted that Yuki would always act in her own self-interest. He couldn't even make that basic claim about Shin. She was more unpredictable than a spring storm.

He believed that they believed they were trying to help. But they lacked discipline. They lacked the guidance of the Path. They had forsaken the sun, and because of that, no matter what they tried, it was doomed to failure. Yuki might have created the demons to protect Samas from the Maramans, but then she'd spent countless lives over countless years forced to protect Samas from her own damned mistake.

This wouldn't end any better, but Sato's hands were tied.

All because the Firstborn had allied himself with these sin. Like them, he was willing to sacrifice the sun in a short-sighted attempt to protect his people.

Sato gritted his teeth and ignored the small, distant voice reminding him that he, too, had allied himself with Yuki and the sin. Before he'd even known the Firstborn had done the same.

"Benson and three other sentinels have been seen skimming goods from the supply line. We have their location and—"

"Benson?" Sato asked, the name capturing his attention. He felt the flames of his anger truly catch.

"Yes sir, he—"

"I arrested Benson two weeks ago. He was awaiting sentencing," Sato said icily.

Crispin shuffled his feet nervously. "Yes, sir. The Firstborn found out and offered him—"

"Clemency?" Sato said quietly.

"Well—"

"Fucking clemency!" Sato roared. Both his lieutenants flinched backward. They both had the good sense to remain silent.

His veins felt like someone had lit them on fire. Anyone could see that the sentinel order here in Versun, which was most of the order left in Samas, was slowly returning to the Path they had wandered from so long ago. With just a little more time, they'd be ready for the most difficult fight of their lives.

He understood that some degree of flexibility was necessary. Crispin had taught him that lesson, and he swore he'd never forget it. But that didn't mean abandoning the Path completely. He'd arrested Benson because his first offenses were egregious enough the man needed to be made an example of.

There was no excuse for clemency. It was no better than abandoning the Path completely, and that was something he would never do, even if the Firstborn already had.

He knew Benson had connections to magistrates. None of that mattered.

The decision came easy.

"Get Roko. We're going to pay Benson a visit," Sato ordered. "If the Firstborn won't administer justice, we will."

Crispin and Alonzo glanced at one another, but they bowed and left the room to find Roko.

Crispin led them to a nondescript building in the port district. Benson was one of numerous sentinels who had been charged with supervising the flow of supplies entering and leaving Versun. Now, more than ever before, the role was vital to Samas' well-being. They had a winter to endure and an invader to destroy. Too many people were packed into too small a space. Distributing food, shelter, and basic necessities could very well mean the difference between victory and defeat.

Corruption was always present in a supply chain. Some

supplies always went missing, and it was too easy for those "missing" supplies to end up in the hands of those that supervised the supply chains. Sato had always punished any sentinel guilty of the practice under his command, but he was well aware other commanders turned a blind eye, so long as the supplies they needed were delivered promptly.

Sato didn't agree, but he could understand.

Smuggling anything from the supply chain, now, though, was unforgivable. Lives hung in the balance.

The building ahead of them wasn't that large, but Crispin reported that Benson had moved in and made it his own little castle. Sato hadn't brought enough forces for a siege, but they would be more than sufficient to bring this edifice down.

He gestured to Roko, and the sentinel kicked the door open. Roko and Alonzo entered first, swords drawn, and Crispin followed with Sato, a dagger in his good hand. He wasn't as dangerous as he'd once been, but Sato had watched him practicing. Crispin wasn't one to be underestimated.

"Halt!" Roko bellowed.

Three surprised sentinels turned to look at them. Sato recognized Benson right away. Tall, handsome and clean cut, he looked every inch the dutiful sentinel. He would look just as comfortable in one of Izuki's famous balls as he did in the warehouse.

The only place Sato couldn't imagine him was on the battlefield.

"Benson, you stand accused of smuggling. How do you plead?" Sato asked.

Benson smiled smugly. "General Sato, there must be a misunderstanding. The First—"

Benson's smug smile was knocked off his face, along with a few teeth, by Sato's fist.

"I'll take that as an admission of guilt. I challenge you to a duel," Sato said.

Benson looked around the room for help. Sato didn't need to see his sentinels to know that they would offer no such service to the man. Sato's reputation was too well-known. "A duel, but you're—I can't—that's a death sentence!"

"Draw." Flames of anger licked at the ice in Sato's tone.

Benson looked around one more time and, resigned, drew his sword. The moment the blade was free Sato drew, knocked away a clumsy block, and ran his sword through the sentinel's heart.

The smell of blood filled the room and Sato turned to Benson's lackeys.

Crispin read Sato's intentions and opened his mouth to say something, but Roko, who had known Sato longer than almost anyone, laid a hand on Crispin's arm.

"Sentinel," Sato addressed the warrior who had been standing closest to Benson when he steeped in the room. "You stand accused of smuggling. How do you plead?"

The sentinel looked to his companion and then at Benson's blood, running down the edge of Sato's sword and pooling on the ground at his feet.

"Please..." the man stammered.

"Draw your sword." The flames of Sato's anger finally ignited into a bonfire, immolating any doubt that remained inside of him.

Versun was his city.

Samas was his nation.

# 16

"Very good, Shin. That's enough for now," Yuki said. Shin moved to get up, but Yuki placed a gentle hand on her shoulder. "Sit and rest. I'll bring some water."

"Thank you," Shin said, grateful to remain seated.

She stretched out her legs and leaned back on her palms. Since she'd fled her childhood home, it felt as though Shin had done nothing but learn new skills and then train them. Stealing, fighting, hiding, sacrifice, and so much more. She'd trained with Harmony until her arms felt like they would fall off. But through it all, nothing had been as intense as the last day spent under Yuki's demanding eye. Sweat soaked through her tunic and trousers.

All that and she hadn't moved once from her seated position. Now she wasn't sure she could even if she wanted to.

As it turned out, Yuki had been going easy on her up to this point. Judging by the sun hanging low in the sky and her growling stomach, the day was nearly done. They'd started just after breakfast and worked on one single skill for the entire day. Shin couldn't remember ever enduring anything like it.

"Corin was asking after you, so I sent him to bring us some food. You must be hungry," Yuki said, handing her a flagon of water that Shin accepted as though it were more valuable than a pot of gold.

"I'm starving. I feel as though I sparred with Hanz for the entire day."

"You sound surprised."

"A little. I wouldn't have thought sitting around *thinking* all day would be worse than a full day of walking stones."

"Your mind is a muscle like any other, although perhaps more important. Additionally, you were engaging in sacrifice, even if you didn't manifest anything, and that taxes your body, too. It's not to be taken lightly."

Shin looked down at her hands. "It doesn't feel like I was using sacrifice. All I did was begin the process of sealing the rifts. I never even touched the realm, just laid the groundwork for the sacrifice."

"And by the end, did you have to spend any effort thinking about it?"

Shin laughed. "Hardly! I think I could construct that sacrifice half asleep now."

"Then we shall work on it some more. You need to have the sacrifice ingrained so deeply in your memory you could do it without a single thought. You need to be able to do it in your sleep."

Shin looked at Yuki in shock. How could someone possibly command sacrifice without being conscious? It took her a few more moments to realize that her mentor wasn't serious. "Was that a joke?"

"Just because I can't laugh anymore doesn't mean I don't

understand what makes a good joke," Yuki said, completely deadpan.

Shin couldn't help but grin at the macabre comment. "Still think it's easier to tell a joke if you can laugh at someone else's."

"I disagree. I'm hilarious."

Shin shook her head and just barely managed not to roll her eyes. She wasn't sure what had gotten into Yuki, but it reminded her of their first times together, before Shin had known who Yuki actually was. "Are you sure you aren't possessed by some new kind of demon? I'm going to need you to make another joke when Corin gets here or he's never going to believe it happened."

Yuki leaned in and whispered, "I'll deny it to my dying breath."

Shin laughed, but the expression on Yuki's faced surprised her so much she stopped almost as soon as she'd started. "Yuki, is that your real smile?"

The older woman nodded. "It is. Every once in awhile I feel something. Usually, it's anger or fear that breaks through. It's been a long time since it's been something pleasant."

Shin struggled to find the appropriate response and eventually gave up. She was still struggling to understand how she felt about what Yuki had revealed during the meeting with Sato. "I don't know what to say."

"There's nothing to say. I should apologize, Shin. I should have shared my past with you long ago. I think it would have given us more time."

Shin accepted the apology. It was still easy to resent Yuki for the secrets and deceptions, but she'd reacted too strongly to Yuki's failures. Yuki was complex, and Shin had seen only the lies. "I didn't want to press you before, especially with Sato around, but if you created the demons..."

"Go ahead, you can ask," Yuki said, the echoes of the smile still on her lips.

"How old are you?"

"Old. Older than I can even remember, if I'm being honest. But I've seen over two hundred summers, to give you a more specific answer."

"How?"

"That's the wrong question, Shin. It's the "why" you should concern yourself with."

Shin was about to answer but stopped herself. It made sense that Yuki would extend her life to protect Samas from the demons within the rift. It's what the sin had been doing for centuries. That was all obvious. "I should ask why you created the demons? But you already explained that to Sato and me. I thought his head was going to explode."

Yuki tilted her head up. "Repeat to me what you heard in that room, so that we may discuss it."

It seemed an odd request, but Shin complied. "When you first discovered the rifts, they weren't filled with demons. In fact, they were pathways through the realm that the Maramans used to travel from Maramas to Samas. You and the sentinels fought off the first invasion, but it was a close and bloody battle, and you knew the Maramans had far greater reserves to draw on. You believed that the sentinel order wasn't yet ready to repel an invasion." Shin's mind still reeled at all the implications of the revelations. "So, you created the demons to populate the rifts so that the Maramans could no longer use them for travel."

"And you feel I was justified in this action? I hear no judgment in your retelling."

"Of course. You saved Samas!"

"I believed the same. Now, let's discuss my decision to extend my life to control the demon threat. Is that justified?"

Shin sensed a trap but answered honestly. "I think so. You had to be certain that Samas was protected."

"I thought the same. But let me tell you how I extended my life, and you can decide just how justified I was."

Shin nodded and waited.

Her mentor sat for a long time, staring into the distance but seeing nothing. Shin was about to ask if she was all right when Yuki finally spoke, "I once had a sister named Rua. A twin, identical, just like Hanz and Jurian were. She had an aptitude for sacrifice, but northing compared to my own. Her skills were primarily martial. There wasn't a weapon she couldn't master nor a tactical situation she couldn't solve. The two of us helped the original Firstborn transform Samas from a land of warring clans into an empire united under the Path of the Eternal Sun. Once the land was united, we set out to form two orders. One to protect it with steel and one with sacrifice. Rua headed the sentinels, and I the sin."

Shin's eyes went wide, although probably not for the reason Yuki would have hoped. "Can I please be the one to tell Sato that the founder of the sentinels could use sacrifice?"

"Most sentinels back then could, to some small extent. It wasn't until we lost control of the rifts and almost lost Samas that the two orders separated entirely. The sin were cast into myth and legend in order to keep the peace. An order built on sacrifice, itself sacrificed for the benefit of Samas. It was then that Rua and I understood what had to be done. Without strict control, the rifts could easily destroy Samas, and maybe the rest of the world. We came up with a sacrifice that would allow one of us to continue on, to supervise the effort."

Shin had an idea where this story went, and she realized now just how much Yuki had sacrificed.

Yuki continued, her voice sounding like it was coming from far away. "We fought for a long time about who should be the sacrifice, but there was only one real choice. There were several excellent candidates to succeed Rua and lead the sentinels. No one in the sin could compare to my power. No one had close to my knowledge of sacrifice. She sacrificed herself so that I might live. The realm happily agreed."

"Yuki..." Shin couldn't think of anything else to say.

Yuki took a long breath, but she didn't seem to be in any distress. Shin reminded herself that to Yuki, this was now just a story. It had no emotion attached. "It hurt for a long time, and I performed some foolish actions in the throes of that pain. That was when I crafted the structure that allows the realm to feed on my emotions. At the time, you can imagine that all I wanted to do was rid myself of the pain, and each time I performed a sacrifice, the memories of Rua hurt a little less. So, I used it liberally. Never superficially, mind you, each spell was useful and always, always justified." Yuki let the word hang in the air and looked pointedly at Shin.

Shin's mind felt pulled in a hundred directions as she tried to absorb everything that Yuki told her. Her deal with the realm, the demons, sacrificing her sister; each decision was a step along a path that brought her to where she was today.

Then it hit Shin.

The realm was bleeding Yuki dry of every ounce of her humanity.

And it wanted to do the same to her. The way it had led her to giving up her memories in order to close the rifts. The fact that her actions only strengthened the realm's foothold in Samas.

"It wants *us*."

"Yes, child. Though I don't believe it to be capable of conscious thought, the realm is certainly not a neutral party. The less of ourselves we maintain, the more likely we are to make a sacrifice that could bring ruin to this world."

"The demons?"

"Maybe, or maybe the realm itself could break through. I don't know what could happen if we aren't careful, but I hope we never have to find out."

Shin's heart ached for everything that Yuki had given up just to keep this world safe. The sadness hurt, but she embraced it because she knew it meant she was still herself. Still human. The memories she had foolishly traded hadn't robbed her of who she was. Not yet.

Shin lurched to her knees so that she could hug her mentor.

She held the ancient woman for a long time and cried silent tears for her. Tears that Yuki would never be able to cry. Shin, having come close to losing her own humanity, still struggled to understand what living a life of such numbness would be like. How hard it would be to keep perspective on those that Yuki worked to protect. Shin swore she'd never take Yuki's teaching for granted.

Eventually, her tears dried and she gathered control of herself. In place of her grief, there was now a grim determination. She let Yuki go and nodded. "After we eat, we train again."

"Of course. You didn't think I was going to let you off so easily, did you?"

Yuki smiled, which came close to sending a shiver down Shin's spine.

It looked so real, yet she knew there was nothing behind it. In a way, it reminded her of the demons, who took shapes close to human, but never quite.

Shin would find a way to use sacrifice to save Samas. She just had to make sure it didn't steal the last of her humanity first.

# 17

Beast woke earlier than normal. He'd drank a fair amount of ale the night before, but not as much as he'd expected. Though they'd won a victory, Beast's mind had been preoccupied with the islanders in general and Keff in particular. He rolled himself out of bed and went looking for the young man.

He didn't have to search far.

Keff was sitting the town square waiting, it appeared, for Beast. "Morning, Keff. Did you enjoy yourself last night?"

"Not nearly as much as you, I'd say. I didn't expect to see you awake so soon."

Beast laughed. "Takes more than a little ale to put me down. Were you waiting for me?"

"I was. I wanted to solidify our conversation from last night. In light of all the celebrating, I felt it would be... prudent."

Beast shook his head. "For Samasian being your second language, you can sure beat around the bush with the best of them."

Keff smiled. "My third language, actually."

"Right, you speak Maraman, too."

Keff answered him with a string of guttural nonsense but stopped when he could saw the blank look on Beast's face. "You don't speak your mother tongue?"

"Samasian is my mother tongue. I didn't even know I was a Maraman until they showed up on the shores of Samas and tried to kill me."

"Truly? I assumed you were a defector. Too bad. I was hoping I could get some answers about the Maramans from you. Those who you defeated were tight-lipped. Sadly, this means I probably know more than you about your own people."

"Possibly. But I'm happy to share all that I do know, so long as you're willing to do the same."

The young man brightened at the idea. "Sure!"

Another thought occurred to Beast. "I can show you around one of their juggernauts sometime, if you'd like. There might be even more to learn there."

Keff shuddered. "I am plenty familiar, but thank you. That's where my linguistics… training was conducted."

"I'm sorry," Beast said. "But the offer remains open, if you ever feel that a study of the ships might prove useful."

"Thank you. Perhaps someday, after the memories have faded a bit, I might take you up on that offer."

Beast gestured at the island. "Care to tell me what happened here? There's plenty I can guess, but I'd like to hear it firsthand, if I may."

Keff shrugged. "They were brutal, but I still count myself fortunate to be alive. Before they reached us, they were destroying everything."

Beast couldn't help but think of the destroyed islands they'd passed on their way here. "We saw. The people on the other islands were all killed. We found no survivors. Were those your people?"

"Yes. Our population outgrew this island, so we branched out to the others. The first reports of the Maramans were from those that had fled the initial assaults. We heard of their overwhelming numbers and the nightmarish monsters they commanded, and those of us here became convinced that our only chance for survival was surrender."

"What if they'd slaughtered you instead?"

"We would have been slaughtered regardless." Keff's face hardened when he saw Beast's expression. "It's not cowardice, though you might see it as such. Life is more valuable than death, and we believed it was our only way to stay alive. As you'll recall, when the situation changed, we adapted quickly and helped you fight the rest of the Maramans—"

"After you went and told on us!" Beast snapped. There were many failings he was willing to forgive, but cowardice wasn't one.

Keff didn't flinch. "We didn't know your strength. Had you come ashore with your full crew, it might have been different."

Beast took a deep breath. It wasn't his place to judge these people, and they *had* come to his aid, with farm tools and knives against the demons. They hadn't acted as he would have, but who could expect constant heroism from your average farmer. He waved away the argument. "True enough, I suppose. You may have surrendered once, but I'll doubt no warrior who attacks a demon with nothing more than a kitchen knife."

"Demons?" Keff tried the word out like he was tasting an unfamiliar food.

"That's what the sin call them."

At Keff's confusion, Beast realized he had to explain the sin to the young man. "The sin are warriors that use sacrifice."

Another blank look.

Beast sighed. "Sacrifice is... never mind. There's a lot for us to learn from one another. What happened after you surrendered?"

"We convinced the Maramans that we could work for them. They seemed pleased to have such a large number of amenable slaves."

"How bad was it, under them?" Beast assumed the answer was bad, but he was curious. The Maramans were his enemy, and he wanted to know them better.

The more he learned, the easier they would be to kill.

Keff said, "They made our lives miserable. The first thing they did was find the strongest men and kill them for sport. They brought the demons down and made our best warriors fight them. The entertainment didn't last long."

Beast could imagine it well enough. The first time he'd seen a demon he'd nearly shit his pants, and he had Yuki there protecting him. These poor fuckers hadn't had a chance.

Keff continued, his monotone voice reciting a litany of horrors. "After that it was beatings, starvation, killing those who moved too slow or looked at them the wrong way. Eventually, they learned that our craftsmen were skilled at understanding new techniques quickly. They also figured out that the more hands we had to farm, the more food they received. It isn't to say any day was easy, but those first weeks among the Maramans were some of the worst of my life."

Beast put one of his massive hands on Keff's shoulder.

"Well, you're free again now, and I'll do everything in my power to keep it that way."

"Thank you, but I'm not sure we can withstand the Maramans if they come back in force. Even your forces aren't strong enough. I fear that all we've earned is a little bit of time and another few weeks of terror once they conquer us again."

"You can always fight. Just because they're bigger and stronger doesn't mean they're unbeatable. If your elders are willing to help us resupply, we can help you defend this village."

"Both villages?" Keff asked.

"There's another?"

"On the other side of the island. It is closer to the fields, so it provides most of the island's food. Here you'll find most of the skilled craftsmen. The two villages work in harmony to serve the island."

"That's where the Maramans were when we landed?"

"They were based there, yes. Although they appreciated the weapons we made, it was our food that made us most valuable to them. So they always kept their main force there."

"Both villages it is, then. You get permission from your elders to help us. At some point, I'd like to meet with them personally, even if it does require you to translate for me. While you do that, I'm going to find Gorou and start putting together a plan to shore up your defenses here. I can't promise you we'll win, but we can give you a fighting chance to remain free."

Keff smiled and nodded. "Let us meet at the great hall tonight. We can discuss the future of our people's alliance. I'll convince the elders to come."

"Speaking of your people, what do you call yourselves?"

"We don't have a name for ourselves. We've never needed one. Before the Maramans came, we were sure we were the only people in the world."

"We should call you something."

"I like mugon. I heard you refer to your crew as that before. Perhaps we too, could be mugon?"

Beast was surprised at the emotion welling up in his chest. "That's a great name."

# 18

Sato's mind drifted to a small, well-protected bay off the northern coast of Iru. It had been a favorite spot for Sato in his younger days, when he wanted to take a break from his sentinel training. It was less than two days' ride from his home in Bulas, but when he paddled out into the center of that tiny cove and looked out at the ocean, he felt like he was worlds away.

"Good morning, General Sato," the Firstborn said.

"My lord," Sato replied with a small bow.

It was hard to keep his voice steady. He'd executed Benson, delivering justice that was overdue, but it did little to quench the raging inferno burning in his stomach. If anything, the execution had focused the fire like a blacksmith's forge, leaving nothing but pure steel behind. On his way to speak with the Firstborn, Sato had felt like an ocean wave, growing in size and power with each step, ready to crash upon the doorstep of his former mentor.

Now that he was here, facing the man himself, he felt as though he were sitting in a small skiff on the calm waters of that cove from his past. His anger still roiled and churned off in the distance, but Sato kept his posture rigid, hiding in the calm bay of his memory.

Normally, the Firstborn would have poured tea or talked about something inconsequential. But he'd always been able to read Sato like a book, and he must have sensed there was no time for him to waste today. They'd had plenty of disagreements over the years, but this one felt different. This one mattered.

"I understand you dealt with Benson," the Firstborn said, jumping straight to the point. Sato wasn't surprised the Firstborn already knew what had happened. The man had always had eyes everywhere.

"Yes. For a second time. My latest sentence will be far more difficult to overturn."

The Firstborn raised an eyebrow. "I see we are dispensing with any pretense of civility."

"When have you known me to bother with pretense of any kind?"

"Fair enough. But I will remind you, General Sato, that you remain a sentinel of the Eternal Sun. And I am the Firstborn. Watch your step carefully."

Sato's anger flared before he controlled it. "With all due *respect,* my lord, I don't believe I am the one who needs a reminder about their place on the Path."

Sato had known the Firstborn his entire life. He'd seen the ruler of Samas upset, frustrated and sad. But he'd never seen the Firstborn furious. If Beast had projected the same rage, Sato would have feared for his life and the lives of those in all adjoining rooms.

But the Firstborn was nothing if not controlled. His eyes flared, but the Firstborn's rage was as cold as Sato's was hot. "It's that very self-righteousness that is going to doom us all if you can't get it under control, General." Sato opened his mouth to respond but the Firstborn held up a hand to silence him. "You've seen what we are up against. You, more than anyone, understand that Samas sits on a precipice and the Maramans are sitting on the wrong side of it, waiting to erase us from existence. Was Benson an ideal sentinel? No, of course not. I'm not the fool you seem to think I am. But do you know what he was?" Again Sato made to answer, but the Firstborn raised a hand. "Don't answer that. I'll tell you. Benson was a sentinel who could wield a sword. We spent enormous amounts of money to train him since he was young to be a sentinel, the most feared warriors in all of history. He was one more brick in a wall that needs to remain standing if we hope to survive." The Firstborn's voice was cold as ice. "*Now* you can talk."

Sato's skiff was drifting closer to the open ocean, to a place where he wouldn't be able to control his rage. "You asked me to rout the corruption out of the sentinel order, did you not? Why charge me with that if you're only going to let that corruption creep back in?"

"Your mission was to make the sentinel order strong again!"

It was the closest Sato had ever seen the Firstborn come to losing control, but the ruler reined in his emotions quickly.

"Yuki warned me that something was coming and that we needed to be ready. For a while, you succeeded wonderfully, Sato. You cleansed Dahl and Versun, while also dealing with an invading force and your growing knowledge of the sin. And you did it by being flexible, by interpreting the Path instead of blindly following it. How can you not see that I am doing the same?"

Sato bristled at the implication that he had strayed from

the Path. He'd used Crispin and Alonzo to do things he never would, true, but he had also brought the two of them back to the Path. They might not be honorable sentinels, but they were sentinels he was proud to have under his command. "The Path is clear about how treasonous sentinels are handled. Smuggling supplies is clearly defined—"

"By the sun, Sato! Tell me where in the Path it instructs us on how to deal with an invading force that has laid siege to our nation with demons from our nightmares?"

Sato had no answer. The answer was the Path itself, not in any detail or line within its dictates.

"Where Sato?" the Firstborn repeated.

"The Path of the Eternal Sun can not be expected to hold our hands and instruct us for any situation that arises. It is a set of principals that guide us so that we may handle those situations the way the Sun intended."

The Firstborn sighed heavily and slumped back in his chair. Sato thought he looked older than he ever had. Weaker. The lines etched into his face appeared like wrinkles on an old piece of fruit rather than a weathered cliff face.

"I had hoped that your time with the Sun Stalkers would show you the value of flexibility and interpretation. No one could possibly doubt your adherence to the Path. You're a model sentinel. Unfortunately, a leader can't be a monolith. There is too much nuance to ruling a nation to be blind to any viewpoint but your own. I'm sorry, Sato, but effective immediately you will no longer oversee the day-to-day ruling of Versun. The Sun Stalkers and their defense of the walls will be your sole responsibility."

The Firstborn's words were a slap across his face. He

couldn't remember a time when the Firstborn hadn't been grooming him as a successor. And that was what this was about, but the man was too cowardly to admit it. "Come out and say it."

The Firstborn looked for a moment like he was going to ask what Sato meant, but thought better of it. "I am removing you from consideration as the next Firstborn. I'm sorry, Sato, but you're not the leader we need when I am gone."

Sato felt his tiny skiff being pulled out into the storm. Seconds stretched out as he drifted past the protection of the coast and into the maelstrom. Only the cold reality of his hand touching the hilt of his sword gave him to some semblance of calm.

He was a true sentinel. Perhaps the only one.

He walked the Path.

He wouldn't sully his honor in the throes of anger.

"Very well, my lord. Am I dismissed?"

Sato was struck once more at how old and tired the Firstborn looked. Too old, Sato thought, for what they were facing.

"Dismissed, General."

Sato turned on his heel and left the room. Crispin, waiting outside the chambers, fell in beside him and the two of them walked through the corridors of the magistrate's tower.

"How did—"

"I don't have time to pretend you weren't listening through the door. Tell Roko to accept any and all requests to join the Sun Stalkers. I also want Helios in my office in ten minutes."

"Understood," Crispin said and took off running.

Sato would follow the Firstborn's orders. The Sun Stalkers and their role in the defense of Versun were his sole responsibility. He could live with that.

It just meant it was time for the Sun Stalkers to expand their role.

## 19

"He's not right. If you're good enough with the second sword, your defense isn't compromised at all," Corin said around a mouthful of stew.

"Corin, he's right. Why do you think I beat you with Harmony all the time?" Shin responded.

"Because it's magic. And since when do you agree with Sato?"

"When he's right. Honestly, I don't know why you're so worried about it. Roko was trying to pay you a compliment by passing on Sato's opinion of you. They're impressed with your skill. They just think you'd be better with one sword."

"What do you think?"

"I think against a sentinel, trained with a sword from birth, you'll lose with two swords. But you don't fight sentinels, do you? You fight demons and against demons the versatility of a second weapon has saved your life. Probably will again."

Corin looked thoughtful for a moment. "Fine."

"Fine, what?" Shin asked.

"Fine, one of these days I'll challenge Roko to spar and show you all the value of two swords."

Shin laughed. "Roko, huh? Not Sato?"

"Well... I mean, he's a general. I can't just go around asking a general to spar."

"Right. Well, I think you'd have your hands full with Roko, anyway."

Corin laughed, but Shin wasn't fooled. The argument bothered him. He'd come so far as a warrior, it made sense that he'd want to prove his worth, that he wasn't just a child playing at being a warrior. Shin could understand that desire well enough. But she wished he saw himself the way she saw him. He meant so much more than his skills with a blade. Or two.

"Is that... Yuki? In the barracks?" Corin asked.

Shin looked around, relieved to have her thoughts interrupted, and saw Yuki in the doorway. She waved to her mentor and the old woman walked over.

"Shin, Corin, how was your meal?" Yuki asked.

"Good. Are you hungry?" Corin asked.

Yuki wrinkled her nose. "No, thank you. I'm not one for stew. Shin, may I ask a favor?"

"Of course," Shin responded.

"Would you care to take me out to some of your favorite taverns? I'd like to have a few drinks tonight," Yuki said.

Shin shared a look with Corin. Then she listened for the sound of demons pouring over the walls. Because nothing short of the end of the world made that request make any sense. "You want to go into a tavern? Wouldn't you prefer a drink in your chambers?"

Yuki smiled her empty smile. "No, child. I wish to go out amongst the sentinels and sin."

Again Shin looked at Corin, who shrugged. She

imagined there were stranger requests Yuki could make, but none came immediately to mind. "Sure, I'm done eating, anyway. Corin, would you like to join us?" Shin asked hopefully.

"Oh, no. No. I've got something really important I forgot about. Thank you though. You two enjoy yourselves." Corin was up and walking away from the table before Shin could call after him. The ass.

She sighed and resigned herself to a night on the town with Yuki. Which sounded only a little less fun than pounding her head against the walls of Versun.

"Lead the way, child. Wherever you would like to go," Yuki said.

Shin shook her head and led the way, wondering if some sort of ambush was waiting for her outside. But the night was as quiet as it ever was in Versun. They left the barracks and turned down the street towards the closest tavern. "Was there something from today's training you wanted to go over?"

"No. You did quite well today. Your grasp of the fundamentals is excellent. Once we got you out of the habit of reacting instinctively to the realm, your progress has been remarkable."

"Thanks." Shin wasn't sure what else to say. If Yuki had something specific to talk about, she would have brought it upon already. She was nothing if not direct.

A few heads turned as they entered the tavern, but Shin was willing to bet that very few sentinels knew who Yuki was. The sin did, of course, but the sin village had been such a tight-knit community that seeing her wouldn't cause any stir.

They sat down at a table and Shin ordered two flagons of ale. Yuki looked at her with her expressionless mask before taking a sip of her drink and glancing around the room.

"Have you thought much about what you'll do once your powers are gone?" Shin asked to break the silence.

Yuki's face was confused for a moment, but just as quickly the expression disappeared. "Ah, not really, no. I think I'll just have to see what awaits me."

"Do you think your emotions will return?"

"No, child. Sacrifice is called sacrifice for a reason. If someone had given their arm in exchange for a sacrifice, would you think it would grow back if they were suddenly cut off from the realm?"

Shin cast down her eyes. Of course, now that she thought about it, the thought was silly. She still sometimes fell into the trap of thinking mental sacrifices and physical sacrifices were fundamentally different, instead of being two sides of the same coin.

Yuki was kind enough to comfort her. "I appreciate the concern, child. What's done is done, and all we can do is look to the future."

Shin was grateful for the kind words, and she tried to imagine what Yuki would be like without sacrifice. Another idea suddenly occurred to her. "Wait, what will losing your powers mean for your age? Will it all catch up to you at once?"

This time Yuki's smile was one of the rare genuine ones. "Do you think I'll shrivel up like a prune before your eyes? I asked the realm to pause my aging. I would guess it will simply resume."

"So you'll get to live out a normal life after that?"

Yuki waved the question away, clearly annoyed by Shin's pressing of the issue. "Perhaps. Even with demons gone, we live in dangerous times. No one's life is guaranteed."

Shin had to agree with that. She had seen Yuki fight and, sacrifice or not, she knew the woman was dangerous. In her heart she hoped Yuki would be able to live out some semblance of a normal life. If anyone deserved it, it was her, but she knew the woman would want to continue to fight.

"Ah, there he is," Yuki said, staring at someone behind Shin.

She turned around. "Who?"

"Hanz. He's refused my summons since he lost his brother. I decided I had to come find him."

Realization dawned on Shin. "Which is why you wanted to go to the taverns."

"Yes, child. Sometimes being a leader means doing things you wouldn't normally enjoy."

Before Shin could decide if she was offended or relieved, the crowd in the tavern roared as Hanz issued his nightly challenges. The betting followed soon after. Shin smiled. She loved watching Hanz fight, but the expression on Yuki's face made her think twice about saying as much. Shin couldn't hear the details of tonight's challenge, but the crowd moved outside and Yuki got up to follow. Shin trailed the older woman.

By the time they got outside, Hanz, clearly drunk, stood in the center of the observers. Arrayed before him were three sentinels, each with swords drawn. Hanz stood there without a weapon.

"Come on!" Hanz screamed.

The sentinels charged, swords cutting through the night air. Hanz slid between the blades, impossibly nimble for a drunk giant. He became harder to see, as though he was covered in shadows. A moment later, one of the sentinels stumbled back from a punch Shin hadn't even seen.

Shin stared, amazed. Hanz was one of their best for a

reason. She wouldn't want to face him with Harmony in hand, even if he was chained to a post. The sentinels were either braver, more foolish, or greedier for some of the betting money than she'd ever be.

"Stop," Yuki said. The words, though not overly loud, cut through the crowd. The mob became silent as every eye turned to her. Even Hanz and the sentinels stopped fighting, though they didn't seem to understand why.

"Yuki?" Hanz said, blinking as if to clear his vision.

"Hanz. You haven't answered my summons."

"I've been busy," the hulking man said. He gestured to the fight as though it were all the explanation he needed.

"I see that. Trying to get yourself killed is hard work," Yuki replied.

"I'm not... I'm just blowing off steam. I—"

"Enough." Yuki interrupted. "I understand. You're seeking punishment for Jurian's death. But it wasn't your fault."

A storm cloud came over Hanz's face, and Shin started to wonder if maybe the safest place to be was somewhere well away from Yuki. "The hell it wasn't. I shouldn't have left him. I should have kept him safe."

"And you think slipping and falling on one of these fools' blades is the answer? You aren't looking for punishment, you're looking for a way out."

"Bullshit! It's not my fault I can't find a worthy opponent."

"If that is all you seek, I am right here. *I* ordered you and your brother to aid Beast. If anyone is to blame for Jurian's death it is me. My orders, my responsibility. If you insist on blaming yourself, however, then I am happy to dole out the punishment you believe you've earned."

As Yuki spoke, the crowd reformed around her and

Hanz. The sentinels, having avoided their fate, vanished like smoke into the crowd.

"I don't want to fight y—"

Again, Yuki cut Hanz off. "Jurian's death is on me. There is no one else to blame. That is how the sin have always lived. Regardless, if you want to battle your way through your feelings, there is no better opponent than I."

Something in Hanz finally snapped. He screamed and charged forward.

Yuki gave ground around the edge of the circle. Hanz's blows were fast and strong, powerful enough to crush boulders, but Yuki was no stone to smash. She flowed around his strikes and redirected the fury of her master-at-arms. When Hanz realized his tactics wouldn't work he tried to grab Yuki.

She slipped out of his grip like water through a sieve and landed a flurry of short punches. They didn't look like much, but each one staggered Hanz. He tried to grab her again with the same result.

Finally, she grabbed hold of Hanz's arm and locked the massive man's joints in a position that forced them to bend against their intended direction. Rather than simply hold the position until he surrendered, she landed kick after kick into the Hanz's exposed midsection, driving him to his knees.

The big man crumpled, and Shin thought Yuki would stop, but she continued her barrage, beating the man long after the fight was over. Only when the giant began sobbing did she stop. Shin thought she heard him crying his brother's name between his shuddering breaths.

Yuki showed no mercy. "Answer me, Hanz. For all your strength and skill, could you stop me? Or were you powerless?"

Hanz sobbed a while longer before answering, "Powerless."

"You see? Sometimes we are powerless. Sometimes we have to accept what happens and move forward. We grieve because we loved the departed, but then we stand and fight, so that others don't have to suffer the same fate."

Yuki knelt beside Hanz. "Can you move forward, or should I kill you now? I'll respect your choice, whatever it may be."

For a long time, Hanz didn't answer. Then he rose to his knees, his face caked with tears mixed with the dirt from the street. "I'll move forward."

Yuki stood, extended a hand, and helped him to his feet. She motioned for two sin in the crowd, and each got under one of Hanz's arms. The trio staggered awkwardly into the night. Shin watched them go before turning to Yuki.

"I thought you were being cruel to him, but nothing else would have worked, would it?"

"No. Leadership must sometimes be cruel. Even to those you love."

# 20

"We had to destroy the... what did you call them again?" Beast turned away from the construction of the spiked wall to look at Keff.

"It's not an exact translation, but the best word in your language is *devastators*," Keff replied.

"That's a good name. Anyway, we had to destroy the devastators, or they would have chewed us up. All that's left are the two on the bow, and we don't have many projectiles left for them."

Keff nodded thoughtfully. "Ammunition shouldn't be a problem. The Maramans had a standing order for us to create the spears that fit this weapon day and night. Even with what we've taken to build our own defenses we'll have plenty to spare. As for the devastators themselves... I'm not sure there's anything we can do. I'd have to take one apart to see how it works, and I'm not convinced I could build them."

Beast frowned. "If we run into another juggernaut as we are, we'll be at a serious disadvantage."

Keff thought for a moment longer. "I'll send a pair of craftsmen to examine them without destroying them. Troy and Abed think a little differently than most. If anyone can figure something out, they can. Don't get your hopes up, though. Likely, your best bet will still be to avoid the Maramans out there."

Beast bristled at the notion of avoiding a fight but kept his thoughts to himself. "Yeah, Colas says the same." He sighed. "The defenses are coming along nicely. Will you have enough materials to finish the project?"

"And then some. The Maramans stockpiled us with everything we might need. Wood, ingots, nails, tools. They wanted a supply station that would help them win a war," Keff replied.

"And now we're using it to kill them. I like that." Beast grinned viciously.

"As do I," Keff said with a dark smile.

Beast watched the villagers, the newest members of the mugon, work together. Gorou had taken over planning the defenses. They had used the natural advantage of the main hall being built on a rise to do some of the work for them. Rather than surround the building with a wall, they had dug out cascading tiers and embedded giant devastator spears in each tier. Any kind of charge on the building would be lethal.

The hall itself was being converted into a keep. Murder holes were being added to the top floor and above that, construction had begun on ramparts from which the mugon could fire arrows upon their attackers.

Of course, they would need archers to do so.

"Let's take a look at how training is going," Beast said.

Keff nodded and led the way through the bustling village. As they walked, the villagers would stop what they were doing to bow to Beast. Though he still enjoyed the respect, it was beginning to feel a little empty. They'd use the time better if they just kept working.

Before long, they made it to the clearing outside the village that had been turned into a training square. Gorou and a few of the most skilled mugon drilled the villagers on basic sword techniques. Gorou had noted that most of the new recruits had picked up the individual skills quickly, but struggled more with the principles of fighting as a unit.

Beast could relate.

Still, as with the village defenses, progress was swift. These new mugon were fast learners. Beast scanned the training ground until he found what he was looking for. Two mugon that Beast recognized as members of Colas's original crew were doing their best to show a group of five villagers how to use the short bows they were accustomed to.

From the arrows Beast could see, it looked like the only thing safe from the archers were the targets they were supposedly aiming at.

The few arrows that left the bow string often flew off in wild directions. One villager yelped in pain as the bow string snapped back onto his hand and threw the weapon to the ground. He stormed over to the instructors and began yelling and shaking what looked like a strap of leather in his face.

"What's he yelling about?" Beast asked Keff

"He's saying your sticks and strings are useless. They already have slings."

"Slings?"

"Yes, it is what we grow up learning to use. Our hunters are quite skilled with them."

Beast walked towards the altercation. By the time they

got there, the crew member was helplessly looking around for a translator.

"Keff, tell him to show me," Beast said.

Keff did, and the villager with the strap bowed deeply to Beast and reached into the satchel that hung at his side, producing a small round stone. He set the sling in motion. Soon, it swung so fast that it was a blur to Beast's eyes. Then the villager flicked his wrist. There was a loud crack, and Beast could clearly see the hole that the stone had punched clean through the wooden target.

He laughed. That was more than proof enough for him. He turned to Colas' crew. "New plan. The villagers use their slings. Tell this man to gather the very best hunters in the village. They're your new keep garrison. They will spend at minimum an hour a day training on the walls with their slings. I want them used to firing from elevation."

Keff relayed the instructions.

"Beast, what about the bows? I know he's good with that thing but if they master the bow, it's a far superior weapon," one of the crew members said.

"And how long did it take you to master that bow?"

"I've been shooting all my life."

"Exactly. We don't know when the Maramans might return," Beast couldn't keep the grin off his face at the prospect of a good fight, "so why not use the skills they have? Besides, maybe Vala can help them make some of those exploding sin pouches small enough to fit in the sling."

"That's a good idea, Admiral! Do you have any other orders for us?" the other man asked.

Beast gritted his teeth. Being in charge was great until you had to find something for everyone to do. "Go ask Colas. I think she was looking for more help with something."

Only when the two men jumped back a step before running off did Beast realize that he'd probably been more forceful than he needed to be. Suddenly, he felt a very strong urge to hit something. "I'm going to go do some sparring."

"Actually, Colas wanted to meet with you once you were done with your inspection of the operations," Keff said evenly.

Beast whirled on the man, his face a thundercloud, and pointed a finger in his face. "You tell Colas she doesn't give me orders."

Keff smiled placidly. "I considered that option, but you know how she can be. Instead, I padded the time we needed for the inspection. I thought you'd want a free hour or so to yourself."

"Then why mention Colas now?" Beast spat.

"Because this way I can take credit for how clever I was."

Beast laughed, louder than he had in a long time. "Oh, Keff, I like you."

"I know, sir. I'm very likeable."

Beast laughed again and walked towards the men sparring hand to hand. Since leaving the sin, he'd felt rudderless. Coming across these villagers had been fun for a time, especially when they'd been leading a small rebellion against the Maramans. Leading a people against a stronger force... it's what he'd always done. Now, though, it all seemed so tedious.

Beast shook his head as he approached the circle of men waiting their turn to spar. "I'm fighting next!" Beast shouted, then looked around the circle. "Better choose two people to fight me."

No one volunteered.

"Fine, three people. I needed a good fight today anyway."

# 21

Sato took the remaining minutes he had before Helios arrived to calm his mind and focus his energy on the task at hand. He was still reeling from the Firstborn's denunciation, but he had little time to dwell on that turn of events.

He had a nation to save.

By the time he heard the door open, he was ready to bring Helios around to his plan.

Instead, Crispin entered, shutting the door behind him.

"Helios is here, but I was hoping to have a word with you before he entered," Crispin said.

"Please," Sato responded. He gestured for the sentinel to continue.

"I'd like to suggest some discretion when you speak with Helios."

"Discretion? I'm not going to pretend you haven't guessed my intentions here. Wouldn't you say that now is the time to be blunt? If I am to make an ally of Helios, then honesty is our best policy."

"What makes you think Helios will be an ally?"

Sato was taken aback at the question. How could Crispin think Helios was anything but an ally? "I saved his family and spared his life. I showed him mercy and gave him a second chance where the Path would have had him executed for his treason. If that isn't enough to earn his loyalty, nothing is."

Crispin shuffled around for a moment, like he was approaching a wild stallion and not quite sure how to keep it from kicking. "Sir, do you believe Helios to be an honorable sentinel? One who views the Path much as you do?"

Sato debated with himself for a moment, but the answer was clear to him. "I do. He has strayed, as do most at one point or another, but he is back on the Path, with a more confident step than ever before."

"Then what makes you think he'd be willing to commit treason now?"

Treason.

The word hit like a slap in Sato's face. He rose from his chair and pointed a finger at Crispin. "Get out! If you enjoy having your head attached to your shoulders, you'll get out of my sight and keep accusations like that out of your mouth."

Crispin bowed low and backed out of the room. He'd looked appropriately cowed, but Sato was well aware of how good an actor his lieutenant was. Still, Sato believed he'd made his point. It wasn't treason to want to save Samas, and it certainly wasn't treason to uphold the laws of the land.

By the time Helios entered the room and gave a respectful bow, Sato was sitting calmly at his desk. "Helios, please sit. How are you and your family?"

"They are faring well. I don't think they ever fully understood the weight that hung around my neck when

Izuki was in charge, but they knew it was there. Now, they can sense its absence."

"Very good. I have also always found a certain ease in living under the tenets of the sun. It is not that life gets any easier, but there is comfort and power in knowing that you are living life in the best possible manner."

"I couldn't agree more. And you? How goes the day-to-day business of Versun, now that you've returned it to the Path?"

Sato snorted. "I fear Versun's return to the Path isn't as complete as I would like. Do you remember the Brunson issue? I believe it was one of your garrisons that brought it to my attention."

"I do."

"Here," Sato said, and slid a report across the desk to Helios.

Helios began reading the report. "Skimming supplies... execution for Brunson. This all adheres to the Path. Ahh, I see the Firstborn granted him clemency."

"The Firstborn insisted that Brunson was too good a sword to lose given our present circumstances."

Helios nodded. "An impending demon siege *is* something to be considered. Perhaps just as important, Brunson's family is well connected. His father served in the Firstborn's honor guard. He has an aunt who was a high-ranking magistrate in Hankala. I can see why the Firstborn wouldn't want him to be made into an example."

"Well, I did, and so I took matters into my own hands."

Helios' eyes narrowed. "A difficult choice. How did the Firstborn feel about that?"

"He was... less than enthused." Sato was about to tell Helios the rest of the story, but Crispin's warning echoed in his mind. "It has made things difficult between us."

Helios was no fool. He understood as well as anyone could. Sato could almost see the wheels spinning in his head. "I'm sorry to hear that, Sato. I know how much you cherish your relationship with the Firstborn."

There was an emphasis on the second line, a subtle warning. Sato heeded it and treaded more carefully. "He has always been my closest mentor."

"And your greatest supporter," Helios said. "I can't tell you the number of times I had to endure some story or another about you whenever we met."

The comment twisted like a knife in his stomach. He and the Firstborn had always been close. What had happened to send them so far apart?

"Helios—"

Helios held up a hand to interrupt Sato. Then he leaned forward. "Sato, I will always be in your debt, and I will always support you. You have remained closer to the Path better than anyone I've ever known, and it is for that reason you can count on me. So long as your steps remain firmly rooted in the teachings of the Path, you can rest assured I will be right behind you."

Helios stared into Sato's eyes, making sure he understood. Sato nodded. The message was clear. "Thank you, Helios. Coming from you, that means the world to me. As always, our conversations are—illuminating. Please give your best to your family for me."

"Thank you, Sato. I will." Helios stood, bowed, and walked towards the door. He bowed again before he left. He looked like there was more he wanted to say, but he let it go. He turned and left.

Sato closed his eyes once more.

By the Sun, he hated when Crispin was right.

"Sir?" Crispin said as he entered the room. He hadn't

been summoned, but there was no chance he was going to miss this opportunity to gloat. "How did it go?"

"He won't support me."

The corner of Crispin's lips turned up in a smile. "Very surprising, sir."

Sato didn't give him the chance to bask in his victory. There was too much work to do. More, now. "I am beginning to think that challenging the Firstborn's claim to the throne directly might not be the wisest course of action."

"An astute observation, sir."

Sato rolled his eyes. "I'm not sure what options are left to us. If we had more time, I would say we could wait it out, but the moment of crisis is coming."

"If I may, sir?" Crispin asked.

"Out with it."

"You're right about acting quickly. If we're going to make you Firstborn, then there isn't time to waste. The moment the Firstborn officially denounces your candidacy as his successor, it'll be too late. No action you take will be able to reverse that."

"What are you suggesting?"

"I have a plan in mind. I just..."

"Crispin, now is not the time to be shy."

"I just don't know how much you want to know about it."

Sato looked at his lieutenant and sighed. He'd known Crispin long enough that he didn't need clarification. Whatever he was thinking would compromise Sato's place on the Path. If Sato didn't know the details...

"You are dismissed, Crispin."

"Sir, I—"

"If I have need of you, I will call, understood?"

Crispin opened his mouth but thought better of it and nodded instead. Sato watched his lieutenant leave the room and leaned back in his chair. His thoughts wandered to the Path and its tenets. They wandered to Samas and the Firstborn. So much was laid out before him that couldn't be answered by the tenets of the Path.

All because the Firstborn had strayed so far.

Samas deserved someone who always walked the Path of the Eternal Sun.

# 22

Hanz's laughter was somehow so full of joy and heartache both that Shin wanted to laugh and break down in tears in equal measure. Looking around the tavern, filled mostly with her own unit enjoying a night together before heading out on campaign, she settled on just the laughter.

There were enough tears in this world. No need to add more.

"You two really fought to a draw every time?" Corin asked.

Hanz wiped away his tears as he chuckled. "Every time. Of course, it was less about us being evenly matched and more that neither of us wanted to beat the other. Yuki saw through it right away and put a stop to the draws."

"She forced you to hurt each other?" Shin asked, not entirely surprised.

"Of course. If we were holding back in training, we wouldn't get any stronger. They were still hard-fought battles. We were always an even match for each other, but eventually we found strengths in ourselves and weaknesses in the other. I'm a little better on my feet, Jurian is... was better on the ground. I'm better with a bow, Jurian... well, you get the idea." Hanz still struggled to speak of his brother in the past tense.

Shin laid a hand on Hanz's big forearm. "Of course we do. I'm not sure I've seen anyone fight the way you two do. Maybe Beast, but his style is still different."

Hanz barked a laugh. "That's a kind way to put it. That man is a force of nature. He taps into a well of primeval violence that I've never seen before. He certainly made us stronger, though."

"I remember watching the three of you train when we first arrived on the sin island. Seemed like you two handled him well," Corin said.

"At first, yes. We countered his anger with calm. It worked for a time." Hanz smiled ruefully.

"And then?" Shin asked.

"Then he learned. He might look as dumb as a cow, but Beast is a consummate warrior. Fighting is in his blood. Once he got over how pissed off he was that we *could* beat him, he learned *why* we could beat him. Then we couldn't beat him anymore."

"Too bad he's the world's greatest asshole," Shin said. "If there was ever a time we needed him, it's now."

"Hanz, you were with him when he made that decision. Do you know why he left?" Corin asked.

Shin knew the question wasn't idle curiosity. She'd liked Beast well enough and loved having him on her side in a fight, but Corin had looked up to him. Beast had been the one who'd always believed in him, even when he barely knew how to hold a sword properly.

Beast leaving had torn Corin up inside.

Just one of many wounds her friend had quietly endured this past year.

Hanz stared into his drink for so long that Shin thought he wasn't going to answer. Finally, he looked across Shin at Corin. "As I said before, Beast was born to fight. Unfortunately, he also has a talent for leadership. Because of that talent, he got the idea that he was meant to lead."

"Wasn't he?" Shin asked. "He was the Bandit King, after all."

"As I said, he has a talent. Without the help of the sin, though, I doubt his rebellion would have gotten far," Hanz responded.

"Benji," Corin said.

Hanz nodded. "Don't be mistaken, we all thought Beast was suited to lead. Benji aided him with the mugon, yes, but he was also grooming Beast to become a leader within the sin."

"So what happened?" Shin asked.

"The burdens of leadership are many, and their weight affects us all differently. Jurian died for the sin, and I wasn't the only one to take that loss hard. Beast can take lives and feel almost nothing, but losing those that he loves? That was a weight he couldn't handle. He'd already watched Benji sacrifice himself for the sin, and then he lost Jurian, too. Colas offered an alternative. As much as I want to be angry at him, I can't blame him for taking it. I almost did."

Shin let the silence hang for a moment before shaking her head. "He's still an asshole."

Hanz laughed, and this time there was only joy. "You're not wrong, but we've always known that." He finished his mug and slammed it down on the table. "Thanks for tonight, you two. I've missed this."

"You're welcome to stay," Shin said as Hanz stood, "I'm going to have one more."

"I appreciate the offer but there's a sentinel that's been offering to buy me a drink for weeks now. I think it's about time I take her up on the offer." Hanz smiled broadly and walked away.

"Seems like he's feeling better," Shin said.

"Seems like it. It is that time of night," Corin said and gestured to around the bar.

Shin could see the patrons slowly pairing off. Some were long time couples from her unit, others were coming together for the first time. "It's amazing what the eve of a dangerous campaign can do for one's sex life."

Corin, in the midst of taking a drink, attempted to laugh at the same time and succeeded in soaking the bar with a spray of ale. "The threat of losing one's life does motivate even the most shy."

"Do you want to go and see Kass? I'm sure she'll miss you," Shin offered and signaled the bartender for another drink.

Corin did the same. "No, I saw her last night. Thought my commanding officer might need some company tonight."

Shin felt a swelling of gratitude in her chest. She struggled for a moment to express some appreciation, but, as she always did, she ended up smiling tightly and lapsing into silence.

They drank for a while longer, but Shin started to feel restless. Something was gnawing at her, but she couldn't say what it was. "This place is dead. Let's go for a walk."

"Sure," Corin said, and downed his ale.

Shin looked at her half-finished drink and pushed it away. She was as drunk as she wanted to be. Much more, and she wouldn't feel much like commanding anyone tomorrow. They left the tavern together and wandered aimlessly through Versun. At one time, the sheer scale of the city would have left her awestruck but now, after almost a year here, it was old hat.

It was amazing what you could get used to.

She stopped as she realized what had been bothering her. She'd spent so long being told she was an elite sin that she'd just gotten used to the idea. "Corin, what if I'm not supposed to be an elite sin? It's like Hanz said, Beast was a talented leader, but he wasn't meant to lead. What if—"

"By the Sun, shut your mouth," Corin said, laughing.

"What?"

"This again? Look, you aren't just talented with sacrifice, you have more power than almost anyone else alive. This is what you're supposed to do. Besides, you aren't even that good at anything else."

Shin stared at Corin for a moment and then burst out laughing. "I can still kick you ass!"

Corin scoffed. "Only because you use that damn sacrificial weapon of yours. Which just proves my point. Maybe it's time to stop questioning the obvious."

Shin ran her hand through her hair, grinning. No one else spoke to her like that. Probably because Corin was the only one she allowed to. But she needed that from him. "What would I do without you?"

"Honestly? You'd still be farming on the sin island. Or you'd be dead. Probably dead. I've had to save your life a lot."

Shin smiled some more. Her doubts weren't gone, but when she was around Corin, they faded to something more manageable. She stared into the night for a few steps before mustering her courage. "Corin, look, I know I don't tell you this enough, but I know I'd be lost without you. You're always there and— whenever I'm lost—you— it's like—"

Corin covered his ears with his hands. "You have to stop. This is painful."

Shin slapped his arms away. "No! I have to say this! It's not fair that you don't know what you mean to me."

"Of course I do. You don't need to tell me, Shin. Besides, expressing yourself is yet another thing you're bad at. Also proving my point, by the way."

Corin kept wandering down the street, his hands in his pockets, whistling some tune Shin was sure he'd just made up.

Shin smiled at Corin's back and, for the first time in a long time, felt at peace. She hurried to catch up with him, and together they walked into the night.

# 23

"Fuck!" Beast shouted as the small rock spinning with the leather sling slammed into the back of his head, right behind his ear.

"You need to hold the sling farther away from you," Keff said.

"No shit!"

Keff put his hands up. "You asked me to show you how to use a sling."

"Right, so do a better job showing me."

Keff rolled his eyes, and Beast wondered if the young man was getting a little too confident in his position. "Might I ask why this is a skill you want to learn? I've seen you fight, and it would be a waste to have you anywhere but in the heart of the fray."

Beast knew Keff was saying things he liked to hear in order to calm him down, but smiled anyway. Everything he was saying was still true. "Flattery will get you everywhere, my young friend. The reason is that I'm more than useless with a bow, and if I'm supposed to be directing forces in battle, I thought it would make sense to learn a ranged skill."

"Gorou and Vala are good tacticians, are they not? Perhaps you are better served to leave command to them. Lead from the front, as it were."

Beast sighed. "Perhaps."

He tossed the sling to Keff and walked back through the training camp and towards the village center. Closest to him, the villagers were teaching the juggernaut crew how to use the slings, while the archers from his crew taught the villagers how to use bows farther on. Some of the villagers were tremendous archers, and some of the mugon were better with the slings than the bows they'd grown up with. For the most part though, practice made perfect, and it was hard to replace a lifetime of training with a new weapon. Beast wasn't sure he'd ever make sense of the sling. Hell, he could probably throw an axe farther than he could sling a rock.

As he walked, Beast saw Vala hunched over a makeshift table with an assortment of powders, plants, and tools arrayed in front of her. She was so absorbed in her work that she didn't see Beast or Keff pass by.

"How's Vala coming along with the explosive rounds for the slings?" Beast asked.

Keff shook his head. "The explosions are too small. She can't get enough of that black powder into the pouches and keep them small enough to fit in the slings."

"Damn, being able to fling explosives over distances would be a great way of killing Maramans."

"Indeed. I do believe she's come up with an alternative, however."

"Really?" Beast said and then cupped his hands around his mouth. "Vala! Come here!"

The small woman jumped in surprise before leaving her workbench and jogging over to them. "You know you asked me to make you something that blows up right?" she asked.

"Of course," Beast replied.

"Then maybe next time don't startle me when I'm working. Sudden movements can be bad for unstable materials," Vala said.

"Noted," Beast said. "Keff says the ammunition for the slings is too small for explosives. He also said you have an alternative?"

"I do. Sin employ a number of powders and herbs that can render people unconscious. Some can be turned into a vapor when burned. These powders are effective in far smaller doses, small enough to fit within the slings." Vala reached into one of the pockets of her robes and produced a small leather ball with a piece of string sticking out of it. "If the slingers light the wick before they throw it, it will land among the Maramans and hopefully knock them unconscious."

"It works that quickly? What if the Maramans throw it away?" Beast asked.

"It's almost instant. Want to see?" Vala asked and produced a flint box.

Beast waved his hands. "No! No! I believe you. That's nice work. How many can you make?"

"A fair number. The wick is the hardest part but the materials are here," Vala said. "It's just a matter of time."

"Good, get started on producing as many as possible. Might as well be ready if the Maramans come back," Beast said.

Vala shared a look with Keff, but nodded. "I'll get a work crew on it. Once I show them how it's done, I'll meet you back at the hall."

"Sounds good," Beast said as Vala moved away, then turned to Keff. "What was that look about?"

"Do you really think the Maramans are coming back?"

"Of course. We took over their supply depot. By now, the emperor is likely cursing my name and sending his best this way."

Keff raised an eyebrow.

"What?"

"You said you fled an invasion of your homeland, yes? A homeland that is far greater than our tiny island."

"Right." Beast couldn't figure out where Keff was taking this discussion.

"The Maramans took what was needed for that invasion and left enough forces to keep us in line. They aren't coming back. Not any time soon, anyway. They have an invasion to worry about. We were only a convenient stepping stone."

It took a few moments for the words to sink in, but then Beast grit his teeth. Keff was probably right. There was no tactical advantage in taking the island back. They probably didn't even know they'd lost it. All the defenses they'd built, the training they'd done, was all for a fight that may or may not happen a long time from now.

And Beast needed a sun-cursed fight a lot sooner than that. He hadn't killed a Maraman in weeks! He swore. How the hell had he not figured this out already?

Beast looked at the villagers being trained to fight by his mugon. They took eagerly to the training, but Beast saw it all in a new light. It wasn't nearly as inspiring as it had been this morning.

"What a fucking waste," Beast growled, "to have all these fighters and no one to fight."

"You've still accomplished much," Keff said, his tone painfully neutral, "this is what it means to lead a people.

Prepare for war and hope for peace. That is what our elders have always said."

Hope for peace.

Beast spat on the ground. "I'm sick of peace! Ever since I sailed away on that sun-cursed juggernaut, the only fun I've had was killing the Maramans that were here."

"You said you wanted to be free, right?" Keff gestured around the island. "You can't get any freer than this. And wasn't it you that said that it was your destiny to lead the downtrodden out from under the yoke of the sentinels? Well, there are no sentinels here, and you freed a whole different group of people from the yoke of the Maramans. Seems to me you should be happy."

Beast whirled around and grabbed Keff by the shirt, lifting the smaller man off the ground so the tip of Beast's beard was pressed against Keff's face. "Well, I'm not! I'm fucking bored! All I want is a good fight. My skin feels like there are bees under it all the time and the only relief I get from it is when I spar, but even then, I don't get to kill anyone."

Beast shook Keff furiously, but the islander just smiled at him, completely unafraid. Beast put him down. What good was he if he couldn't even intimidate one scrawny kid?

"Finally. I thought you'd never figure it out," Keff said.

"What?" Beast asked, his anger partially spent, still simmered.

"I haven't known you that long, but it's clear that you are a warrior. You can lead and inspire, sure, but in the end, you need to fight. It's who you are. And there is only one enemy that's worthy of your skills. Only one enemy that provides you the challenge you seek."

Beast knew where Keff was going, and he didn't like it. "The Maramans."

Keff grinned wolfishly. “The Maramans. Sure, we might fight them here, but if we do, it means they took over Samas. We could hold out for a while, especially with you here, but we’d eventually fall. No matter how much we train or prepare, their forces will always be too substantial.”

“You think we should go to Samas,” Beast said.

“If we’re going to win, we need more forces than what’s here. Why not join with the sin and the sentinels? It’ll be the biggest fight this part of the world has ever seen.”

“Will your people come?”

“Why do you think they’re so eager to be trained? Life under the Maramans is something no one else should have to experience. The best way for us to prevent the Maramans returning is to defeat them on Samas.”

Beast considered Keff’s argument. He poked at it, hoping to find some flaws but finding none. The young man was, as usual, right. “Fine. I agree. We’ll have to convince Gorou and Colas, though. They were as eager to leave Samas as I was.”

Keff smiled strangely but only nodded.

They hurried back towards the hall. They had a midday meeting planned anyway, but Beast’s mind raced as he came up with arguments that would convince his captains to agree to a return to Samas and the death and destruction that waited for them there.

When Beast and Keff entered the hall, everyone else was already seated and eating. A plate of fowl, along with vegetables and potatoes, awaited Beast but, hungry as he was, he didn’t sit. Instead, he went straight to Colas and Gorou.

“I need to talk to you two about something. You might not like it, and I won’t force either of you to do anything you don’t want to, but I have to say it.” Beast looked at each of his captains' expectant faces. "I need to go back to Samas to fight the Maramans."

Beast braced himself. He should have taken more time to create good reasons to go. How was he going to convince them?

"Fucking finally," Colas said.

Beast's mouth dropped open.

"Agreed," Gorou said. "It's about time."

"How'd you convince him, Keff?" Vala asked.

"He came to it all by himself," Keff said, the sly grin still on his face.

"What are you all taking about?" Beast asked.

"It's obvious you wanted to go back, Beast. I'm surprised it took you this long to figure it out," Colas said. "But I suppose you never were the brightest."

"Obvious?" Beast was so dumfounded he didn't even get upset at the insult.

"Beast, you need a fight. A real fight. Ruling a people? That's not what you're built for," Gorou said, smiling.

"Why didn't any of you tell me? You could have saved us some time," Beast said.

"No one can just tell you anything, Beast. You're too damn stubborn," Colas said.

"That's not true. You can tell me things!" Beast said.

Colas just shook her head.

"Fine, fine. So, will you join me?"

"It doesn't feel right to sit by and let Samasians be slaughtered by Maramans just because I don't like how the sin and sentinels are operating," Gorou said. "I'm in."

"I've become accustomed to a certain lifestyle," Colas said with a smile. "I just want a juggernaut of my own. I get the sense travelling with you is going to be bad for my health no matter where we go. Once all this is done, I'm going to take anyone that wants to live until they see old age and sail the open seas. On my own juggernaut."

"I'd like to see old age with her," Vala said and gestured to Coals. "I also don't want to see the sin wiped out. Whatever else you say about them, they keep this world safe from dangers few others even know about. Or, at least, used to know about."

Beast looked around and grinned. He took in the islanders eating in the hall and considered all those training outside. They had an army, resources, and a will to fight.

"Well then, what are we waiting for? Let's go kill some Maramans!"

# 24

Sato was exhausted and, as much as he hated to admit it, a little defeated. He laid in bed willing sleep to come, but sleep fought against him. Each time the warm tendrils of slumber started to pull him into unconsciousness, cold thoughts of the Firstborn yanked him back to the waking world.

Inevitably, such thoughts led to those of Crispin and whatever deviousness the young sentinel was planning.

Sato gave up and opened his eyes. He rolled onto his back and stared up at the ceiling of his sparse chambers. Years of a soldier's life had given Sato the ability to sleep under almost any circumstances. He'd spent countless nights out in the elements on rocky ground and slept soundly. The concept of struggling to sleep was as frustrating as it was foreign.

"Fucking Crispin."

Sato stretched his arms over his head and flexed the fingers on his disfigured hand. In the dim moonlight cascading into his chambers, the ethereal pinky finger that he'd earned at the hands of one of those sun-cursed sin rifts seemed to glow slightly.

As much as he detested it, that lost pinky was the key to his own plans. At the very least, he needed to learn how to send those demons back to the realm they came from. As yet, however, he'd not had either the time or the inclination to actively pursue the knowledge. Not since his first failed attempt. He'd observed the process several times. He'd felt the realm but hadn't attempted the spell himself again.

Even though he knew he could do it, it was of no consequence. Simplicity itself, if the method was known and the price paid. Even now, he hesitated as the necessity grew. If he did this thing willingly, it would be the same as admitting how much he now shared with the sin.

No. Sato was being foolish, and he knew it. The Firstborn's mistakes were not his own. The sin were a tool to be used against a common threat. In the same way, his ability to use sacrifice was now a tool. He would be a coward not to use it.

Taking a deep breath, Sato closed his eyes and searched out with his mind for the shared generational spell that was a part of him.

It didn't take long.

The spell, of course, need not be cast without a demon nearby. Thankfully, there were none, but allowing his mind to trace a spell that it understood brought Sato closer to the realm. This close, the power it promised was seductive. The spell to send back the demons was so simple, so small. Behind that veil laid possibilities beyond measure. They tugged at his mind.

They were all right there.

His for the taking.

*Stop,* a voice in his mind said, and Sato realized how close he'd been to opening a connection to the realm.

*You aren't ready for that just yet,* the voice said.

Had Sato been doing anything other than attempting to reach out with his mind to another realm in order to test the mechanisms of casting ancient magics, he might have been taken aback by a voice in his head. Under the circumstances, he barely questioned it. "Who are you?"

*Rua. And you are Sato.*

"How do you know that?"

*When you opened your mind to the realm, you opened it to me as well. Don't worry, I mean you no harm. I'm here to help you.*

Sato scoffed. "I need no help."

*Are you so certain? Sacrifice is a difficult and dangerous skill to master, and I doubt a sentinel has many teachers available.*

Sato was about to ask how she knew he was a sentinel, then stopped himself. If she was in his mind, then he had to assume she knew everything. "Why? What's in it for you?"

Sato wasn't sure how, but he got the distinct feeling that Rua was smiling.

*I'll show you.*

Before Sato could react, his stomach sank the same way it had when he'd been a boy jumping from cliffs to test his courage. His mind was pulled from his body, but instead of leaping upwards, it was pulled through the veil that separated Samas from the realm.

*Calm yourself. You are safe in your chambers. I merely draw your perception into my own. I want you to see.*

Sato was about to demand she stop when his mind abruptly halted. Instinctively, he knew he was looking out through Rua's eyes.

Right at Yuki.

She was a little younger than the woman he knew, but not by much. The smile she wore, however, was so full of real emotion that it made the smile Sato had seen before look like the mask it was.

"We did it," Yuki said. "It's finally over."

"I didn't think it was possible," Rua answered, and the effect was like hearing an echo in a cavernous chamber. "I figured we could unite the clans on Iru, but the other islands as well? I'll admit I had my doubts."

Yuki laughed, and Sato was shocked to see real joy in her face. "That's why he's the Firstborn. He's the embodiment of the Sun in Samas. Just as he always told us."

"I guess, but how does he plan to keep it all together?"

Sato's mind lurched again, and even though he knew what was happening, the effect was no less jarring.

Now Sato stood before a small, regal looking man. His perspective turned and he could see Yuki beside him, adoration in her eyes.

"Do you accept your charge, Yuki? Can you lead an order to protect Samas from the unseen threats that lurk within the realm?" the Firstborn asked.

"Yes, my lord. We will stand guard in the night, so that Samas can shine under the sun," Yuki said.

"Eloquently put, as always. Our ancestors used to call the moon the sin. Since you will guard the night, perhaps that should be your name?" the Firstborn suggested.

Yuki's eyes shone. "Yes. That's perfect."

"Good. Rua, without you leading our forces, Samas would remain a disparate collection of clans. It is my hope that you will be as adept at keeping peace as you were at making war." The man looked at Rua, but he stared into Sato's eyes just the same.

In his heart, Sato knew this was a man he would follow without question. This was the Firstborn they deserved.

"We will stand like sentinels against any who threaten to undo what we have created here, my lord," Rua answered and, in spite of himself, Sato couldn't help but be awestruck at seeing the foundational moment of his order.

His mind lurched again, and he was thrown into a pitched battled. He watched as Rua's sword arm flashed again and again. It took a moment to realize that she was fighting against Maramans. They were being forced backwards into a rift, but all around Sato could see the bodies of sentinel and sin alike.

"Whatever you're going to do, Yuki, do it fast," Rua's voice said, echoing in his head.

"I don't know if it will work!" Yuki responded.

"Don't do anything you don't understand. We know where they're coming from now. They're big and fight like monsters, but a choke point is a choke point. My sentinels can defend against them."

"Forever? Rua, look around. They almost wiped out our best forces."

"I trust you, Yuki. Just know we'll hold this line forever if we have to. If you can stop them safely, then do it."

Yuki nodded and closed her eyes.

Sato was back in his chambers.

*You know what happens next.*

"She doomed Samas to a life of vigilance against demons," Sato whispered.

*And then sacrificed me so she could oversee it forever.*

"So what, you want revenge on your own sister?"

*No. I want you to become exactly what Samas needs. What it didn't get back then, when it was needed most.*

"What's that?"

*A sentinel with the power to stand against any foe. A sentinel that doesn't need the sin.* A Firstborn *who doesn't need the sin. Who has all the strength needed to save Samas on his own.*

# 25

Shin hunched low in the bow of the skiff with Corin beside her. Behind them, her mixed unit of ten sin and sentinels waited. Beside their skiff, a matching boat cut through the water as quietly as possible. Through the dim dawn light, Shin could make out the outline of Hanz's hulking form in the other boat. She knew that Yuki would be crouched beside him, but she couldn't see the diminutive sin elite from her vantage point.

"Almost there," Corin whispered to the unit, "prepare to make landfall."

There was no acknowledgment of the order, but Corin didn't need one. The moment the bow of the vessel hit the ground, Shin heard ten tiny splashes behind her. She and Corin also leaped out, and they all dragged the skiff onto the beach. To her left, the other half of their assault team was doing the same.

Without further orders, the two separate groups melded into one and moved into the cover of the nearby woods in a holding formation.

So far, so good.

She ran through the plan one last time in her head.

They expected the most resistance from coastal patrols. There was no reason, with the rift sealed, for the Maramans to have many patrols in the interior. But that didn't mean Shin expected to sneak through. There weren't that many places to put ashore on Iru, and the Maramans patrolled the island well. Her teams would make all possible haste, but they would most likely be spotted. Their one goal was to fight through and get Yuki to the rift. Then they had to hope she could complete the sacrifice quickly enough that they weren't still at the rift when the Maramans responded.

If they were truly fortunate, they might even have a chance to escape.

It wasn't a reassuring plan, but it was the best they had, and their troops were the best around. It would have to be enough.

Weapons drawn, Hanz and Corin led the sentinels with Yuki and Shin in the safest position, near the center of the group. The sin melted into the woods and moved ahead to scout their route.

Yuki drifted closer to Shin. There was something different about the ancient sin tonight, but it took Shin nearly a quarter mile to figure out what it was. There was an ease to Yuki's movement that wasn't like her. Yuki had always had a light step, but tonight it was even lighter.

"Are you ready?" Shin whispered. She felt silly asking the question, but Yuki was key to their plan. If anything was off, Shin needed to know.

"I am," Yuki said. "Sometimes, I feel as though I've been waiting for this night for a very long time. Are you ready?"

Shin didn't understand what Yuki was talking about. "Of course."

"Not for tonight." Yuki swept her hand across the group.

"But for all of this. Tonight you command this group, but someday, all of the sin will look to you for guidance. Are you ready for that?"

Shin shook her head. "No. There's still too much I don't know. Too much I need to learn. But I promise I'll be ready when the time comes."

Yuki smiled. It struck Shin as being surprisingly genuine. "I think you will be, too. You've surrounded yourself with good people. Corin, in particular, is a treasure worth holding onto. But even those like Sato have lessons to teach us."

Shin wanted to scoff, but she recognized the truth in Yuki's advice. She would never take orders from Sato, but he was brave, and honorable in his own way. He'd also inspired a loyalty in his Sun Stalkers that was impressive to witness. "I will."

"Good. You've always had great potential for power, Shin. All that matters now is you continue to learn how to control it. But I'm proud of what you've already accomplished."

Their whispered conversation ended when their scouts reported contact up ahead. For a while, Shin had thought they might get lucky and avoid the Maramans altogether, but the size of the island and the sheer number of Maramans eventually brought about the inevitable.

A sin gave their report. “Patrol headed this way. There’s a summoner leading them with one of the chained demons.”

Shin consulted her knowledge of the maps she’d memorized for the mission. “The path is narrow ahead. Take your sin and work your way behind the patrol. Kill as many as you can before they notice, then escape. We’ll deal with the rest,” Shin ordered.

The sin disappeared back into the trees. Shin nodded to Hanz, who motioned their unit forwards. Shin moved up beside Corin and readied Harmony. This battle needed to end quickly and running into a summoner wouldn't help that.

They heard the cries of warning from the Maramans before they saw them, and Shin broke into a sprint. She didn't run long before rounding a bend and coming upon the patrol. A crimson glow surrounded the summoner, who was standing with his back to them. A moment before Shin threw Harmony, the spiked end of Yuki's weapon flew at the summoner's exposed back. Before the weapon could slam into the summoner, though, he turned and blocked it with glowing red hands, three times the size of normal ones.

The weapon bounced off harmlessly, but Shin adjusted Harmony's trajectory and the spinning blade sliced into the unfortunate Maraman's exposed groin. The crimson hands vanished as the summoner released a scream of pain that Yuki silenced with the deft placement of a throwing knife.

Unfortunately, the death of the summoner did nothing to control the demon, which charged toward them.

The tight quarters of the path that had served the sin so well now prevented them from surrounding the demon. Yuki and Shin held the beast at bay with the speed of their attacks, but they were wasting time and couldn't allow any of the remaining Maramans to flee.

Shin heard a primal shout from behind her and then she was knocked out of the way as Hanz charged forward, sword raised. The demon advanced to meet the attack. It slashed with its long claws, but Hanz slid forward on his knees, beneath the blow, and sliced the tendons off the demon's lead leg. When the creature tumbled forwards, Hanz stood and sliced his sword into the demon's bull neck. The blade embedded itself halfway, but before the demon could attack Hanz, Corin's twin blades slammed home and the head rolled off.

Shin immediately sent the demon's mist form back to the rift and opened her eyes to rejoin the fray.

It was already over.

The sin and sentinels, with a year of training together, were deadly efficient. The Maramans had been taken by surprise, and Shin's unit survived without any losses. She hoped it could continue, unlikely as it was. But this was a promising start.

"Maybe we can win this thing after all," Shin said to Yuki.

"This was a small patrol, and we took them by surprise. On an open battlefield I fear the Maramans still maintain the advantage," Yuki responded.

"You sure know how to kill a mood," Corin said.

"Yes, she'll do that," Hanz agreed.

"Please focus. The rift is ahead, but we are running out of time," Yuki said.

As if to punctuate Yuki's sentiment, a horn peeled a loud alarm in the night from behind them.

"They've found the boats. Let's move!" Shin shouted.

The sin still moved ahead to scout, but the sentinels moved along the path at a brisk jog. Yuki took the lead when they were close to the rift and led them up the hidden path. The sin were already waiting within the clearing when they got there, and the sentinels took up a formation around the entrance. The high rocks surrounding them would provide some protection against attack, but would also slow their escape.

They weren't leaving by the same path they entered.

"Are you ready?" Yuki asked Shin.

"Yes."

"Whatever happens, whatever you feel, you complete that spell. Understood?"

There was a weight in Yuki's words that went beyond the gravity of their situation, but Shin couldn't guess what her master was getting at. Still, preventing the realm from taking control of Yuki was the most important thing. She wouldn't hesitate. "Understood."

Yuki closed her eyes and Shin felt her touch the realm. The spell she was weaving was so complex that Shin could hardly follow it. No wonder Yuki was the only one that could get rid of the feral demons. Shin continued to watch in amazement as Yuki created her spell.

Then the first Maraman appeared in the clearing.

They were out of time.

# 26

Far off in the distance, a small speck of land broke the monotony of the water.

Iru, the southernmost island of Samas. The place where Beast had grown up, and the place where he'd built a loyal following of mugon.

It was as close to a home as he had.

He was glad to see the old place. More than he'd expected, if he was being honest with himself.

The slightly unexpected problem was that there was a Maraman juggernaut directly in between him and his grand homecoming. And it was sailing toward him at speed.

Vala and the rest of the command crew stood next to him. “Do you have a plan to fight it?” she asked.

Beast made a show of pondering. “Probably best if we sink it,” he said after a lengthy pause.

“I know you’re enjoying this, Beast, but we need a real plan,” Colas snapped. "They'll be better armed and better crewed than we will. I'm sure you'll want to charge straight ahead, but we're outclassed."

Beast shrugged. “That's fine. I wanted to save our

broadside devastators for an emergency, anyway. They might not be expecting an attack, so I say we use the bow mounted weapons to do as much damage as possible head on, then we turn hard to port, and hit them with the rear placements. After that, we can circle back around and hit them from the front again. Then—"

Colas stopped him. "First, we can't turn like that. This is a floating city. We can hit them from the front, but then we have to decide between ramming them head on or passing by them. Anything else is physically impossible. Two, while we're spinning in circles, they'll just hit us with volley after volley from their broadsides. It's not a great plan."

"Neither is passing by them. We'd be open to their broadsides," Beast said.

Colas rubbed at her temple. "Yes, and they'll be open to ours. That's how this works."

"We'll have the advantage of striking first, however," Gorou added.

Beast considered. The devastators were the question. Kef and the others had done a remarkable job rebuilding them from the original wreckage, but no one was certain if they'd last more than a single launch. He'd hoped to save them for more dire circumstances. "I suppose there's really no sense in dying with a quiver full of arrows."

"Perhaps there's an alternative," Vala said, and Beast nodded for her to continue. "We hit their bow mounted positions as you say, then when we pass alongside them, we use the slings with the gas to take out the Maramans operating their broadside weapons. If we have some archers firing flaming arrows at the same time, we can sow enough chaos to move past the ship and then we can hit them again from our stern. After that we'll be able to put distance between us and them before they can even turn around."

"We don't guarantee we destroy them that way," Beast said. "And that's placing a lot of hope in those slings."

Beast considered for another moment, but he had no good ideas. "Colas, I think this is your call."

"It is?" Colas sounded shocked.

"Yes. As much as I've learned about sailing, this is your area of expertise. I think you should tell us what to do," Beast said.

Colas put her hand to her forehead, as though taking her own temperature. "Do my ears deceive me?"

"Shut up and tell us what to do," Beast said.

Colas looked to Vala. "You're sure that stuff will knock out the Maramans?"

"I made a few different batches. This stuff isn't going to knock them out, it's going to kill the assholes. We'll just want to make sure we pass by them on the upwind side." Vala grinned.

"Alright, let's do it," Colas said sand smiled at Vala. She shouted her orders, and the deck became a hive of activity.

"I'm surprised you gave up control like that. You know she's going to get the idea that she's in charge now," Gorou said.

"Better get used to it, because you're going to be making the battle plans once we're fighting on dry land," Beast said in response. "Tactics, strategy, all that shit."

"I see, and what will you be doing while I'm so busy?" Gorou asked.

"I'll just lead by example."

Beast clapped his old friend on the back and went to help prepare in any way he could. He offered words of encouragement and helped move ammunition to the bow placements. In truth, his role in this fight would be small.

He looked out and saw the Maraman juggernaut had

closed the distance quickly. Once everything was prepared, there was nothing to do but wait. The juggernaut fell unnaturally silent as the warriors waited at their posts.

Beast found Vala standing among the slingers. "It's hard to wrap my head around just watching this all unfold."

"You are usually far more hands on," Vala replied. "But if you need something to do, you can stay here and watch my back."

"Sounds good. Wouldn't you prefer to be father from the action, though?"

"This was my plan. I'd like to be close enough to do something if it goes awry."

"You mean with your..." Beast gestured randomly in the air.

"With sacrifice, yes." Vala chuckled.

"That stuff seems dangerous. To you, I mean, I know it's dangerous for the people you're using it on."

"The cost can be high, yes, but that's a risk we accept when we embrace our aptitude for sacrifice."

Beast still didn't like sacrifice. It had cost him his closest friend in the world, but what could he say? This was an arena in which he knew even less than naval combat. He'd just have to hope, for Vala's sake, that her plan went off without a hitch.

When they were close enough, Colas gave the order to fire.

"Firing!" The crew members manning the devastators called out, but their voices were immediately drowned out by the hissing and popping that accompanied the firing of the giant weapons.

From his position, Beast could make out most of the enemy juggernaut and he couldn't help but give a shout of joy as he watched the giant spears cripple the weapon placements of their foe. His crew rushed to reload their still-intact devastators, but they hadn't practiced much and one volley was all they had time for before they were passing beside the enemy ship.

"Step one complete," Beast said.

"Now the hard part," Vala said.

Beast watched the slingers, positioned high up in the rigging to add as much range as possible, prepare their weapons. Beast gripped the gunwale tightly in front of him as the ships came closer.

"Shouldn't they be… slinging?" Beast asked.

"A little closer," Vala said tightly.

The enemy's broadside devastators crept closer, and Beast readied himself to leap to the deck, for whatever good it would do. Finally, he heard the call to fire and a dozen projectiles, trailing white smoke, flew from the rigging and landed on the deck around the Maraman weapons. The Maramans ignored them at first, but when they started choking and coughing, they futilely tried to pick up the projectiles and throw them overboard. The closer they got, however, the faster they succumbed. Soon, there was a deadly cloud of smoke surrounding the weapon placement that no Maraman could enter.

Beast almost felt sorry for the poor bastards. They'd never had a chance. "Those really work," he said.

"We aren't done yet." Vala was staring at the next placement.

It came up fast, and the order was given to throw. Again, the projectiles flew across the gap between the two ships and Beast allowed relief to swell in his chest. He'd seen how effective the poison smoke was. They were in the clear.

Movement on the Maraman ship ripped the relief from Beast's chest. The Maramans, led by one of those ink-black fuckers, charged forward and batted the projectiles out of the air with their hands before they could land. The few that got through were kicked off the deck or picked up and thrown. A few of Maramans collapsed, coughing up blood, but there were enough of them to clear the deck.

And leave the devastator in perfect working condition.

Beast immediately put a foot up on the gunwale. It was a long gap, but he was sure he could make it. Probably. Once he was there, he'd charge the devastator and —

"Stop. I'll deal with it," Vala said.

Before Beast could protest, she raised a hand and pointed it at the Maramans. A crimson glow started at her fingertips and then a gout of flame shot forwards from her outstretched hand. Beast recoiled from the heat as the fire smashed through the Maraman commander and into the devastator. The structure went up in flames, and then exploded when the fire reached the black powder that powered the projectiles. Maramans dove out of the way but anything Vala's flames touched caught fire with a speed Beast had never seen.

Then he noticed she was screaming in pain.

Beast watched in horror as the crimson glow that had started at Vala's fingers worked its way up her arm. It had already moved past her hand and was now creeping up her wrist. Behind it, Vala's flesh was left blackened and crisp. Between the cracks that formed every time she moved, blood seeped out and Beast could see raw, red, flesh.

"Vala stop!" Beast cried.

"I can't," Vala sobbed through ragged breaths. "Not until it's done."

Beast could do nothing but watch as the glow moved up past her elbow. Vala, with a strength of will Beast couldn't fathom, continued to direct the flow of fire to where it would be most effective. She burned the sails closest to them and then directed the fire to burn a hole through the hull of the ship. By the time they were moving past the ship and the spell had run its course, the Maraman ship was an inferno of chaos. A burning tomb for those aboard.

And Vala's arm was blackened and bleeding from shoulder to fingertips.

The tiny women collapsed, and Beast caught her. "I need a healer!"

Beast's cries caused a chain reaction in the crew as his request was relayed across the giant vessel. Vala's eyes fluttered, and she whimpered in semi-conscious pain. All Beast could think to do was stroke her hair.

"Vala... Beast, what happened?" Colas asked.

"They stopped the poison gas. They were going to fire on us and she..."

Beast trailed off as Colas sat down beside him and cradled Vala's head in her lap. The healer was close behind and immediately slathered a poultice on Vala's arm. Beast had to stop Colas from drawing her dagger on the healer when Vala sat up and screamed in pain.

"It's going to help her," Beast said. "It'll hurt now, but it'll help."

Colas ignored Beast, but left her dagger sheathed. "Vala, I'm here. What do you need?"

"I'm fine. I'll be fine," she whispered.

"What were you thinking?" Colas asked.

"They would have killed so many of us. Maybe crippled the ship or worse. I had to," Vala answered.

"You saved us, girl. Well done," Beast said.

Colas looked like she was about to yell at Vala some more, but Beast gave her a pointed look. Instead, she leaned forward and kissed Vala on the head. She whispered something in Vala's ear.

Beast left the two women. He looked out over the stern and watched the juggernaut behind them burn. It was a good start.

But Beast was ready to watch all Maramas burn.

Especially their damned emperor.

# 27

"Unfortunately, I think all the answers you're looking for lay in the libraries of Bulas," Helios said as he sipped his tea. "And I'm afraid the Maramans probably aren't going to let you browse the shelves anytime soon."

Sato stifled the urge to sigh. Hoping Helios possessed the answers Sato sought had always been a gamble. But he had few better ideas. "Sometimes I'm not even sure the truth was written anywhere. I'm beginning to think that the history of our order is different from what we've been taught," Sato responded.

The courtyard of Helios' home was bathed in warm sunlight and Sato leaned back in his chair, trying to enjoy the day. His mind, however, hadn't stopped racing since Rua had shown him the visions. And then she'd left, making him to wonder if she'd ever been there at all. Or if his exposure to the realm was causing his own madness.

"Oh?" Helios said and raised an eyebrow.

"I..." Sato trailed off. He couldn't well say that a voice in his head had shown him scenes of the long past. Not even Helios' gratitude extended that far. "I know you have a reputation for being well read. I'm just wondering if you know of anything I don't concerning our order's founding."

"Forgive the rude question, but I need to ask: why the question, and why now? You've chosen a terrible time to be focusing on history instead of the present."

Sato fumbled for an answer for a minute before finding one. "Lately, I've been struggling to understand what it means to walk the Path. As you well know, I was very literal when I was younger, but my lieutenants, and the discovery of the sin, have made me question everything I thought I knew. It seemed to me that perhaps going to the very beginning might help. That if I understood exactly how the Path came to be, I might understand it better."

Helios seemed to accept the explanation. He closed his eyes and thought for a while. But when he opened them again, he shook his head. "I don't think I know anything that would help you. Rua Tanaka founded the sentinel order after she helped the first Firstborn unite Samas. We've been following the tenets of the Path that she created ever since. There isn't much room for interpretation."

"I'm not talking about interpretation. I'm.... have you ever read anything about the founding of the sin?"

Helios laughed. "Sato, until a year ago I would have told you the sin were a myth made up to scare children. Like I said, any forgotten tomes that speak of them would be found in the Firstborn's private library in Bulas, and you've spent more time there than I have."

Sato nodded and took a sip of his tea. Of course, what Helios said made sense. None of the books or lessons on the sentinel order made mention of the sin. The sentinel order had been formed in the service of Samas. Who knew why the sin order was formed? If he really wanted to, he could ask Yuki when she returned, but he didn't know if he could trust her. He also didn't want to do anything that might indicate he was listening to a voice in his head.

But the visions last night had been so real.

“What’s this really about, Sato? Don’t get me wrong, I enjoy drinking tea and talking history, but you seem preoccupied.”

Sato sighed. “To say the least. It's nothing more than I've said. We feel like we're in our time of greatest crisis, and I want to be in a position to lead us well. It's difficult, when my own center is shifting."

Helios bought the story. "For what it is worth, Sato, I believe in you. If there is anyone who can chart the course through the Maramans and into the future, it's you."

*He’s a little stuffy, but he’s right. You have a chance to shape the future for all sentinels.*

Sato clenched a fist in frustration at the voice in his mind, but kept it hidden beneath the table so Helios wouldn’t see it. Thank you, Helios. I do feel better after speaking with you, and I appreciate you making time to speak with me. I’ll let you get back to your day.”

Helios stood when Sato did, and the two men exchanged bows. Sato waited until he was a fair distance away from Helios before addressing the voice in his head. “So, you are real. Perhaps next time, don’t surprise me in front of someone like that.”

The voice snorted in derision. *If you can't keep me in your mind when talking with an old sentinel, you don't deserve my gifts.*

“What gifts are those? The ability to interrupt conversations?”

*You can't even imagine.*

Sato dreamed of wiping out the Maraman emperor and all the demons.

The laughter in his head was soft. *You dream so small.*

Sato swallowed hard. "You can see my thoughts?"

*I know most of what you know. Though I've done my best to keep out of your thoughts that don't concern me, as a courtesy.*

"That's very considerate. And if I want to be rid of you?" Sato asked.

*Then I'll go, but I think it would be a mistake. I'm your ally here. Perhaps the most important one you have.*

"And what is it you want?" Sato snapped, causing a few people around him to hurry about their business and away from him. Sato swore. He ducked into an alley where he wouldn't be seen.

*I want to see the sentinel order, my order, continue on. Under the current Firstborn, I'm not sure that will happen. Are you?*

"No," Sato answered.

*Unfortunately, simply attempting to take power for yourself would only guarantee your execution for treason. And if you survive that, you won't survive much else. Your ascension to the throne must be without question, so that those under you have no chance to question your integrity. I do not know what your lieutenant has planned, but perhaps it's time for you to let him do what he does best.*

"I will not compromise my place on the Path in order to achieve my goals. That leads only to the same flaws I am seeking to remove from the current Firstborn."

*But you wouldn't be compromising. Crispin is a tool, one you've used in the past, that serves a specific function. All you would be doing is pointing that tool in the right direction. Then, your only responsibility would be to act according to the tenets of the Path once the consequences of that tool's actions come to fruition.*

"Is that truly adhering to the tenets of the Path?" Sato asked.

*Of course! Your hands are clean. A true leader knows when to let those who serve him take initiative. Especially when it is time to clean the corruption from the land.*

Sato was silent while he contemplated Rua's words. They sounded true, but they might also just be what he wanted to hear.

*Sato, I wrote the tenets. I've seen few sentinels in my time that walk the Path as honorably as you do. You wouldn't be straying.*

Sato shook his head as if the action would make his decision clear. He was the only one that could lead Samas. The current Firstborn had compromised too much, strayed too far from the Path to continue to lead the sentinels against their enemies.

And the founder of his order, the author of the tenets of the Path, had just told him his course of action was just.

Perhaps. Just maybe, she was right.

Sato left the alley, squared his shoulders, and walked to the carriage that was waiting to take him back to his office. Since Crispin had made his offer, Sato had avoided the lieutenant and Crispin had done the same. Alonzo stood by the carriage door and opened it when he saw Sato.

"Alonzo, find Crispin. I want him in my office as soon as he is able," Sato said.

At the very least, it wouldn't hurt to explore his different options.

# 28

Shin felt as though her mind was split in two and each half was occupying different places at the same time.

In the physical world, she watched the first Maraman that stepped into the clearing fall to Hanz's sword. Then two more took his place, and her warriors formed a wall of flesh and bone that stood between the Maramans and Yuki.

In the realm, she gaped as Yuki spun a complex weaving with such speed that Shin could barely follow. Fortunately, Shin needed only to wait for the signal from Yuki to do her part. Had she been required to fully understand Yuki's weaving, all would have been lost. Still, she focused more on Yuki than she did the battle around her. She would never have this experience to learn from again. When this was all said and done, she was determined to make up for lost time with her mentor.

Now, more than ever before, she realized just how much she didn't know.

"More coming. I think we need to join in," Corin said.

Shin snapped her focus back to the clearing and saw that her unit was giving ground as the press of Maramans increased. Every step back allowed more of Shin's unit to join the fray, but opened the mouth of the choke point a little wider. "Not yet. We need to protect Yuki."

Corin was about to protest, but the sounds of something large crashing through the trees surrounding the clearing interrupted him. A moment later, as if to punctuate Shin's point, a feral demon tumbled down from the tree lined rock face that surrounded the rift and landed awkwardly on the ground.

Corin dashed over to cleave the head off the demon-wolf before it could rise. One of the adepts from Shin's unit sent it back to the rift.

"Hanz, hold the line! Corin and I will deal with any demons that get through," Shin called, expecting no response.

"Actually, we might need some help," Corin said. "If they start pouring over the sides, there's not all that much I can do."

"The trees are dense, and the fall is steep enough that it should slow them down. Besides, Yuki's almost done. Then we won't have to deal with the ferals at all."

Corin nodded and readied his swords. But nothing else followed the demon wolf, and Shin dared to hope it had just been a lone feral drawn to the sounds of battle. She turned her attention back to Yuki and, while Shin still couldn't understand everything her mentor was doing, she recognized that Yuki had thrown up a mental barrier against something. Shin couldn't feel what it was, but it was strong. Her first thought was the emperor, but this power was emanating from inside the realm.

And it was wearing down Yuki's strength.

"Yuki, what is that?" Shin asked.

"Nothing I can't handle. Ready yourself. It is almost time," Yuki said.

Shin couldn't help but notice the dead tone with which Yuki spoke. It seemed as if the last of her humanity was draining away with each word.

Shin wouldn't waste it.

Again, she felt as though her mind was divided. Two more demon animals crashed into the clearing, but Corin was ready for them. Unfortunately, Shin could hear more coming. The fight was about to become desperate.

In the realm, she felt the final preparations of Yuki's spell become clear. She wasn't so much creating something new, as she was mirroring her old work and attaching new strands to it. As they attached, Yuki gathered the ends of the strands close to herself.

A sin demon appeared on the edge of the rock face and deftly jumped into the clearing. Corin leaped forwards and Shin tossed Harmony so that the moment it landed, the demon was forced to deflect her blow. Corin landed two more cuts right after and put the creature on the defensive. Rather than wait for Harmony to return, Shin ran towards it and settled into the fight beside Corin.

As her body fought the demon, another surge of energy pulsed against the shield Yuki had created. It bowed inwards but held. Yuki had gathered the last of the strands of her spell around herself. She was almost ready.

Corin pressed the attack furiously and Shin stepped in to block an unseen blow. The long arms and legs of the creature, mixed with its stolen martial skill, made it almost a match for the two of them. But they only needed to hold on a little longer. Around her, Shin could hear the leaves rustling above the cliff face. There were a lot more demons coming.

The signal pulsed and Shin snapped her prepared sacrifice into place. The realm demanded a memory. Her memories of first meeting Corin in Dahl, but Shin refused. She offered instead her right pinkie, a more conventional trade that the realm reluctantly accepted.

Pain shot up her arm as the finger cleanly vanished. She almost sank to her knees, but there was still a battle to be fought, even as her vision swam.

Corin, deprived of her support for a moment, was cut open from the swipe of a demon's claws. He gave ground, and the wound didn't look fatal, but he was losing. She tried to grasp Harmony, but it was hard to hold.

Behind her, two large thumps landed in the clearing. There was no one between them and Yuki, and Yuki's weaving consumed all her focus. They only had moments left, if that.

Shin felt Yuki heave with her mind, as if she'd gathered all the strands attached to her old spell in her hands and pulled them towards herself. There was resistance at first and then the old spells ripped free and gathered in a ball in front of Yuki. Once they were gathered, she compressed the ball until it became smaller and smaller. With one last groan of effort, Yuki collapsed the ball completely.

Shin expected a dramatic explosion of light and sound in the real world but, with the spell gone, the feral demons simply vanished. Corin swung at where he expected one to be, then stumbled forward as it wasn't there.

Shin turned her full attention to the realm. It was time to execute her spell.

With everything in place, Shin simply willed her spell forward and, in her mind, saw a glowing curtain of light envelop Yuki. When it touched her, the crimson light tumbled down and gathered at her feet. Slowly it wrapped around Yuki and made its way upwards. Shin could feel the curtain leaching the power from Yuki as it went.

Another minute and it would be done. Yuki would be cut off from sacrifice for good.

Then the sin leader fell to her knees. She looked weak, unable to stand.

Shin stared, uncomprehending. Then she looked at Yuki through the eyes of the realm. Tendrils of power spiraled away from her. But that wasn't all Shin's sacrifice was taking.

It was also taking her life.

"No!" Shin shouted. She focused on her own weaving, forcing it to slow.

"There is no other way," Yuki said. "This was always the plan. I just couldn't let you know it. I'm sorry for that."

"We need you." Something caught in the back of Shin's throat. "I need you. There's so much I have left to learn."

"And you will. I wish I could be there to guide you farther down your own path, but you'll have to find your own way from now on."

Shin shook her head. "I'm not going to lose you." The way was easy enough to see. Another sacrifice, to unravel the one she'd already put in motion. She didn't care if it cost her another finger, or even a limb. Yuki was worth all that and more.

They still had an emperor to fight. A land to save.

She couldn't leave them behind now. Shin prepared the new sacrifice.

"Shin." Yuki's voice was quiet, but it commanded her whole attention.

Shin forced herself to look up, to meet her mentor's gaze.

"Feel it for yourself. It's coming for me."

Shin didn't have to look far. In the physical world, the night was clear and cloudless, the moon and stars shining overhead. But the realm was coming, pounding against the walls that separated the realities. Dark tendrils stretched toward Yuki, hoping to wrap her in one final embrace. The crimson curtain of Shin's sacrifice protected Yuki for the moment, but it wouldn't last much longer.

And if she used another sacrifice to save Yuki's life, the shadow would consume her mentor.

It was what Yuki had always feared. The reason Shin was here. To protect Samas from what Yuki could become if the realm captured her.

Tears streamed from Shin's eyes, and she fell to her knees beside Yuki. She reached out and took the older woman's hands. "I don't want to lose you."

Yuki pulled one hand away and pressed her finger against Shin's temple. "I'll live on, in here," she put her hand against Shin's chest, "and here. That's enough."

Shin knew what was necessary. But she couldn't bring herself to lose Yuki.

“Please, Shin. I’m so tired. You’re ready for this fight. Help me end mine.”

It was less the words Yuki said and more the weariness in her voice. She sounded every bit as old as she was.

"I'll miss you," Shin said.

"And I you."

Shin didn’t try to say any more. Already, the shadow was close to breaking through the last of Shin's sacrifice. She finished her weaving, stealing the last of Yuki's life. Yuki collapsed forward into her arms. Shin rocked back and forth with silent tears streaming down her face, as Yuki died with a smile on hers.

# 29

Beast was still watching the carcass of the Maraman juggernaut burn as it floated listlessly towards the endless expanse of open ocean. Beast wasn't sure if the faint screaming he heard was real or imagined, but, in either case, it made him thirsty for violence.

"We aren't done yet, Beast." Any concern for Vala in Colas' voice was overridden by steely determination.

"Of course we aren't. We're just getting started. But what are you talking about?"

"The ship bays on that juggernaut were empty. Stands to reason they're trying to choke the islands off from one another, which would mean they have some nearby."

Beast grinned. "Well, we can't have that, can we?"

"No. We can't. We need you to take *Warhammer* and deal with any ships that are still disrupting the supply lines. The juggernaut is far too big to sail between the islands. Gorou will take *Cutter*. Get your crew ready and prep your ships. Got it?"

"Well, you've certainly taken to your promotion quickly," Beast said.

"I'll take that as yes. Get moving," Colas ordered.

"I hear we're in charge of clearing up the riff-raff out there," Gorou said as he fell into step beside him.

"Yes, thank the Sun! Standing on the deck and watching other people fight is no fun."

As they ran, their respective crews were joining them. Orders were being relayed up and down the giant ship, bringing in warriors from every corner.

Gorou held out his hand, and Beast enveloped it in his own. "Good luck out there," Gorou said.

"You, too."

Gorou and his crew broke to the port side of the juggernaut where *Cutter* was berthed. Beast moved starboard and boarded *Warhammer*. He took his position and shouted orders as his warriors prepared for this new battle. There wasn't much for him to do yet, but he could inspire anyone who wasn't reaching their place quickly enough.

"Lowering!" The order echoed down from the deck of the juggernaut and *Warhammer* lurched into motion.

His ship hit the water and the crew got them under way. Beast was wise enough to leave the operation of the ship to those better suited, but the lack of a task left him antsy. His leg was bouncing up and down as he sat and he reached back to touch the haft of the great axe strapped to his back.

Some of the crew noticed his movements, so he grinned viciously. "Are you lot as tired of watching the action as I am?"

A cheer rose in agreement.

"Are you ready to cut open some sheep fucking Maramans?"

Another cheer.

"You're damn right. Anyone that can kill more sheep fuckers than me gets free drinks for a year!"

This time, weapons began to thump along the side. *Cutter* drew up beside them and the cheering became infections. They opened their sails up as far as they would go, and the ships sliced through the water at unbelievable speeds. It only seemed to enthuse the sailors more. By the time the two ships were in sight of the shipping lanes, their crews had taken up a bawdy song that went back and forth between the ships.

Fortunately, it didn't take them too long to find their first enemies.

"Beast, two more ships, closing fast," a crew member said and passed Beast a looking glass.

Beast looked through the device and saw two Maraman ships closing.

"Signal Gorou to head towards the coast. We'll break out to sea. If they don't split up, whoever they don't follow can flank them."

The crewman nodded. He relayed the message to the *Cutter*. Gorou ordered his ship toward the north coast of Iru.

Beast and *Warhammer* turned tail and ran towards the open sea and, as he had hoped, the Maraman vessels split up to address both threats. Beast told the helmsman to keep the ship steady, but to bring some of the sails in. He wanted the Maramans to catch them. The ship tailing them leaped towards them, a predator that believed it had found wounded prey.

As the ships neared, archers from both crews launched flaming arrows. Though many hit their target, the crews were adequately prepared, putting out any fires before they became problems. The Maramans grew closer, and Beast grinned as he saw them prepare to board.

The two ships finally came together, and boarding hooks were tossed from each side. Beast braced himself as the two ships slammed together one last time.

Then his pent-up violence was unleashed.

He jumped across to the other ship and split the skull of a Maraman nearly down to his nose. He pulled his axe free and moved on to the next Maraman. Around him he heard a battle cry rise from his crew and they poured onto the enemy ship. For a moment, the Maramans seemed overwhelmed by the sheer intensity of the warriors they faced. The moment of hesitation allowed the mugon to press onto the Maraman ship.

But then years of battle experience kicked in and the Maramans began to push back. The ferocity of the assault might have caught them by surprise, but they were no sentinels that ran at the first sign of danger. They were true warriors, worthy of Beast's axe.

Today, he thought of Vala, and his rage had no equal.

He stalked the battlefield like a wolf among sheep. Anywhere he saw his mugon pushed back, he would step in, killing Maramans until his crew could press their advantage against the remaining enemies.

He wasn't sure how long he moved across the ship. His hands were slick with blood and his chest heaved. For every dead mugon, he saw two or three Maramans. Finally, he looked around and only his mugon remained. "Come! We need to help Gorou."

His crew ran back to *Warhammer*, disengaged the hooks, and turned the ship around. They were bloody and exhausted, but they had the fire of victory in their eyes. They didn't need another fight, but if they found one, they'd jump into it without question.

But by the time they found *Cutter*, the Maraman ship

was listing out to sea with a cloud of white smoke clinging from its deck all the way up to the rigging. Beast's helmsmen gave the ship a wide berth and then pulled up alongside *Cutter.*

"Did you have fun?" Gorou asked, taking in Beast's blood-soaked visage.

"You didn't even leave your ship, did you?" Beast asked.

"No. It was suggested to me that we could take care of the Maramans with the remaining poison ammunition for the slings," Gorou said and gestured to a very smug looking Keff.

"I thought you were supposed to be on board the juggernaut," Beast said.

Keff shrugged. "I figured Gorou would be more amenable to listening to my suggestions."

Beast thought about jumping over and punching Keff in the face. But the young man had the right of it. Beast wouldn't have listened anyway.

He squeezed his fist until his knuckles turned white. If Keff had thought Beast would have listened, lives on the *Warhammer* would have been saved.

For now, he pushed the problem aside. There would be time later.

"We should make landfall. We need to assess the damage to the shipping lanes," Gorou said, and Beast suspected his old friend had changed the subject on purpose.

Beast agreed. "I don't think we'll need to bring everyone. Let's leave the ships out here, in case any more Maramans try to cut off the skiffs. Gorou, you and I can go to Iru and see how they're holding up."

"I would like to join you, if I could?" Keff asked.

Beast nodded, the orders were passed around, and soon

Gorou and Beast were in a longboat with Keff heading toward the port outside of Dahl. Gorou, wisely, kept his own counsel, allowing Beast to work through his own problems.

Beast didn't have any answers. They'd destroyed two more Maraman ships, so the day had been a success. But he still could have done better.

Even though he ran from leadership, it didn't mean he wasn't responsible.

As the longships were dragged up on shore, a cadre of sin and sentinels met them with weapons drawn. At their head stood a familiar, if expressionless, face.

"You look like you had a good time," Sheryic said.

Beast smiled at his old friend, and for a while, all his problems were gone. "Just happy to help."

# 30

"Alonzo said you wanted to see me?"

Sato looked up at his most trusted lieutenant. For a moment, he was lost in the history they shared. From their first antagonistic meetings to their march through Versun as criminals. A pang of guilt shot through Sato as he took in the young sentinel's missing hand.

Crispin had given up much in service to the Path. Hard to believe, at times, but true.

"You're sweaty," Sato said.

"I was training when Alonzo found me. I don't think I'll ever be the swordsman I was with my good hand, but I'm working my way towards not being entirely useless."

"Cleanliness is one of the tenets of the Path. You should have cleaned up before you answered my summons."

Crispin arched an eyebrow. "That always felt like more a suggestion to me."

"It's not. Especially when you smell like that."

"And here I thought you appreciated my interpretations of the Path," Crispin said.

The quip brought a smile to his face, though he

squashed it quickly. As much as he'd like to keep the mood lighthearted, he'd summoned Crispin about serious matters. Seeing Crispin training so hard, after all he lost, reinforced his decision. He owed Crispin. And for that, he would help preserve the young sentinel's honor.

As well as his own.

"I'll not mince words, Crispin. Whatever plan you have in mind for the Firstborn, I want you to forget it."

Crispin kept his face neutral. For several long moments, he was silent. But Sato recognized the sentinel's sharp mind at work. "You're giving up."

"My destiny remains to be the Firstborn of the Eternal Sun, but I will not get there this way. We cannot stray this far from the Path."

"Then you won't get there at all."

"Trust the Path, Crispin. As sentinels, it's all we can do."

"Sometimes I get tired of you lecturing me about the Path," Crispin snapped. He held up his maimed arm. "I'd like to think I've sacrificed enough to earn some reprieve."

"Careful, Crispin. My patience has its limits." As much as he trusted Crispin, the sentinel still had a way of worming under his skin.

"Good! Because now is the time to be impatient. That's the only way you're going to achieve your so-called destiny. If you stay patient, then the Firstborn has already decided your fate. There's no honorable way for you to become what all of Samas needs!"

"If I can't become the Firstborn honorably, then I don't deserve to become Firstborn."

Crispin couldn't control his frustration. "I'm so tired of your sun-cursed honor, Sato. You're the only one playing by the rules anymore! I thought you'd figured that out when we took care of Izuki, but here we are again.

Ramming our heads into the same damn wall over and over."

"Enough!" Sato stood up and placed both hands on his desk. "I tolerate a lot from you, Crispin, but there's only so much insolence I'll let slide."

Rather than be cowed, Crispin stood too, surprising Sato. "And how would you punish me, *sir,* take another limb? Force me to change my whole life, *again*? What else can I do for you?"

"Don't play the petulant child, Crispin. It doesn't suit you. You're a sentinel. You weren't doing anything for me. You were doing your duty."

Sato was surprised to see his words take the fuel out of Crispin's anger. His lieutenant sank into his chair and looked at him with hurt in his eyes. "Is that really what you think? That you showed me the way back to the Path and everything else I did was in the service of Samas?"

"Yes. When we met, you were as corrupt as they come. You lived comfortable and easy. I simply led you back to the Path."

Crispin shook his head. "No, Sato. Before I met you, I was on a path, but it would have consumed me. I would have worked my way up through the ranks and continued to use my power to gain more power. I would have used my money to earn more money. Before I met you every town had a friend I knew I could call on for a special favor, and I called on many. Had you not shown up, I would have wrung the people of Samas dry until the Maramans or the demons or the sin showed up and burnt the husks to nothing. Who does that sound like?"

"Izuki," Sato said softly.

"But I would have been so much worse than her. Because I was so much better than her at what she did. I wasn't there yet, but I would have taken her seat, or a seat at Dahl. I was already on the Path, Sato, that's what you don't understand. The Path that the Firstborn created. However honorable the Firstborn might be, he's a creature of half measures. Of compromise. He's the light of the sun, casting shadows in which beings like me can grow. It's you, Sato, that can make the difference. That can hold us all to a higher standard while still doing what needs to be done. That's what I want."

Sato was stunned. For a long time, he didn't have any answers. "You don't have to go back. The Sun Stalkers can still do what needs to be done to save the people of Samas. I still have the Firstborn's ear. I can influence him. Help him the way I helped you. Trust me."

As quickly as it had arrived, all the vulnerability in Crispin's face was gone. "If you say so. Just understand that my plan has a time limit. I can't hold things in place much longer without acting. If you're sure you want to leave the Firstborn to rule, then fine, but if you think that you need to stop him, you only have a few days left to do so."

"I understand, Crispin. I do. You'll see. Yuki and Shin are removing the feral demons as we speak. Then we can strike a true blow against the Maramans and take Ilos back."

Crispin seemed to sink into his chair and shrugged. "If you say so. May I go?"

Sato hesitated for a moment. He wanted to say something to make Crispin feel better, to make him understand that they were doing the right thing, but he couldn't find the words.

"You may."

Crispin stood and nodded before walking out of the room. Sato sat down heavily in his chair and laid his head in his hands for a moment.

Assassinating the Firstborn was treason, no matter how clean he kept his hands in the process. If he walked down that road, he'd be no better than the traitors he'd sentenced to death. Sato felt a brief flare of frustration from the visitor in his head but it was gone so fast he wasn't sure if he had imagined it. He was letting everyone down today, it seemed.

"Nothing to add?" Sato asked Rua.

*You must do what you think is best. As I said, you are a true sentinel. You'll find your way.*

Sato shook his head. He recognized a placating tone when he heard one.

A knock drew his attention and Roko poked his head through the door. "Sir, it looks as though the Maramans dispatched a juggernaut to Iru. Based on our most recent reports, it's been disrupting the supply lines."

"We're cut off from Iru?" Sato asked. As if the day hadn't been lousy enough already.

"If we aren't already, we will be shortly."

He steeled himself. At least this, he understood. This was the chess match of battle. They'd made a move against the demons and now they were attacking the Samasian supply chain. The war had entered a new stage.

Roko clearly had more to say. Sato could read it in his posture. "Give me the good news."

Roko smiled. "We've just heard word. The attack succeeded. The ferals are no more."

Sato permitted himself a brief grin. Battles never went the way one planned. But they always advanced, favoring whoever could adapt best.

It was time to take the sentinels on the offensive.

# 31

"What happened to her?" Corin screamed.

Shin opened her eyes and saw Yuki's motionless form wither before them. The ageless face became shrunken and wrinkled. The black hair turned gray and then white. Had she been alive, Shin imagined the suffering would have been intense. But there was no soul in the body. Not anymore.

She felt empty inside, like someone had come by and hollowed her out. A flicker of something burned hot in her gut, but it was weak and intermittent.

"She's gone. Come on, we have to get out of here," Shin said and produced a rope ladder from her pack.

Corin stared at her for a moment in disbelief, then nodded. He took the ladder and wrapped the end around his arm. Then he scrambled up the rock face surrounding the clearing. Shin turned to the trail head and saw that the last of the Maramans were still pressing their attack. They had the look of crazed animals who'd just watched their food be taken away.

"Hanz, time to go," Shin called.

The big man turned. Shin watched him take in Yuki's now decaying form and grimace. He looked sad, but not surprised. It seemed Yuki had shared her plan with someone.

"Pull back!" Hanz called, and her unit began a methodical retreat.

Shin didn't have time for methodical.

She thought of Yuki's last smile and something inside her snapped. The flickering warmth in her stomach exploded.

With a scream, Shin threw Harmony at their attackers again and again. Each time she caught the weapon, blood spattered on her face. Every time she only held it long enough to throw it again, curving it in ways that defied understanding. Soon, the Maramans broke against her relentless attacks that came from everywhere at once. Her unit broke into a full retreat and ran towards the ladder that Corin had secured.

The Maramans didn't follow, but she wasn't done.

She sprinted towards the trail head. She would exact blood from every one of those monsters.

Two big arms grabbed her and lifted her in the air.

"You just became the only one who can stand against the emperor. I'm afraid I can't let you run off and get yourself killed," Hanz said.

Shin struggled for a few seconds and then the fire inside died as though it had been tossed in the ocean. Her rage turned into sorrow and her muscles into jelly. She allowed Hanz to drag her towards the ladder. Tears came unbidden.

"Can you—" he began, but then reconsidered and picked her up and draped her over his shoulders instead.

When they reached the top, rather than put her down,

he carried her as if she was a child. She turned her head and sobbed into his shoulder.

"Is she hurt?" she heard Corin ask.

"She'll be fine. Come on, this plan only works if we aren't where they expect us to be," Hanz said.

Shin didn't hear Corin's answer. A low hum seemed to be closing in on her. She had killed Yuki.

Killed her.

All because some emperor wanted to take Samas for his own.

The hum continued, but Shin's tears dried as a goal formed in her thoughts. Her mind cleared, as did her vision. Over Hanz's shoulder, she saw Corin's worried face.

"Put me down, Hanz," Shin said.

The big man did so, but before he let her go, he wrapped her in a hug and whispered in her ear, "You're going to make her proud."

Shin fought down a fresh bout of tears and nodded. Yuki had believed in her, which meant Hanz did too.

The words were more of a salve than any platitude could have been.

"I'm fine, Corin," Shin said after she'd composed herself, everything is going to be fine."

"How?" Corin asked.

Shin smiled without humor. "I'm going to kill the Maraman emperor."

Corin briefly recoiled from the intensity of Shin's visage, but soon his grin was a violent mirror image of her own. "Sounds good to me. How do we do that?"

Shin breathed in deep, seeking some sense of peace. Every fiber of her being called for violence. She wanted to unleash Harmony on her enemies. To rend and tear flesh with the same feral abandon as the very demons she had just helped banish. She wanted to visit upon the emperor the same fear and pain he'd delivered to Samas, with her teeth and nails if she had to.

But that wasn't the way.

"With patience," Shin said quietly.

Corin arched an eyebrow and even Hanz turned and looked at her with a funny smile on his face.

"Patience?" Corin asked. "You have to be running a fever. Or did you sacrifice some part of your head?"

Shin ignored the jibes. "Patience. Right now, I am no match for the emperor. His ability to manipulate the realm is so great that even Yuki feared him. I need to learn more. About sacrifice, yes, but more importantly about him. He must have weaknesses. Something we can exploit. No one is invincible, and I intend to prove that. When the time is right.

"Making her proud already," Hanz said without turning around.

They continued their moonlit retreat from Egzuki in silence. The sin scouted ahead, and all Shin had to do was follow quietly. She was grateful for the opportunity to abandon her responsibilities, if only for a while.

Yuki's death was a fresh wound, one she suspected would take considerable time to heal. But every step she took was one in the right direction.

They hiked through the night, covering miles quickly despite their exhausted state. Their hope was that the Maraman emperor would need time to recover from the sudden loss of so many of his forces. Their window to slip away lasted only as long as the Maraman confusion.

Fortunately, it seemed to be enough.

"Almost there," Hanz said.

"Good, I don't think they'll catch us." Shin could hear

the Maramans in the distance behind them, but the sentinels leading their party grew up in these mountains. They knew every pass and shortcut to get them to the coast.

"I think you're right, for what it's worth," Hanz said. "We need to take this one step at a time. When we return to Versun, we're going to have to figure out our next steps with the sentinels, and they've never been good at listening to others."

Shin looked up at the giant and, for a moment, saw the placid smile that used to adorn his face at all times. She knew exactly who he was talking about. "They really do think highly of themselves, don't they?"

Hanz laughed. "Well, you're the leader of the sin now. It's your job to keep them in their place. Whoever they might be."

Hanz let the implications hang in the air. It didn't matter if Sato would listen to her or not, she needed to convince the Firstborn to give her the time to find a way to beat the Maraman emperor.

She needed to make Yuki proud.

# 32

"How long were you under the Maramans' thumb?" Sheyric asked Keff.

"Too long. But Beast killed them," Keff responded.

Sheryic smiled. "Yes, he has a tendency to do that."

Beast grunted but said nothing. Keff and Sheyric got along like long-lost friends and had been chatting all the way from the beach. Beast had no idea how the young man did it, but Keff had somehow pulled out Sheyric's personality. Beast hadn't even been aware Sheyric possessed one.

"I'm sure there will be plenty more killing to come. If they're cutting off the shipping lanes, can we assume they'll be trying to attack Dahl next? Force us to defend two places at once?" Beast almost rubbed his hands together at the thought.

Gorou shook his head while Sheyric answered. "I doubt it. They would make us split our forces, but they would split theirs as well. Cutting off the supply lines would have collapsed the Samasian resistance, but now that they've lost another juggernaut, I can't see them trying again. I would guess their focus will turn now to Versun."

Their discussion came to a stop when Keff passed through the gates into Dahl proper. "Wow," he said as he took in the city before him.

Beast grinned at the sight of Keff in a new city. Then he turned his own attention to the gates. The walls here had been freshly painted, and the gates themselves were obviously new. Try as he might, Beast couldn't find any signs of the damage done by the siege.

"For a city that got the shit kicked out of it, this place looks pretty good," Beast said.

"Yes, the walls are stronger than never. Repairs within the city moved quickly under the sin and sentinel alliance. On the surface, it's like nothing changed," Sheyric said.

Beast recognized his friend's tone, "But?"

"But there is unrest everywhere. The city is overcrowded because people are afraid to live outside the walls," Sheryic was about to continue but Beast interrupted.

"Didn't Yuki implement the patrols I suggested?"

"Yes, and they're working. Iru has been quiet as of late. But every day when the warriors leave, people grumble about us not protecting Dahl's population. Food continues to flow into the city from the farms, but when people see most of it leaving to supply Versun, they fear that there won't be enough for Dahl if there's another siege," Sheryic said.

"But with the sin forces bolstering the garrison, as well as food coming from their village, we should have more than enough, shouldn't we?" Beast asked.

"Yes, but fear makes people irrational. Not to mention there are those calling themselves 'true Samasians' who are furious about an alliance with the sin. They outwardly speak against taking any help from the sin," Sheryic said and shook his head. "Or the mugon, for that matter."

Beast took another look at Dahl, now through the eyes of his new information.

On the surface, the city looked the same as it ever had. People bustled from one place to another, going about the business of their day. Under that surface, though, was a furtive energy that plagued every mundane action. People looked over their shoulders or up at the walls without even noticing they were doing it. Arguments broke out over things that would have been brushed off under better circumstances.

It looked new, but Dahl was a pot of boiling water and Beast feared what would happen if they couldn't turn down the heat.

"We're managing as best we can, and in terms of military resources we've never been stronger, but I fear what will happen if we rely solely on the threat of violence to keep people in line." Sheryic's statement had the whisper of a request in it.

"Sheyric, from what I can see, you're doing an amazing job running the city. I'm sure you can figure it out," Beast said.

"Thank you, but now that you're back I—"

"Oh, I'm not back. I'm here to kill Maramans. If you don't have any here, then I'm going to go find some," Beast said.

Sheryic's face remained expressionless, but Beast knew he was disappointed. "I see."

"Look, you want to fix things here? Then we remove the threat of being ripped apart by a foreign invader and their demon pets. So tonight I'm going to go get drunk, then tomorrow I'll leave for Versun and see what I can do about ending this invasion." Beast smiled and clapped Sheryic on the back.

"Of course. Is there anything else you need from me?" Sheyric asked. He knew better than to try to push Beast in a different direction.

"Yes, get a message to Colas. Tell her to find me in the tavern where we first met. Gorou, Keff, care to join me?"

"I think I'll stay and catch up with Sheyric," Gorou said.

Beast chose to ignore the judgment in Gorou's tone and instead grinned at the two reserved men. "Well, that sounds like it'll be a wild time. Don't get into too much trouble. Keff?"

"I think I'll join you. I'm interested to see why you love these taverns you keep talking about so much," Keff said.

"Great!" Beast said, but in his heart, he knew his joviality was just an act. He felt bad for leaving Sheyric without help, but what could he do? He'd already proved he was best suited for fighting. Whatever success he'd had uniting the bandits didn't apply here. Gorou and Sheryic were better served fixing things without him.

Besides, it had been too long since he'd had good Samasian ale.

By the time Colas walked in, Beast was entirely too sober.

He'd planned to get roaring drunk, but instead he'd nursed a few mugs of ale while talking to Keff. The young man seemed enamored with the tavern. Ale wasn't his favorite, but the din and chaos of the crowded room held his full attention. There was a musician playing a lute in the corner that seemed to be of particular interest to Keff, even though Beast didn't think the man was all that good.

“Are you corrupting this youth already?” Colas asked, and motioned for a drink.

“It’s pronounced *educating*, Colas. This poor boy has lived his whole life without spending a single night making poor decisions in a smelly room full of other people making poor decisions. That’s just no way to live,” Beast said.

“I am learning a lot,” Keff added.

“Keff, he took you off the island already. You don’t have to kiss his ass anymore!” Colas responded. “Now, why did you call me here?”

“I needed to drink with someone who wasn’t going to try to recruit me to the cause of saving Dahl,” Beast said.

“Well, that’s me. I will, however, try to recruit you into sailing away from this war,” Colas replied.

“Maybe after I get a good fight in. The open seas are boring, though. Not sure it’s for me,” Beast said.

Colas looked at him for a moment. “So do you want to talk about why I’m really here?”

“I already said.”

“Sure, but the truth is you want to head to Versun but you can’t leave Dahl in a lurch, as much as you’re pretending you can,” Colas said.

Beast raised an eyebrow. “How did you possibly figure that out?”

“Gorou's note was thorough. So, let’s get it figured out so we can get drunk,” Colas said, and took a sip of her ale.

“I don’t want to leave Sheyric on his own, but I don't think I can help. He wants me to be the bandit king again, but I don’t think that's what's needed,” Beast said.

Colas snorted a laugh. “Of course it’s not. These aren’t disenfranchised bandits living on the fringes of society. I don’t think you’re going to inspire the local blacksmiths and bakers to rise up in violence. Unless it's against you. I do think..." Colas trailed off as a woman approached Keff and whispered in his ear before handing him a small note. "What's this?"

Beast looked. "Oh that? That's been happening all night."

Keff added the note to a pile of others on the table. "I like taverns."

Colas grinned. "I'm sure you do. Look, Beast, you don't need to be the Bandit King to help Sheryic, but you're a local legend. The man that united the bandits of Samas and took on the sentinels. The man that helped save Dahl from the demons. Just be that."

"I am that!" Beast said in frustration.

"So show them," Keff said quietly.

"What?" Beast asked.

"You want to fight, and they need something to hope for, right? So let's give them hope. On the island, we would have big parties every full moon. There would be drink and food and we'd put on a performance that told the history of our people," Keff said.

"Sounds nice, but what does that have to do with Dahl?"

"Have a big party... a..." Keff was searching for the word.

"A festival," Colas said.

"Yes!" Keff said and pointed at Colas. "A festival. The city is afraid, so distract them. Have a performance, like him, but better," Keff said, pointing at the musician.

Beast smiled. "We could have a tournament. Unarmed, of course. I'll take on all comers and then when I win, I'll announce to the city that I'm going to fight the Maramans."

"I don't want to fill your head with anymore grandiose ideas about yourself, but that might actually work," Colas said.

"Of course it will! Then I can go and deal with the

Maramans. We can show them the juggernaut as well. Promise them that you'll be sticking around in case the Maramans attack again," Beast said.

"So, I'm on guard duty?" Colas asked.

Beast smiled. "Well Colas, it's your juggernaut. You can do what you please with it, but I was hoping you might be able to stick around and help us out."

"Mine?" Colas asked.

"Yours," Beast replied.

"Keff, you heard that, right? In case he tries to go back on his word?" Colas asked.

"I heard it," Keff said.

"Good. Then let's get drunk."

Beast drained his mug.

# 33

"Dead?" Sato repeated the word back to Shin after she finished recounting their expedition on Ilos.

"Yes," Corin answered, so the Shin wouldn't have to say it again. "After she gave her last sacrifice she demanded that Shin—"

"I killed her, Sato," Shin snapped.

Sato held up his hands. Shin had always been prone to anger, and whatever had happened on Ilos hadn't done anything to change that. She was dangerous. In his calmest voice, he said, "I'm sorry, Shin. I'm just trying to make sure I understand everything you told me. From the sounds of it, she trusted you with a terrible task. You didn't let her down."

As was her customary reaction to kindness from him, Shin fixed him with a glare before pointedly looking in another direction. Sato took advantage of the silence to wrap his head around Yuki's death. His feelings were mixed at the news. She was, at her core, the antithesis of everything the Path taught.

But she'd earned his respect.

She was their most powerful weapon against the

emperor. Although he had always planned to kill her at the conclusion of the war, he would have much preferred the elder sin over her apprentice. Now, all he had was Shin, and she wasn't ready.

"Shin, I'm sorry for your loss. Yuki was an impressive woman," the Firstborn said. His voice was as soothing as a babbling brook, and Shin looked at him with immense gratitude. Sato pushed down a wave of anger.

"Thank you, but she wouldn't have wanted us to waste time mourning her. Not now. We struck a blow against the Maramans. Now we have to be ready for what comes next," she replied.

Sato used the opportunity to contribute his thoughts. "I agree with Shin. We've spent almost a year preparing our combined forces for this exact moment. With the ferals cleared, our path is clear to begin an assault on Iru," Sato said.

"Assault?" Shin asked. "No, we need to prepare our defenses here. Without the ferals to harass us, the emperor has to commit his actual forces to any attack. We can start bleeding him dry. Here we have the thick walls, the people, and the supplies."

Her words made him cringe. She had no idea about managing a campaign, and he spoke before he'd considered his words. "With all due respect, girl, whatever power you have does not qualify you to speak on the intricacies of war."

"Call me girl again and I'll show you exactly what kind of power I have," Shin said evenly.

"Excuse me?" Sato said, standing up.

"I have every right to be in this room making these decisions. It's exactly what Yuki groomed me for. So, if you have a problem with my plan, let's argue it, but you will *not* dismiss me out of hand." Shin never raised her voice, but

Sato was suddenly very aware of how little he knew about sacrifice.

Despite his anger, he was impressed. Shin's current composure was new, something he'd never seen from her before.

*You need to be careful about this one*, the voice in his head agreed.

Sato kept his reaction to nothing more than an eye twitch. The last thing he needed was another voice to argue with.

Before Sato could respond to Shin, the Firstborn stood up calmly. "Sato, please sit. Shin, I understand that you're upset, but I have found in the past that strategy meetings tend to be more productive when the strategists aren't threatening one another."

Sato mastered his anger. He wouldn't display less composure than a peasant. If the Firstborn wanted her here, he was in no position to say otherwise. "I am sorry, Shin, but I disagree. We need to press our advantage now. The people here in Versun and back on Iru need us to reclaim Ilos."

"Yuki wouldn't want my first act as leader of the sin to be throwing away the lives of my people," Shin said.

The Firstborn cut Sato off with a gesture. "First of all, Shin, this may be hard for you to hear, but I don't recognize you as leader of the sin—"

"You don't get to decide that!" Shin shouted. Her composure dropped, and Sato wondered if the Firstborn knew just how close he walked to a very dangerous confrontation. Especially with Corin here. Those two were young, but plenty formidable. Sato didn't think he could kill them both in time to save the Firstborn if it came to that.

The Firstborn remained unperturbed. "Listen, Shin. I do not doubt your power, nor your intentions, but you do not have the experience to lead. I will listen to your council, but until further notice Hanz will run the day-to-day operations of the sin—"

"How dare you?" Shin interrupted again but this time the Firstborn held up a hand with all the authority of the eternal sun behind it.

"How much do you need from the coffers for next quarter's rations?" The Firstborn asked.

"What? I don't know."

"Which of your units needs its weapons repaired? How many arrows do you need from the fletchers?"

"I... I'm sure I could find out. There's someone to handle all of that," Shin said defiantly.

"That's true. Who?"

Shin stared and Sato smiled smugly.

The Firstborn concluded his argument. "Hanz knows. And what he doesn't know, he knows how to delegate. I'm not saying you can't do it, I'm just saying you aren't ready and now isn't the time to learn."

For a long moment, Sato wasn't sure what Shin would do. Behind her, Corin was a tense as a loaded coil, ready to lash out if necessary.

Shin took a deep breath. "I understand," Shin said. "I will speak with Hanz and we'll discuss the best way forward."

The Firstborn nodded. "Good. Now, for point two. As I said, I will listen to your council, and in this case, I think you're right."

"Right about what?" Sato asked.

The Firstborn turned to him. "An attack isn't in our best interests. We are strongest behind these walls, and with the ferals removed we've finally given ourselves a chance to breathe and plan."

*He doesn't trust you as much as he does the girl.*

Sato composed himself. "Sir, I think that's a mistake. We can't afford a prolonged siege. The ferals may be gone, but they still have their pet demons. You didn't see them at Dahl. They scaled the walls like they were nothing," Sato said.

"I saw them when Bulas fell, General. I understand their power. But they'll be no less dangerous if we attack. And the emperor himself is still an unknown. Shin, it will be up to you to explore what sacrificial options we have. Report to me when you know more," the Firstborn ordered.

Shin, seemingly mollified by the Firstborn taking her side, accepted her orders without complaint.

Sato felt a cold wave of realization crash over him.

"So, you're giving orders to the sin now?" Sato asked.

"Hanz will oversee the day-to-day operations—"

"Yes, you said that. And when Shin's ready, she'll lead them. Until then, what? The sin have been absorbed into the sentinel fold?" Sato's words were slow and measured.

"Yes. We are at war, Sato, with Yuki gone, it's up to me to lead our combined forces." The Firstborn's tone was equally measured.

*He's turned from the Path. He wants to embrace the sin.*

Sato swallowed hard. The consequences were dizzying, and he needed time to understand. But one thing was clear. The Firstborn had gone too far. Even if this war ended tomorrow, he'd do nothing to eliminate the sin.

Sato regarded his old mentor, his old friend, and nodded sadly. Even after everything, he couldn't believe it had come to this. Before, he'd disagreed. But this?

This was wrong.

"With permission, sir, I would take my leave. I need to prepare my Sun Stalkers for a siege.

"Of course, Sato. Thank you for your time," The Firstborn said.

Sato wondered if the Firstborn knew the course of his thoughts. He often had in the past. If so, what would he do? Sato needed Crispin, immediately.

Sato bowed, then took one last look around the room. He fixed Shin with a look that told her he wasn't done yet. He didn't want her to believe he was embarrassed by what happened here. She was still just a peasant. When he left the room, he allowed his fists to clench tightly but kept himself under control otherwise. She remained, to talk further with the Firstborn.

About the sin.

He was furious, yes, but with that fury there came a clarity that he hadn't felt for a long time.

For the first time in what felt like forever, since before the Firstborn had put him in charge of the Sun Stalkers, his personal path was clear.

# 34

"I think it's good," Hanz said evenly.

"Good?" Shin thought she was imagining his answer. "He thinks he can just take over the sin because I'm not as experienced a leader as Yuki!"

Shin had left the meeting with Firstborn torn in two. The Firstborn had heeded her council, and Sato was on the outs with his old mentor. But as she made her way through Versun and back to the barracks, she worked herself into a fury at the way she had let the Firstborn take charge of the sin without a fight.

"Is he telling you how to use sacrifice? Or how best to fight the emperor?" Hanz asked.

"No," Shin replied. She tried to match Hanz's calm, but it was hard.

"And he took your advice about readying our defenses rather than attacking?"

"Yes, but you're missing the point! He said he was taking the sin into the sentinel fold! Yuki never would have allowed that." Shin's heart broke at the thought of letting down her old mentor.

Hanz smiled. “No, she wouldn’t have, and you don’t have to either.”

“So what do we do? We can't pull out of Versun. We need to stay to fight the Maramans.” Her first decision as the sin leader, and it might doom them all.

Then Hanz laughed at her.

She was sure her glare would have cut a sword in half.

“I think you’ve spent too much time with these sentinels,” Hanz said.

“What’s that supposed to mean?”

“Not everything is black and white, and we're certainly not followers of the Path. We need the Firstborn’s leadership and the knowledge of his generals so we can fight the Maramans. They need our skills to fight the demons and the emperor. The Firstborn can say whatever he wants, but this is an alliance, and nothing more. When what's needed is done, all that matters is we are ready for what comes next.”

And if he plans to maintain control of the sin?”

A look of realization crossed Hanz’s face, and he looked at Corin, who had been silent since they left the meeting. “She doesn’t realize it yet, does she?”

“No, but are you all that surprised?” Corin asked Hanz in return.

“What are you two talking about?” Shin asked.

Hanz grinned. “The sin will follow you, no matter what the Firstborn says.”

Shin looked over at Corin, whose expression made her feel like a fool.

Hanz's claim loosened something in her chest, and her breath came easier than it had for months. "Is it really that simple?"

"Yuki said so. And you've commanded your unit well since we escaped Iru the first time."

Shin clenched her fist. That, at least, made what came next easy.

The Firstborn wouldn't take anything from her.

"Thank you, both. I'll need both of you in the coming weeks. More than I have before."

"Of course," Corin said. "That was always our plan. What do you want to do next?"

Shin thought for a moment. "We need to be ready for the Maramans' possible responses, right? So, food should be a priority—"

"No," Hanz interrupted, "I'll take care of all that. What Corin means is, what are you going to do about the emperor and his summoners?"

"Right," Shin said. She trusted Hanz, and he was better suited to the task anyway. Her focus was on the sacrifice. "I want every adept to meet me at the southern gates tomorrow. Whatever assignment they previously had can wait."

"Done. What are you planning?" Hanz asked.

"We're going to go for a walk," Shin said with s smile.

"A walk?" Corin looked confused.

"A walk. We need to clear our minds. The sin have been using sacrifice in a very specific way for a very long time. It's a power that needs to be used in moderation. Every decision made needs to be weighed and calculated because there's only so much one person can give up."

"But now?"

"Now our backs are against the wall. The threat that we've been carefully rationing out our power to defend against is here. It's time we change our mindset. We need to be careful, but we can't let that care stop us from reaching our full potential. The summoners are willing to siphon every ounce of their life into the realm in service of the emperor. I would never ask that of the adepts, but in order to fight enemies possessed of such conviction, we will need to do more than we are now."

"Is that... safe?" Corin asked nervously.

"Probably not. We call it sacrifice for a reason. But there has to be a way to mitigate the risks of using more power. Yuki spent so long regretting the path she took to gain her strength that I think it clouded her judgment when it came to forging new ways to use sacrifice. I think she knew that at the end."

Shin realized that Hanz and Corin were staring at her and felt her cheeks flush. "Sorry, I got lost in my own thoughts there."

Corin beamed at her. "You should probably memorize what you just said. I'm convinced, and I can't even use sacrifice."

Hanz seemed equally pleased. "Everything we've done to fight the Maramans has been reactive. The sin send back demons that others have killed using the same safe spell that's been used for centuries. I'd wager they're ready to shake things up a little."

Shin felt a rush of excitement and pride that was replaced with searing guilt as quickly as striking a match. "Yuki's not even dead two days and I'm already planning to tear apart what she built."

"Exactly like she planned," Hanz said.

Shin hugged Hanz around his neck, not trusting herself to speak. She felt Corin's arms wrap around them both and for a few minutes, all was right with the world.

"To Yuki," Corin said, and raised his mug.

"To Yuki," Shin and Hanz said in unison.

The sin were hers now, no matter what the Firstborn thought. She could handle him. Besides, it could be worse.

She could have to deal with Sato.

# 35

The crowd roared as the fierce battle between the two mismatched warriors raged on. The air was thick with tension, as the two combatants exchanged blow after blow, each one more powerful than the last. That either was still standing seemed an incredible feat.

Suddenly, the much smaller sin made a devastating move, catching the big sentinel off guard and sending him flying. As the big sentinel landed flat on his back with a thud, the crowd erupted in even louder cheers. The sin threw his hands in the air and began to strut around victoriously.

Beast observed the exchange, but most of his attention was on the crowd. The sin was a clear favorite, and Beast didn't think it was only because the crowd loved rooting for the smaller fighter. They were cheering against the sentinel. Though the order was still supposedly in charge, Beast sensed the change in the air. Generations of grievances had built up, and only now were finding release.

For a moment, it seemed like the fight was over, and the crowd started to stand, satisfied with the outcome. But the big sentinel was far from finished, and he quickly recovered, springing to his feet and launching himself at the sin with a vengeance.

Once again, the crowd fell silent as the two warriors clashed in a flurry of punches and kicks. As the battle intensified, it became clear that the big sentinel was determined to make up for his previous defeat, and the small sin was just as determined to prove it hadn't been a fluke.

As the two warriors continued their fierce battle, the crowd held its breath. Suddenly, the big sentinel swung too hard, leaving himself open to a devastating blow. The sin delivered, knocking the big sentinel backwards. As the sentinel tried to regain his balance, the sin struck once more with lightning speed, forcing him to the ground.

The crowd erupted as the sin stood over his fallen foe and threw his hands in the air victoriously.

Beast joined in the adulation as he finished his ale in one long drink. His original thought had been to fight in the tournament along with everyone else, but Gorou suggested it was better for him to act as the final reward for the event. Beast had to agree. Facing him in single combat would be an honor for anyone. A painful honor, admittedly, but still an honor.

"This is going well," Gorou said.

"I told you not to doubt me," Beast said.

"I didn't doubt you. I just knew you wouldn't help with the logistics. Fortunately, I had Sheryic and Keff to help me while you... wait. What did you do?"

"I inspired the masses of Dahl to participate in an event unlike any they'd seen before. To shake off the malaise of their everyday lives and celebrate what it means to be a Samasian!" Beast argued.

"What he means is that he walked around Dahl for a few days telling people that we were throwing a party while the rest of us did all the real work," Keff said.

"Sounds about right," Sheyric said.

"Ungrateful. The lot of you," Beast said before hopping down from the makeshift dais and walking towards his challenger.

Beast had to admit that his friends had done well. The festival was a success. There had been food and entertainment throughout the day. Keff's people who'd come with Beast mingled freely with the Samasians as though they'd always been on Ilos. As dusk settled the sin put on a fireworks display. Colas showed off the juggernaut and its accompanying warships by staging a mock battle.

And then there was the tournament.

Beast couldn't believe no one had thought of it before. People had signed up in droves to test their mettle against the best warriors in the city.

And now one lucky winner got to fight Beast.

"What's your name, son?" Beast asked.

"Darien," the young man replied.

"You're quite the warrior. Where have you been?"

"Recovering. I lost a fight, badly, and it took me a while to get back on my feet."

"Well, I can promise you're going to lose again, but I'll make sure you're not hurt too badly this time. Sound good?"

In response, Darien darted forward and threw a whip-fast kick that almost connected with Beast's head before he could dodge out of the way. Beast only had time to laugh at the gall of the man before he was blocking blows once more.

Beast danced with Darien for a while, throwing some strikes while blocking others. His opponent was fast and sharp, and the crowd cheered when he made a particularly acrobatic move. Beast, always one to put on a show, indulged both the crowd and Darien while getting some cheers of his own.

Then a kick slipped through Beast's guard and made his ears ring.

"Fuck," Beast shouted and shook his head.

Sensing blood in the water, Darien sprang forward and threw a punch meant to put Beast down for good.

His fist caught only air.

Beast ducked the blow and, as he had so many times before, wrapped his massive arms around the man across from him. Beast lifted Darien into the air with ease before slamming him on the ground. Darien looked dazed.

"Yield?" Beast had positioned himself well, trapping Darien under his bulk, and had a fist raised.

"Yield!" Darien said.

Beast stood and helped the younger man up. When Beast raised his opponent's hand, the crowd erupted into applause and cheers that Beast was sure could be heard all the way in Versun.

"You cheer the might of Dahl. The might of Samas!" Beast roared.

The crowd roared right back in agreement.

"I know it's been hard. The Maramans, the demons, your entire way of life changing. But here, tonight, you can see the true strength of Samas!"

Beast knew he had their attention. It brought him to his true point.

"So, why not lend your strength to that cause? Who cares if you aren't a sentinel or a sin? We've seen tonight that we can all fight. Colas needs those with knowledge of the seas to join her on the juggernaut. She seeks new lands and new opportunities and welcomes all who would join her.

My mugon need strong, brave Samasians to soak the soil of our land in the blood of its invaders! Join us!"

Beast left the ring to the sounds of cheers and applause. As he left, he saw mugon moving amongst the crowd, signing up any who wanted to join. Before long, they were surrounded by eager volunteers.

"Told you it would work," Beast said to Sheyric.

"Actually, Keff told me it would work. You told me you were going to kick the ass of whomever won the tournament."

"Beast?" Darien's voice was tentative.

"What?"

"Are you heading to Versun next?" Darien asked.

"I am. Likely within the next few days. But first, I plan to be very drunk."

"I would like to accompany you, if I may," Darien said.

"Of course, you'd be welcome! Anyone who can beat up on the sentinels the way you did is more than welcome to join us."

Darien bowed. "Thank you."

Beast watch Darien walk away. Although he'd looked small next to his larger opponent, and even smaller next to Beast, he was of a medium build and walked with the grace of a fighter. Beast had seen firsthand how good he'd been. "He'll be a valuable addition."

"Agreed. But enough of this. You go drink. I'm going to make sure that all our volunteers have somewhere to go by tomorrow," Sheryic said.

Beast thanked Sheryic, then went off in search of food and ale. He found both before long and sat at a table away from the festivities to eat. Although he hadn't fought a battle today, the distinct feeling of winning a victory settled over him.

And the loneliness that often accompanied it.

Keff plopped down beside him with a drink in hand. "Mead, Beast, mead is my drink."

"That fruity shit? No thanks."

Keff laughed and took another sip. "I was impressed today. I don't know if it's just your size, but people seem to flock to you, even if it isn't good for their health."

"It's beginning to feel like more of a curse than a blessing."

"Why?"

"Because they come expecting me to know what to do, when all I really know how to do is fight. Which is fine for me, but most people who try to follow me have a habit of dying."

"Dying and dying for a cause are very different."

"Are they?" Beast asked. "Seems to me like dead is dead."

"I bet most people who have died following you would agree with me."

"I'd like to believe that," Beast said. His hand drifted, as it often did, toward the hilt of Benji's sword.

He looked out into the masses of people who loved him but would never be close to him and sighed deeply in appreciation of those who were.

# 36

Sato's eyes snapped open.

Though he hadn't yet identified the sound that had disturbed him, a lifetime of being a soldier meant he shook off the shackles of sleep instantly.

"What is it, Crispin?" Sato said. No one but Roko or Crispin would have the gall to wake him, and Roko always knocked.

"I have news about the Firstborn," Crispin replied from the dark.

"Go ahead."

"He's taken ill. He was found on the floor of his chambers unconscious but breathing. Apparently, a light could be seen coming from his chamber, but there was no answer when an attendant knocked to check on him."

"Who found him?"

"Captain Harris was the first on the scene, sir."

Sato nodded, though Crispin likely couldn't see him in the dark, and stood. He began to dress. "Has anyone else been to see him yet?"

"No one. We thought it best if you were the first. We have

already sent for a healer," Crispin said and held the door open.

Sato briefly debated the best action to take. "Of course. Send for Helios as well. If this illness is serious, then we'd best be ready."

It had only been a couple of days since his meeting with the Firstborn and Shin. The meeting that proved to Sato that the Firstborn's willingness to compromise had led him irrevocably from the Path.

*Ill or not, he's still the Firstborn.*

Sato smiled grimly at the uncertainty in Rua's voice. He didn't bother answering the old sentinel. He appreciated her wisdom but didn't want to share his head with her or anyone else. He still had much to attend to, but getting her out of his head would soon be a priority.

They reached the door to the Firstborn's chambers. Harris was standing guard outside, as pale as a sheet.

"He's alone inside," Harris said. "It doesn't look good, sir."

Sato looked at Harris and saw the sadness in his eyes. He'd served directly under the Firstborn for years. He laid a hand on the man's shoulder. "I'm sure he'll be fine. When Helios arrives, you may come in with him."

Sato was surprised at the strength of his own sorrow. Whatever his flaws, however far he'd strayed from the Path, the Firstborn was still one of Sato's oldest friends. If he was to die here, the man would leave an emptiness in Sato's life when he was gone.

It took a moment for Sato's eyes to adjust to the dim light of the Firstborn's chambers. Once they did, he saw the Firstborn on his bed, his chest rising and falling in rapid, erratic movements. Sato almost broke when he heard the ragged breaths that accompanied the Firstborn's chest, but he steeled himself.

Sato knelt beside the Firstborn's bed. He'd intended to rest a hand on his old friend and offer some comfort. None could escape his throat, so tight it felt as though he was choking. He knelt by the Firstborn and did nothing to stop the hot tears that ran down his cheeks. Sato wasn't even sure if he blinked. All he could do was watch the Firstborn's chest rise and fall and listen to his breath try to claw its way out of his throat.

The door opened behind him, and Sato's body unlocked itself. He reached out as if he were going to lay a hand on the Firstborn, but his arm stopped in midair as Helios arrived.

"Helios, I'm sorry to wake you." Sato wiped the tears from his cheek as he stood to face the old sentinel. He had to be strong.

"Nonsense. How is he?" Helios asked.

"We don't know. Crispin has sent for a healer, but one hasn't arrived yet. The attendant that found him was able to get him into bed, but I don't think he's woken since," Sato said.

"I sent for a healer of my own," Helios said and raised an eyebrow at Sato.

"An excellent idea. The more help we have, the better. I know little of healing, but I'm no stranger to death. I fear I can hear it in his breaths," Sato replied.

Helios considered the two men for a moment before turning to Crispin. "Thank you for acting so quickly, Crispin. What do you know?"

Crispin bowed respectfully. "Very little, sir. I did my duty and nothing more. The attendant reported to Harris, who found me. I was working late in Sato's office, and Harris was looking for him."

Helios looked again between the two men. Then he looked down at the Firstborn, a man he'd known since childhood.

"Helios, I'm sorry to bring this up now, but there's another reason I called for you first," Sato said.

"What?" Helios asked.

"While the Firstborn is ill, it would fall to the magistrate of Versun to take over in his absence," Sato said. "It should have been Bulas, but she died in the invasion, and Versun's magistrate is next in line."

Realization, and suspicion, dawned on Helios's face. "And you want me to make sure that the rest of the sentinels in Versun support you?"

"No!" Sato almost shouted. "My only mission now is to protect Samas from the Maramans. You should take command. Then, if the worst happens and he should pass, you can take over as Firstborn."

Helios stared at him, and Sato let the silence hang.

But Sato could see the skepticism that had been growing in Helios fade at the offer. They all had to work together if the Maramans were to be defeated. Helios would understand.

"No," Helios finally answered.

Sato felt as though he'd broken the surface of the ocean after being submerged and realized he'd been holding his breath. He let it out slowly. "Why? Helios, you're the obvious choice. You have experience as a magistrate in Versun and have been a long-standing sentinel of influence. There's no one better!"

"And everyone here knows I was Izuki's pawn. It wasn't

until you came along that I had the courage to do the right thing. By the sun, I'm only alive by your mercy! No, I appreciate your confidence, but it must be you. The Firstborn has been grooming you for this moment since you were a child."

Sato shook his head. "I'm not ready."

"No one ever is. But you'll succeed. I know you will."

Sato looked over at the Firstborn. "It would be better if he recovered."

"I hope he does, too, Sato, but I have also seen my share of death. I think you'd best prepare yourself for a long rule," Helios said.

As if on cue, the healer Crispin sent for burst into the room. The three men turned to look at the woman who wasted no time rushing over the Firstborn with a large satchel slung over her shoulder.

"My lords, if you please, I'll need the room," the healer said in a tone that offered no space for argument.

"Do you know who you're speaking to, healer?" Sato demanded.

"Sato, it's fine," Helios said. "Let her work."

Sato, his face a thundercloud, nodded curtly and turned to leave the room. Once they were out in the hall, the second healer arrived and Helios gestured him towards the chambers.

Sato rubbed at his eyes. "I think sleep will evade me for the rest of this night. I'm going to start planning for tomorrow. The people will need to know what's happened here. Helios, would you mind helping Crispin find the records of succession that the Firstborn created? I doubt he was expecting to use them so soon, but he was nothing if not organized."

"Of course, we'll stay here until the healers are done. Any updates I'll pass along to you," Helios said.

"Thank you." Sato began to turn when Helios stopped him with a hand on his shoulder.

"Is there anything else you need?" Helios asked.

Sato looked back at the room they'd just left. "I'm going to miss him dearly."

Helios nodded before giving Sato a brief, fatherly hug.

Sato strode down the hall, towards his destiny as Firstborn, tears streaming down his face.

# 37

Shin stood with her back to the ocean and felt the slight breeze rustle through her hair. Assembled before her was every sin on Egzuki that had the ability to touch sacrifice. There were about eighty sin in total, mostly adepts with a handful of elites scattered throughout.

Shin had chosen a path that would lead them to this spot on the northwestern coast of the island. They were far enough from Versun and the port that it was quiet, but they still had a view of Iru to the north. The day was clear, and it was easy to make out the coastline of the occupied island across the water.

And even easier to see the two juggernauts looming between them and the capital city of Samas.

"Everyone enjoying the view?" Shin asked the crowd.

There was some murmuring from the group and a few people shouted out that they didn't.

"Good. Neither do I. I know the sin have spent most of our time hiding from the people of Samas, encouraging the belief that we are nothing more than a myth, but this is still our home," Shin said and then pointed out towards Iru, "and they're trying to take it from us."

Shin's tone had been subdued, and she was met with a grim silence from the sin before her. While deadly, this was no group of soldiers that Shin wanted to whip into a frenzy. The true danger of these sin lay in their measured response to danger.

The silence before her was pregnant with murderous intent.

"So, the question becomes what are we going to do about it?"

Shin could sense the confusion amongst the sin and smiled. She needed to get them thinking differently than they ever had.

"Well? They're coming for us. What are we going to do about it?"

A tentative hand went up in the crowd. "We send the demons back, like we always have? Isn't that what we've drilled alongside the sentinels for?"

"Yes, and I think we're ready for that. But what about the summoners?" Shin asked.

There was murmuring from the crowd, but no one seemed to be sure what answer Shin was looking for.

"What about the summoners? Do any of you think we're a match for them?"

This is time she was met with timid silence.

"Who saw them at Dahl? During the first attack?"

Hands went up.

"And? One for one, can we stand against them?"

"No," a voice said from the crowd.

"You're right. As of this moment, right now, we aren't prepared for the summoners. We've prepared for the demons, but now the ferals are gone. It's time we figured out how we're going to deal with those summoners."

Every eye was on her. Every sin was expecting some a direction, some answer to the problem Shin had presented.

She said nothing.

Finally, a voice came out of the crowd. "So, what do we do?"

Shin smiled at the question she'd been waiting for. "I don't know."

Sin heads turned and looked at each other.

"I'm not Yuki." Shin let the words sink in for a moment. "I may be a match for her power, but there's no way I can match her experience. No one here can. At least not alone."

Now, she had their attention.

"Yuki led the sin from the time she created the order. She was the first to wield sacrifice, and it was she who oversaw its teaching through generations. Every piece of scaffolding that supports sacrifice as we know it was put in place by Yuki. But she's only human. She made mistakes, and many of her teachings were colored by those mistakes."

There was some angry grumbling from the crowd.

Shin held up her hands. "I'm not here to disparage Yuki needlessly. I loved her as much as any of you, but if we are to survive this, we need to do so by thinking differently than she did. She knew this at the end. She knew it and that's why I'm here. So, I want to ask all of you to think of new ways to use sacrifice. New tools that we can use against our enemies. New ways to break the rules that we've lived by for so long."

The silence from the crowd was deafening. Slowly, sin began looking at one another and some whispered questions were asked. Finally, a woman that Shin recognized as an elite, Lyla, raised her hand. "The rules are in place to protect us. If we sacrifice too much, we could damage ourselves or others."

"I know, and Yuki was always careful to strike that balance. But now, with the Maramans on our shores, we need to take risks. I know some of you must have had ideas that you've dismissed before. Things that seemed unsafe or not worth the risk. Now is the time!"

Another hand went up. "Adepts can only create existing spells. Even if we had ideas, how would we know if it could work?"

Shin was surprised to hear Lyla answer before she could. "Don't be afraid to have ideas that won't work. The elites have the capability to be more creative with sacrifice, but that doesn't mean we *are* more creative. Shin is right, we need to lean on our experience as a group."

Shin smiled as the crowd began talking among themselves excitedly. It was chaos at first, but then the group got into a rhythm of presenting an idea and then dissecting it. Some suggestions were dismissed out of hand as impossible. Some were filed away to be parsed some more. Most, unfortunately, suffered from the same issue: the price was too high. The sacrifice demanded to defeat a summoner or two would put the adept out of commission or even kill them. In the end, they would have no sin left to stand against the demons.

Or worse still, the emperor.

Shin could sense the sin getting discouraged. "Just because we haven't found the answer yet, doesn't mean we won't find it at all. Look at the power we've created here, as a group, by simply supporting each other's ideas. We'll find it."

"That's it," Lyla said.

"What is?" Shin asked.

"We're supporting each other as a group. Remember the portal the summoners tried to open on Dahl? They did that together. Divided the cost."

"They called the realm as a group," Shin said.

"Exactly. We always think of sacrifice as the cost to us as a person, but our most effective spell is one that is divided amongst all sin, for all time." Lyla held up her ethereal pinky for the group to see.

Sounds of realization bounced through the crowd and then an adept spoke up. "Yuki created that spell, though. Can we do something like that again?"

"I think so. We would just need to decide how much we are willing to give up and see what the realm offers. First though, what do we want? How can we use our power as a group?" Shin asked.

There was some more discussion among the sin. Lyla seemed particularly animated in her discussion with the other elites. The crowd settled and Lyla had some final words with her cohorts before turning to Shin. "What if we asked for limitless access to the realm, for one battle, one final fight against the Maramans, where our imagination was our only limit?"

Shin liked the idea. "What would that cost?"

Lyla looked back at the other elites for confirmation before nodding. "Our lives."

Shin considered the idea for a bit. Many of their decisions would lead them here. "We can't rule it out, but we can't leave Samas defenseless," Shin said. "There will be other battles down the road. Samas will always need the sin."

Lyla cleared her throat. "I spoke poorly. Our lives wouldn't be forfeited today, but they would be shortened. The realm would get half of our years. It could savor all the joy, sadness, love and fear we could possibly feel in the days after the midpoint of our lives."

"Would that be enough? For those assembled here to live to what, forty years at most? Then the realm takes us?" Shin asked.

Lyla shook her head. She looked uncertain. "Not just us here, all sin from now until forever. Any of us touched by the realm— adept, elite, or just a warrior. A cap on our lives, so that Samas can survive."

The scope staggered Shin. Some part of her had started to hope that if it came down to it, the realm would only demand another finger. The enormity of this shook her. What right did she have to make this decision for so many? There was only one way to choose, one way to prevent her from going mad with the grief of the choice. "This has to be unanimous. If anyone here doesn't agree to this, we won't do it."

Looks passed back and forth between the warriors, but no one raised an objection. Shin wasn't relieved. Part of her mind was racing for other ideas, but another was already planning what came next.

One hand finally went up. "I'm fine with it, but what can the adepts do with that power? We're limited to spells that we've been taught. We'll need some kind of weapon to make this worthwhile."

The assembled adepts all voiced their agreement and Shin was humbled by the commitment of those surrounding her. To this, she finally had an answer.

"I think I've got just the spell. One that would make Yuki proud."

# 38

It took Beast longer to recover from being drunk than he'd expected. Of course, he'd ended up being drunk for a day longer than he'd planned, but what was the point of life if you couldn't celebrate a little? It was good to be back home.

Gorou and Sheyric had been happy to let Beast drink. They told him it kept him out of their hair while they dealt with the sudden swelling of their ranks. Apparently, organizing hundreds of people to fight took longer to iron out than one evening. Beast was just happy none of that minutia fell to him.

"Have you been to Versun?" Keff asked.

"Once or twice, when I was younger. Once I became the Bandit King, I kept away. Sentinels breed there like rabbits," Beast answered as he struggled to get comfortable in the transport skiff.

He missed the wider decks of Warhammer and the juggernaut, but the trip was short, so he ignored his discomfort and focused on the prospect of spilling more Maraman blood.

"I can't imagine a place that's bigger than Dahl," Keff said.

"Well, start imagining, because Versun makes Dahl look like a village." He paused, and knew Keff would be annoyed, but he had to say what came next. "Remember your promise, though. If we find out Maramans are on their way, you stay off the walls and somewhere safe. I know you're good with that sling, but you're too valuable to the cause to be lost to some Maraman's spear."

Keff did look annoyed. Beast had mentioned this three times already today. "Valuable to the cause or valuable to you?"

"Both," Beast grunted.

Judging by the look on Keff's face, Beast guessed he was thinking of teasing Beast, but, likely because he didn't fancy swimming the rest of the way to Egzuki, he kept his mouth shut.

"Hopefully Gorou will have more information for us when we make landfall. I sent a raven before we left, instructing him to meet us at the port. I'd like to know how Yuki and the Firstborn are feeling about me before I meet with them," Beast said.

"Because you deserted them?"

"I exercised my freedom." Beast's response was a low growl.

"Of course." The sarcasm dripped from every word.

Beast glared. "I'm not sure if I admire your bravery or pity your stupidity for talking to me like that."

"It's your fault for showing your cards. You just told me how valuable I am," Keff said with a shrug.

Beast grunted. "Not too valuable for a swim, I'd wager."

"True enough. Why do you think I waited until we were so close to shore?"

Beast glanced toward the port of Egzuki and realized Keff was right. There wouldn't be much satisfaction to be gained by tossing him overboard now. There was barely a mile left, and Keff swam that distance for fun.

"You might be too clever for your own good," Beast said.

"I figure I'm fine as long as I'm around imbeciles like you."

Beast shook his head and picked up his axe. As the skiff came to a stop, he stood and strapped the weapon to his back. At the end of the dock, Gorou waved at them. Keff raised his arm in response.

Beast shoved him into the water.

The small islander went flying off the boat and into the water with a yelp. It turned out Beast had been wrong; there was plenty of satisfaction to be gained from tossing Keff overboard.

"I'll assume he deserved that," Gorou said in greeting.

"And more," Beast replied.

Gorou nodded. "Come on, I got us a drink at one of the dockside taverns."

"That bad, eh? Who's angrier? It's Yuki, isn't it?"

"No, she's dead."

Beast was used to Gorou's even keeled delivery of any and all news, but he was still taken aback. "Dead? How?"

"She went to Iru with Shin to remove the threat of the feral demons. It worked, but it cost her her life."

Keff returned in time to hear the conversation and was doing his best to look solemn while dripping wet. "Should we go get that drink?"

"Yes," Beast said.

Gorou led them to a table that looked out onto the ocean. There were three mugs of ale sitting on it. Beast drained all three before sitting down. "Did Shin make it back?"

Gorou motioned Keff to the bar before sitting across from Beast. "Yes. She and Corin led the raiding party home."

Relief swelled in his chest. "So, is Shin is leading the sin, then?"

"She's their leader, yes, but the Firstborn absorbed the sin into the military structure of the sentinels. He didn't feel she was ready to lead."

Beast took one of the mugs of ale that Keff had bought back. This time he took a more measured approach and leaned back in his chair. A lot had changed since his time in Samas. "So the Firstborn is making the decisions for the sin and sentinels alike?

Gorou grimaced. "No, he's fallen ill. From what I can gather, they aren't sure if he'll survive. From what I can gather from the darkest corners, it might not be a natural illness."

Beast pinched the bridge of his nose with his thumb and forefinger and squeezed his eyes shut. "That's a lot of things, Gorou. You're telling me a lot of things right now."

"I'm aware. But I fear you're going to like the last thing least of all."

Beast didn't bother opening his eyes. "It's about who's ruling in the Firstborn's stead, isn't it?"

"It is."

"Shit. We're doomed."

"Are you thinking you might be fleeing again?"

Beast shook his head. What was it with his subordinates these days? "I was exercising my freedom." He sighed heavily. "Well, I'm going to need some time to prepare before I go see Sato. Yuki and the Firstborn were going to be hard enough."

"He's already asked that you meet with him soon. I was only able to buy you a little time."

"How much time?"

"Long enough for a drink."

Beast looked at the now empty mug of ale in his hand. "Word of my arrival travelled fast."

Gorou pointed at a sentinel sitting at a table on the other side of the tavern's outdoor patio. "You can thank him for that. Crispin, one of Sato's lieutenants, but as well connected as I've ever seen. He'd have given Benji a run for his money. Just as devious, as well. Maybe more. His name isn't being explicitly whispered in those dark corners I mentioned, but I can connect the dots."

The sentinel saw them looking his way and gave a wave with an arm that ended in a stump. He looked to the sun and gestured with his own mug of ale in the universal symbol for another drink.

"Looks like we have a little more time," Beast said and motioned to the bar for another round, "so let's make use of it. How do you think this is going to go with Sato? The self-righteous little prick is likely to order my execution on the spot."

"I doubt it. They need all the soldiers they can get and, given that you aren't a sentinel, even his strict view of the Path might allow for a little leniency. I've been talking with people and thinking, and my proposal is that the mugon remain a separate force under Shin's command. We don't have the time to properly integrate with the sin and sentinel units, and I think we all know working with Shin will be an easier proposition for the mugon to accept than Sato."

Beast thought for a moment but couldn't come up with a better plan. It reminded him too much of Dahl, though. Once again, he'd collected all these people willing to fight, only to surrender them to someone else. "So long as the mugon remain separate. That's the only way this works."

Gorou didn't argue.

"Fine. Let's go see Sato and see if he managed to pull the stick out of his ass."

Crispin joined them. "It's a pleasure to see you again, Beast. You're looking...just as imposing as always."

After a beat, the memory of Crispin's face snapped into place. "You're the one that got us out of the cells in Dahl. Betrayed that ass of a magistrate. Never thanked you for that."

"Technically, I was there to save Sato, but after watching you tear through those bandits, I was happy to see you, too. Now, we should go. Sato will be getting impatient," Crispin said.

Beast grunted and motioned for Crispin to lead the way. As they walked, he watched Keff take in the different districts of Versun. The young man did his best to hide the awe on his face, but he was looking everywhere at once. "Impressive, isn't it?"

"Sure, but it's different from Dahl."

"I told you it would be."

"No, I mean the soldiers. In Dhal, they were gathered on the walls. Here it looks like they're preparing for something else. Like they're getting ready to leave."

Beast was taken aback by Keff's observation. He didn't know all the right words, but Keff's sharp eyes had caught the difference in the soldiers' behavior. Sato was getting ready to launch an assault.

They went up a set of stairs and into a waiting chamber. Beast's eyes lit up when he saw a whip-thin woman sitting in one of the chairs.

"Shin!" Beast exclaimed and moved forward to hug his former protégé.

Shin stood up and took a step to meet Beast.

Then his vision swam and his head rang as Shin's fist connected with the side of his face. She punched a lot harder than she used to. They grew up so quick.

"Bastard!" Shin said.

# 39

Sato looked up from his desk when he heard a commotion in the waiting room. Alonzo met his gaze and grinned.

"Sounds like Beast is back," Sato said.

Alonzo made a gesture that Sato recognized as roughly meaning chaos or disaster.

"Indeed. Let's go see if we can put a bridle on a tornado," Sato said and gestured Alonzo out into the antechamber.

When Sato stepped out of his office, he saw Beast rubbing his cheek. An angry red welt was already forming on the skin visible beneath his beard, and Crispin stood between Shin and Beast like a judge separating the contestants of a sparring match. At first, Sato thought he was trying to defend Shin from the much larger man, but one look at Shin's face made him realize she was the aggressor.

"You left us! You motherless sheep fucker. Samas was burning, and you just *left*." Shin's words were measured and calm, but they tore like jagged metal.

"I'm no one's puppet, girl. I go where I please," Beast responded with anger, and a little surprise, in his voice.

Crispin flashed a few quick gestures to Alonzo, who nodded. Sato caught enough of it to understand. Beast had expected a friendly greeting from Shin.

Sato ran his eyes around the room. He recognized Gorou from Crispin's reports. By all accounts, he was a more than competent military sin mind who had left with Beast. The other man, a boy really, slight of stature with chestnut dark skin, was a mystery to him. Whoever he was, he noticed the sign language that Crispin, Alonzo, and Sato used right away. Sharp, whoever he was. Beast had always been smart enough to surround himself with people smarter than himself.

"And it was your pleasure to leave your friends to die? Like a coward?" Shin shot right back.

"I got you off Iru. I'm here now. What more do you want?"

*These allies are tenuous at best. It would be in your best interest to keep them at odds with each other,* Rua's voice said.

"I hate to interrupt this squabbling, but we have pressing matters to discuss," Sato said, and was met with two equally angry glares. If there was one fact they agreed on, it was how much they both hated him.

Sato didn't care. Politics was not his game. He would lay out his plans. They need not agree with him. He was acting in his capacity as the Firstborn's designated successor and therefore his word was law.

They had to see that his word carried as much weight as the Firstborn's. His stomach still twisted a little at the thought, but he charged forward.

"I'm sorry for my direct approach, but time is of the

essence. We just struck a great blow against our enemy. It would be foolish to think the Maramans won't seek to strike back," Sato said.

"We anticipated that," Shin said. "The whole point of removing the ferals was so that we could better withstand the inevitable siege. We've already talked about this, Sato."

He bristled at the casual use of his name. He was the Firstborn! In practice, if not yet official. He tamped down his anger, grateful it was Beast who jumped into the argument.

"A siege? Did you get rid of those chained up demons the Maramans are so fond of, too?" the giant man asked.

"No, Yuki could only cleanse the rifts of the ferals. The demons controlled by the summoners are something else," Shin responded.

Beast scoffed. "Then hunkering behind these walls is a bad idea. You were at Dahl. You saw how useful walls are against those demons."

Sato added to Beast's argument. "The Maramans will also expect us to remain on the defensive. They already took one of our major cities and know we can't afford to lose another. They sent ships to cut off our supply lines from Dahl. They aren't expecting us to attack."

Shin didn't back down. "You also aren't considering the summoners. At least the walls give us some protection from their spells. Who knows what they can do on an open battlefield?"

"Do you know what they can do against the walls?" Beast asked.

Angry as she was, Shin was forced to concede Beast's point.

"We also have the supply line issue to deal with," Sato pressed. "We can't hunker behind the walls."

"Hold on," Beast said. "I don't want you thinking I'm siding with you over Shin. I'm still getting caught up here. But your supply chain problem is fixed. I took care of the Maramans blocking the shipping lanes and Colas is patrolling with the juggernaut and our stolen ships, making sure no one else slips past us."

"Thank you, Beast. I can't say for sure what the summoners will do, but taking a defensive position will give me more time to find out." Shin said. "Anyway, all this arguing is pointless. The Firstborn already agreed with me. We need more time to better understand the emperor's abilities. That's why we're waiting. So why do you have us here, Sato?"

The surprised look on Beast's face told Sato that Crispin had passed word to him already. That was good. It made this next part a little easier.

Sato stood as straight as he could. "The Firstborn has fallen ill. Healers are with him now, but I fear it doesn't look good. In his stead, I am making decisions on the defense of Samas." He watched his words sink into Shin and forced his face to remain neutral. Now she finally understood who she was dealing with.

"And if he recovers?" Shin asked.

"Then he will resume his rule, of course. That is the outcome we are all hoping for, but until that time, we need to keep the best interest of Samas in mind," Sato said, and almost believed the words himself.

"And the best interest of Samas is to go against the Firstborn's final orders?" Shin asked. "We *decided* this, Sato."

"In this case, yes. But that's not just coming from me. My advisors, and even Beast here, understands that striking the Maramans now is our strongest play. We don't have time to be as cautious as the Firstborn." Sato looked at Beast. It was a gamble, but he thought he understood the terrifying warrior well enough.

Beast looked as though he'd eaten something bitter. "I'm sorry, Shin, but I think he's right. They weren't expecting my return with a juggernaut. We've negated their naval advantage and bolstered our numbers. Unless you have a good reason to believe that their summoners will be easier to stop from behind the walls of Versun, I'd have to agree with Sato." Beast looked like he wanted to spit on the floor but thought better of it.

*Good, the big one is more important. The girl is strong with sacrifice, but unpredictable. If she refuses to come, so be it.*

Refuses? No one refused the Firstborn. Whatever Rua thought, Sato would make Shin help, one way or the other. "Do you accept your orders, Shin?"

Shin held his gaze with the same hateful glare that she'd always reserved for him. She didn't answer, and Sato was about to ask again when she finally lowered her head. "Fine. We need to be united against the Maramans. I won't be the one that weakens the chain."

Before Sato could answer Helios burst into the room.

"I'm sorry to interrupt Sato... my lord, but the Firstborn... he's gone."

Sato's world narrowed to a very small point of light, and all the air rushed out of the room. He wasn't sure how long the ringing in his ears lasted, but when it cleared Helios was looking at him expectantly. "Sorry, what was that?"

"I said that you're the Firstborn."

Sato's smile was heavy with sorrow for his lost friend, but he'd never had any illusion that his mentor would still be alive when he was named Firstborn. That just wasn't how it worked.

Especially not with Crispin around, Sato thought and

immediately pushed the thought, and the guilt that came with, it out of his mind.

He was Firstborn.

Now, it was finally time to return Samas to the Path.

# 40

Shin sat on the ramparts of Versun and looked out to the sea. The small waves broke on the stone beneath her, their pounding rhythm slowly unknotting the tension she'd carried from the meeting with Sato. She was hiding here, and she knew it, but staying within the walls would have driven her mad.

Every time she started to recover from one blow, life dealt her another. She still teared up, and her breath still caught in her throat, every time she thought of Yuki.

If the death of her parents had taught her anything, it was that grief was a complex process. It was even more true for Yuki, as their relationship had been far more complex than Shin's childhood love for her parents. She could go a whole day feeling almost normal, and then something would trigger a memory. A face in the crowd that almost looked like Yuki's. Any mention of the feral demons. Then the whole world would crash on her shoulders. In those moments she wanted to shout at the sky, hoping Yuki's spirit would feel her anger at being left to fight the Maramans and the traditions of Samas. A moment later, she'd be on the verge of weeping, mourning the loss of the woman who had shown her what she could become, who had died with so much left to teach her.

All Shin could do was push everything down. She didn't have the time or the strength to properly mourn the woman. The sin needed to be prepared to fight the summoners and their demons. She needed to be prepared to kill an emperor. And now, Samas would need someone to save it from Sato. Her own emotions mattered little against such a backdrop.

She hadn't confessed this, even to Corin, but there were times when she considered making another sacrifice, offering up her memories of Yuki in exchange for anything else. Sometimes, it felt like the only way she would be able to lead without breaking. Even though she understood well the foolishness of such a plan, the idea of washing away her grief was so tempting the realm didn't even have to entice her. She wouldn't do it, even if it seemed the only way to go on. For now, she would just keep pushing it down, locking it away with her lingering guilt over the mistakes she'd made with the rifts a year ago. Someday, when there was peace and more time, she would sort through it all. Until then, there was only the next step. And the one after that.

She heard footsteps behind her. Not so soft that someone was trying to sneak up on her, but soft enough that they were trying not to disturb her. It was kind enough, she supposed, but meaningless. She couldn't help but be disturbed by the various challenges facing them. A low grunt came from behind her, and she knew who it was.

She clenched her fists. For a big man, he had always been light on his feet. She'd thought he was just another one of the endless messengers that were always seeking her out. Without looking back, she asked, "Come to apologize?"

"No." Beast said. He sat next to her, and like her, dangled

his feet off the side of the wall as he looked out to the sea. "Came to talk."

"Most people would apologize."

"I'm not most people. And if you put me in the exact same situation, I'd do it again."

Shin shook her head. She wanted to punch him until he was senseless, but suspected her arms and fists would be bloody and broken before he even had the good manners to be dazed by her blows. And though she was furious at him, it was also hard to stay angry. Beast was Beast. "So, what did you want to talk about?"

"Being under your command. I don't like it. I'm not great at taking orders."

"No shit." She waved away his concern. "I'm not going to try to integrate your mugon the way the sin and the sentinels did. That took us the better part of a year of training to make work. You'll command them as a separate army, but we'll all be working toward the same goal." It wasn't an ideal solution, but with Sato ordering them to attack tomorrow, trying anything else was even more a disaster. It meant Beast and his mugon would get chewed up, but in so doing, Shin hoped they would give the better-trained units a chance to break the Maraman lines. "Do you want me to find a few sin to protect you?"

Beast waved away her concerns, mirroring her previous gesture. "We'll be fine." He paused and sighed. "We should talk about Sato."

"You mean the Firstborn? Eternal light of Samas and all that?"

"That's the one."

"What about him?"

"You don't like him."

Shin barked out a harsh laugh. "I *hate* him. He's so tied

up with his notions of following his precious Path that he'll destroy us all. Everything we've fought for will be meaningless if he's allowed to have his way."

"Agreed. You're not going to try anything foolish, are you?"

Shin wondered if he'd somehow seen into her thoughts. And she worried if her thoughts had been so transparent even Beast had been able to guess at them. If so, Sato would have as well. "No. I'm still uncertain about the wisdom of attacking Iru, but I understand his reasoning well enough, and I won't be the reason we fail against the Maramans. My battles with Sato will come after the Maramans are gone."

"Good. For what it's worth, if Sato seeks to undo all the progress we made, I'll help you kill him."

Just like that, Beast was in her good graces again. Sometimes, he knew just the right thing to say. "Thanks."

Before they could move on to more pleasant subjects, something twisted sharply in the back of Shin's neck. For one terrifying moment, she thought she'd been stabbed. But the pain was inside her skin. She focused on it, grimacing as she noticed it connected to the realm. The ocean swam in her vision, and suddenly she was falling forward, pitching off the walls of Versun. She tried to catch herself, to hold onto anything, but her body refused to answer any of her commands.

Two strong hands caught her and pulled her to safety. She thought she heard someone calling her name, but it sounded as though the call came from a distant shore. She tried to focus on it, but the pain bouncing around in her skull took all her attention.

Shin followed the pain, traveling along the threads that connected her to the realm. In a way, it reminded her of her first days training with Yuki, learning how to sense the realm in their world. Had the forces then been as powerful as these today, she would have mastered the skill in a heartbeat. This was so strong anyone should have felt it.

A wave of fresh agony crashed over her senses, and it felt as though her mind was on fire and melting. She wanted to run and hide, to shield herself from the realm in some way. But there was no hiding from this.

She gathered her strength and sought the source of the struggle. The realm itself screamed as it was used as a weapon between two incredible forces. Visions flickered across the back of her eyelids, glimpses of the fight happening both in the realm and in the physical plane.

One of the combatants was the Maraman emperor. He was big enough that he made Beast seem remarkably average. The strength and power emanating from him were incredible, and he fought against a small woman. At first, Shin thought it was Yuki. Her heart leaped as she saw her mentor fighting the battle she'd so dreaded. Somehow, Yuki had defeated even death.

But then the vision pulled Shin closer, and she saw it wasn't Yuki. The features were similar, but not the same.

Rua. It had to be Rua.

She and the emperor fought on a dark plain, illuminated by a blood-red sun. One moment they grappled like wrestlers, a sight made even more bizarre by the difference in size. In Shin's world, a slight woman like Rua would have no chance against a man of such size and raw power. Here, though, their strength seemed matched. Then the image flickered, and they were dueling, Rua's sword crafted like a sentinel's blade.

The vision wavered and flickered, and the realm was wrapping thick strong arms around her. Embracing her and holding her close, but not squeezing the life from her. She wanted to be in those arms, to let the worries go.

The arms weren't the realm's. They were Beast's, and she grasped onto them, using them as anchors against the vision that threatened to pull her away in its powerful currents. She opened her eyes and found herself on top of the ramparts at Versun, staring up into the sky. Beast's concerned face leaned over hers.

"What happened?" he asked.

She blinked, and thankfully the vision didn't reappear. The pain remained in the back of her head, but it had faded a little. She didn't dare follow it again. She sat up. "Thanks for catching me."

"What happened?" he repeated.

Shin put together all the pieces, then sighed. "As much as I hate to admit it, I think Sato was right. The emperor just started a battle I'm not sure he can win. He's weaker than ever. We need to attack Iru now."

The sun had been falling by the time Shin and Beast had left the ramparts and now, standing on the prow of *Cutter*, it rose on the opposite horizon. The battle between the Emperor and Rua raged on, and everyone even slightly attuned to sacrifice could feel it. Shin couldn't believe the reserves of strength that the emperor drew upon. They were like nothing she'd ever felt before. Even Yuki wouldn't have had a chance had they met in a duel.

But she had to put that out of her mind for now. She had all the power of the sin behind her. Or at least, she would soon.

Her focus was on what was to come. The sacrifice that

she had created, with the help of the elites, was unlike anything she had ever attempted.

It also demanded more than she'd ever dared.

Shin felt the ocean air, heavy with moisture, on her face. She closed her eyes. She reached out to the eagerly waiting realm and made her offering. At first the realm balked. A request for so much power demanded a price that no single person could pay. Shin continued the complex process of negotiating and presented her sacrifice.

The terms were laid out.

It wasn't like negotiating with a human, or anything of equal intelligence. The realm was vast and cruel, and it wasn't particularly logical. It was all desire and instinct, used to getting its way because of its incredible strength.

But she stood firm, like a supplicant before the Firstborn, laying out her sacrifice and trying to show how it would benefit the realm. She imagined all the lives to come, their lives cut short. The happiness and sadness they would have felt in the missing years. Not to mention the sharper emotions they would feel, knowing their lives would be shortened.

The realm accepted. It would come to collect when this battle was over. Shin opened her eyes and looked at the elites gathered around her. Their eyes were wide as they experienced power like they'd never had before.

It had to be worth it.

"By the sun, Shin, the power you're giving us is like nothing I could have imagined," Vala said from behind her.

"It is," Shin responded. "We'll only have one chance at this."

"Vala, are you sure you can handle this on your own?" Lyla asked. "We could spare another elite or two."

Shin shook her head but said nothing. They would need

every sin they had on the shores. Vala knew it, too. They all did.

Vala waved them away. "You all go kill an emperor, I'll make sure their juggernauts can't help them."

There were embraces all around and calls for luck. The sin began to separate, leaving for the longboats that would take them to the shore. They would make landfall just after the sentinel forces. After the emperor had committed his summoners.

Once they revealed themselves, Shin and her sin would cut them down.

# 41

Beast felt useless sitting in the skiff transporting him to the island of Iru. In the distance, he saw Colas's juggernaut moving towards the emperor's own juggernauts. *Cutter* and *Warhammer* were closer, protecting the mugon skiffs from any intervention from the Maraman navy. In the other direction, the sentinels sailed in their fancy military transports, filled with horses and all the shit that came with them. Beast couldn't care less about them, though he hoped plenty of sentinels died to keep him safe today.

Beast's eyes kept traveling toward the *Cutter*. All the sin elite were on there, doing whatever mad shit they did when they called upon the realm to give them strength. He'd learned a little of what the sin intended, and the enormity of the sacrifice impressed even him. Shin was many things, but one description he'd never use for her was "coward." Would the others have enough courage to follow her? That, as far as Beast was concerned, was the first and most important question of the battle. They'd have no chance if the sin couldn't stand up to the enormous might of the summoners.

Finally, Beast saw the longships drop from *Cutter*, and he

breathed a sigh of relief. Shin and her elites were on their way. They'd done it. And now, thanks to their tremendous sacrifice, the rest of them might just have a chance. Flesh and blood, Beast could kill, but who knew what those summoners might throw at them?

Honestly, he'd rather not find out.

"The mugon are frightened of the battle to come," Gorou said. He'd been harping on the same problem since they'd left Versun. He didn't believe they had the same courage as the sin. "Remember that most have never seen an actual battle. If they break as soon as they hit the shore, they'll be worse than useless."

Beast stared at his old friend. "They won't break. Not so long as they follow me."

Before Gorou could answer, they were interrupted by the peals of Maraman horns echoing across the water. It was expected, but it still chilled Beast to know they were walking into a battle that the Maramans were prepared for. If it had been possible, he would have much preferred to ambush them. In response to the horns, the sin adept assigned to each of the skiffs moved to the bow.

Beast guessed they would make the beach in minutes, but it wouldn't be in time to disembark without danger. The Maraman defenders were already massing on the shore. Siege weapons intended for the walls of Bulas and Versun were being brought down to the water, and Beast tried to guess if they would make it to land before the monstrous weapons unleashed their destruction.

A crimson glow to west drew his attention away from the beach.

The Maraman juggernauts had moved to intercept Colas's ship, and a dozen of the smaller warships were being dispatched. Beast could hear the hissing pops of the bow-mounted devastators as Colas fired on the attackers. She rained devastation on the advancing ships, but the juggernaut was vastly outnumbered.

But only for a moment.

Giant crimson tentacles appeared at will around the Maraman warships. A lone figure stood on the bow of *Cutter*, the source of the otherworldly light. Vala defended them, and the Maramans got the first taste of the sin's new abilities. Tentacles wrapped around the ships and squeezed, and the crack of the ships breaking in half echoed across the water. Rough shouts followed soon after. Beast didn't know the language, but he understood a cry for help whenever he heard one.

A few ships escaped the tentacles, but Colas and her crew were prepared for the survivors. The devastators hissed again, chewing up the warships as though they were children's toys.

The tentacles turned their attention to the first Maraman juggernaut. Even the enormous tentacles couldn't wrap around the floating city, and the body of a giant crimson beast rose from the water as it sought to destroy the vessel. Tentacles ripped and tore whatever they could grab as the Maramans returned fire with their own devastators. Beast couldn't be sure, but it seemed like the magical construct was reacting to the blows.

"I hope that's enough to stop them," Beast said.

"We have our own concerns," Gorou said. He pointed towards the beach.

They'd made it close to the shore, but not close enough. A few of the siege weapons had come within range. Giant spears flew towards the Samasian forces, and for a moment Beast thought the battle would be over before it had even properly started.

Then a crimson tentacle batted away the first of the spears. Another tentacle caught another, twisted it, and hurled it back at shore, shattering one of the ballistas. The adepts were surrounded by crimson glows.

All of them.

Beast watched in awe as the adepts on each of the skiffs sprouted crimson tentacles from their back. The tentacles extended and caught or deflected the projectiles before they could hit. A few spears made it through, but the worst of the disaster was averted.

"That looks like what Yuki did at Dahl," Beast said.

"It does. Whatever Shin came up with, it's giving the sin an incredible level of power," Gorou said.

Their skiff landed, and Beast roared at the Maramans who charged the boat.

He didn't have time to organize his forces. The Maramans hoped to kill them all as they attempted to disembark across the sandy beaches.

Beast leaped from the skiff and charged headfirst into the Maramans. He swung his axe in a deadly arc that maimed and killed as he moved unerringly towards his target. The huge, ink-black Maraman commander led his own forces with a giant sword in one hand. The two deadly warriors grew inexorably closer. Finally, Beast threw his axe with both hands directly at the Maraman leader, who knocked it away with a disdainful swipe of his sword.

It was all the opening Beast needed.

He dropped his shoulder and planted it directly into the Maraman's chest. The man staggered but kept his feet. Beast followed up with savage blows to the man's head and body. He knocked the sword out of the Maraman's hand and then kicked him in the balls with such force that the Maraman was lifted off the ground for a moment before falling to his knees.

With a massive twist, Beast snapped his neck.

Beast's mugon, who had been fighting to catch up to him, redoubled their efforts at the sight. The Maramans that had been following behind the now dead Maraman commander faltered at the sight of their painted leader being taken apart so savagely. It wasn't much, but it was enough for the mugon to secure the beachhead. Beast picked up his axe and rejoined the fray, strengthening any part of the mugon line that seemed close to breaking.

Soon, there was little left for him to do. Gorou shouted orders and the mugon formed up in a defensive ring that would allow Shin and the elites a safe landing spot.

As they battled on their corner of the beach, Beast saw the sentinels fighting a similar fight to the east. Unlike the frenetic charge of the mugon, the sentinels formed up and moved forward with a ruthless discipline that was twice as deadly. The Maramans, whose style more closely mirrored Beast's mugon, crashed like a wave of flesh and steel against the sentinel's formations.

Beast wasn't sure which one would break first. The Maramans were pure strength, the sentinels unrivalled discipline.

"How was that?" Beast asked as Gorou appeared beside him.

"Better than I expected. Lots of fight ahead of us, though."

Beast grinned. "Good." He was as happy here as anywhere he'd ever been. Battle called to him like nothing else.

There was a disturbance farther up the shore. Beast looked up the incline that lead to Bulas. The crimson-robed summoners had appeared, and they'd brought their damned demon pets. The summoners released the chains, and the twisted imitations of Maraman warriors charged the Samasian line with silent, bloodthirsty grins. Behind them, the dawn sky lit up with crimson as the summoners prepared their own attacks.

Beast glanced behind him and saw that Shin's forces had made the beach.

The final battle for Samas had begun.

# 42

Sato sat atop Nightmane, well back from the main battle, and watched the violence unfold on the beach before him. Despite the ringing of steel clashing against steel and the shouts of furious sentinels, his trusty horse stood without fear. It might have been grazing in a meadow, judging by the beat of its heart.

His practiced eye ran over the battlefield, taking note of the details that would guide his judgement. The Maramans surged against his sentinels, their giant forms rushing headlong into the spears the leading sentinels thrust ahead of the line. A few didn't even bother trying to slap the spears away. It was as if they took a twisted sort of pride in impaling themselves on the spears and fighting on anyway.

The Maramans were as human as he was, but they were damned hard to kill. One berserker had broken through the line. Sato counted three spears lodged in his chest, but he still tried to smash in the skull of a nearby sentinel with a war hammer. The other sentinels surrounding him cut at artery and tendon, but it wasn't until one brave soul thrust a sword through his neck that the Maraman died.

Up and down the line, Sato saw similar scenes repeated over and over. None of the Maramans Sato saw had the skill of Beast, but most of them had the same raw power.

If they ever learned to organize themselves, they'd be a force even the sentinels couldn't stand against.

As it was, though, his lines held, at least for the moment. Berserker strength met sentinel discipline, and no clear winner had yet emerged. Sato swallowed the lump in his throat as he watched another Maraman kill two sentinels with one swing of an enormous axe. Another sentinel lost his life avenging those he had fought beside.

He'd ordered many sentinels to their deaths before. Such was the burden of command, and one whose weight his shoulders were used to carrying. Never on this scale, perhaps, but it was a burden he knew how to bear. They fought for the future of Samas. For all the sentinels yet to be born. For the glory of a Path only he could lead them to. His legacy began here, as they drove the Maramans from their land forever.

He shifted his weight in the saddle so that he could get a better view. As violent as the battle before him was, it was almost a comforting scene after the last year of nightmares. He had been born and raised a sentinel and the battlefield was where he belonged. The ebb and flow of combat, the screams of pain and the smell of blood were all as familiar as the sword at his hip. This was a war he knew how to wage. A fight he knew how to win.

The battle happening within a different realm, though, was anything but familiar. And at the moment, far more concerning. It tore at his attention when he needed it focused. There was nothing he could do about the realm. Not now. That task fell to Shin, and he had little choice but to trust her.

General Roko's voice pulled his full attention to the physical plane. "Alonzo's unit has secured his beachhead, sir."

Sato nodded. He'd seen the same minutes ago, though it was reassuring to hear the report. Up and down the beach, the forces of Samas dug in and fought against the giant invaders. For a moment, it had looked like the mugon would fall before they established themselves, though that was little loss in Sato's mind. But Beast, as was his way, had single-handedly carved a bloody path forward.

The battle in this area went better. As frightening and dangerous as each individual Maraman was, they couldn't match the cohesion of a sentinel unit. Discipline meant more than strength. He and the other sentinels had trained for a year for just this fight, and their tactics were paying off. Spears at the front of the line prevented Maramans from crashing through, and the sharp swords behind the spears fought together to bring down the Maramans who were foolish enough to challenge them. As much as it was possible, no sentinel faced a Maraman alone. Just as they had trained.

Their advance up the beach was bloody. The cost in lives would be felt for a generation, but they advanced all the same, one relentless step after another.

Sato's immediate concern wasn't the remaining Maramans on the beach. It was currently gathering on the crest of the hill that led to Bulas. Another unfamiliar element.

Roko thought the same. "Our formations won't be in place in time to repel those demons," he said. His words became an immediate prophecy as the grotesque monsters started their charge down the hill.

"We only need to hold them back long enough for Shin

to join the fray. Roko, buy us time. But make sure you come back. I don't want to be forced to promote Crispin to general out of sheer lack of options."

Roko grinned and bowed quickly before signaling his unit of mounted sentinels into action. Sato gripped his reins tighter. He wanted to be there, leading his warriors. Not sitting back here, watching others risk themselves. He knew his place, but it stung all the same.

"You'll get used to it, sir." Crispin read his thoughts, as he often did.

"I don't have to like it, though." He turned to Helios. "Let's move forward. Our lines are solid, and I want to make room for the reinforcements coming from Versun," Sato said.

The orders were given, and they inched forward. Sato's eyes were only on the demons as they came down the hill, gathering speed even as Roko and the cavalry rode to meet them.

Much to the sentinel's credit, they didn't run even in the face of the terrible attack. They planted their spears firmly and held the line. The demons struck with inhuman ferocity. Spears cracked as they broke, and sentinels screamed as the demons sliced through flesh and bone with equal ease. One demon swiped at an unprepared sentinel, raking talons across his face and gouging out his eyes.

Roko and the mounted sentinels joined the fray moments later, the combined power of horse and sentinel together enough to halt the demon advance. The mounted sentinels could attack the demon necks with greater ease, and the first of the terrible creatures turned to mist as the sentinels reformed their line. Sato felt the realm being accessed as the sin adepts amongst his sentinels sent the demons back to their sun-cursed realm.

For now, the sentinels held. They had to hold. They had no other choice.

He turned his attention to the other battle, the one that frightened him even more than the demons. Deep within the realm, two tremendous forces dueled. The emperor's power originated in Bulas, and it was beyond anything Sato had considered possible. But the force that dueled him was just as strong, if not stronger.

And familiar, too. He'd sensed that power before. In his own head.

Why would Rua and the emperor be fighting?

Sato wanted to believe Rua was helping him, but she struck him as far too self-interested for that. There was something more at play. But for now, the emperor was distracted. That was all that mattered. It gave them the opening to attack.

Far off to his right, Shin accessed the realm, and the power of it almost unhorsed him.

Whatever she was doing, it was more potent than Yuki's considerable strength. It was on par with the emperor and Rua. What had she done?

Sato couldn't guess, but when this was over, she would have to die. That much strength couldn't exist outside of the sentinels. For now, though, he was glad to have her by his side. The demons attacking his sentinels broke off in ones and twos, far more interested in Shin and her sin. It gave his lines a chance to plug their gaps and prepare for the next advance. Taking the hill would come next, and that would be a bloody affair.

Still, all was going according to plan. Or at least, as close to plan as any battle could. Sato dared to hope that their bold gamble would work. He ran his eyes over the line one more time, preparing his next set of orders.

Then the sentinel line broke in the space right in front of him.

The shouts and screams drew his eye, and he saw the cause of the problem right away. One of the so-called Unnamed commanders Beast had told them about. The emperor's elite. He was a giant of a man, tattooed until he was dark as night. He had two of the larger demons following him like belligerent pets. The man carried a great sword so large even Beast would probably think it was a little much, and it cut through sentinels like they were made of paper. No sword that large should move so fast.

The Unnamed was staring straight at him, wading through sentinels like they were no more than a tangle of bushes in his way. His eyes were just as dark as his skin, and even Sato had to fight the urge to flee against such a foe.

There were only a few ranks of sentinels between him and the Unnamed, but they'd do little to stop the monster. Sato's honor guard would be the better choice, and they were already closing around him. He was the Firstborn, and he didn't seek out this battle. But when the fight came to him, there was only one choice to make.

"Clear the way," Sato bellowed.

The startled sentinels did so, leaving a space between Sato and the Unnamed. He kicked Nightmane into motion, and the Unnamed smiled an empty smile as he spun his enormous sword over his head.

"Sato!" Helios called behind him, but it was too late for his general to do anything but follow.

Sato drew his sword and pushed forward. With his honor guard following behind him, he plunged into the gap. Then the Unnamed swung his sword, and Sato realized the monster intended to cut through Nightmane's neck and

Sato's torso in one slice. Given what he'd already seen, it didn't seem as impossible as it should be.

Sato pulled sharply on the reins, and Nightmane came to a stop. Sato leaped from the saddle.

He rolled to his feet and quickly reoriented himself. It wasn't hard to find his opponent. The Unnamed stepped forward, eager to finish what he'd started. By the time Sato knew where he was, he was standing face to face with the monster.

Well, face to chest.

The Maraman grinned viciously and swung his giant great sword in an arc that would have cut Sato in half.

Sato wasn't fool enough to block. He wasn't strong enough to stop that sword. He leaped back, and the wind from the passing blade was like a gale coming off the ocean. His honor guard arrived, but their attention was focused solely on fighting the demons. For the moment, Sato had the Unnamed to himself.

For a few precious moments Sato stayed outside of the Maraman's reach and avoided blows. After a few cuts, he thought he had a sense of his opponent's style.

The giant sword tip whistled past his face, and he darted forward with a thrust. He grinned in triumph.

And then somehow, the Unnamed wasn't there. Sato blinked in time see the foot catch him in the side. The kick sent him flying to the side, and he tumbled into the beach.

Sato stood unsteadily as sentinels launched themselves at the Unnamed. They were brave, and Sato was grateful for the time they afforded him, but they were fools. The Unnamed cut them down like weeds.

Sato steadied his breathing. He'd underestimated his opponent, thinking him no more than pure muscle. He was as good and as fast with his sword as Sato was with his.

They met again in a duel unlike any Sato had ever fought. In reach and strength, there was no contest. But as they passed and passed again, Sato believed he had the slightest of edges in speed.

His world narrowed to the one Maraman. The longer they fought, the longer the Samasian warriors went without a Firstborn to lead them. But Sato could find no opening.

It was Crispin, of all people, who did.

Sato might not have been able to defeat the Unnamed, but he did attract all the Unnamed's attention. He saw Crispin move behind the giant, making one cut with his left hand. It was an impressive cut, all things considered. Sato's only thought at the moment was that Crispin's training had paid off handsomely. Crispin got the back of both the Unnamed's ankles.

Sato struck as the enormous Maraman collapsed to his knees.

Even in his agony, the Maraman moved his weapon quickly, but not quickly enough to fully block Sato's thrust. Sato felt his sword cut deep into the flesh of the Maraman's side. The warrior, like a demon, made no sound. He swung a backhanded blow with his off hand at Sato. Sato drew his dagger and plunged it into the man's wrist.

This time, the Maraman roared with pain. He raised his sword above his head, ready to make one more powerful cut.

Sato wasted no time piercing his heart. Even then, the Unnamed refused to die for several long moments that felt like hours. Finally, the impossible sword dropped from his hands, and he fell forward in the sand. Sato was panting, more tired than he'd been in as long as he could remember.

He looked around, searching for the demons that had accompanied his opponent, and saw that his honor guard were holding them at bay. One was already dead and sent back to the realm, and his surviving guards were fighting against the last.

Sato stumbled forward. Crispin called to him, but the voice was coming from far away.

The demon knocked one of the honor guards off his feet. The guard struck Sato, still in the air, and they both went tumbling back.

Sato ended up on his back, unable to find his breath. Then he looked up to see a giant, crimson hammer descending upon him. He had just enough time to realize that the summoners had joined the fight when a crimson falcon caught the head of the hammer in its talons and tossed it backwards.

Sato wondered if he was dead, and if that he was seeing things. It took him too long to decipher what his senses were telling him. But the battle had been joined, both on this plane and in the realm. He pushed himself to his feet, finding himself in the eye of the storm.

Crimson glows lit the daytime sky, both from the hill and now on the beach. Shin and the others had arrived.

The elites had joined the fight.

# 43

Shin cursed out loud. In the distance, like a beacon pulsing across the island, Shin felt the emperor battling Rua within the realm. Their powers twisted and warped that dark mirror of the real world, and her own connection to the realm ached in response. Shin pushed that aside to focus on the one fact that mattered. In the midst of it all, the emperor was weakening. There would never be a better chance to strike.

She swore then and there she'd never admit this out loud, not even to Corin when she was drunk.

But attacking Iru now had been the right choice.

Sato, asshole that he was, had been right.

An army of giant berserker warriors and their even larger demon allies stood between her and the emperor, but if she could get to him while he fought Rua, she might just be able to kill him.

First, she had to get there.

"Should we engage?" Lyla asked.

"No, we wait until the summoners engage. We may have levelled the playing field a little, but they're still powerful.

I'd rather add the element of surprise to our small list of advantages."

Lyla didn't argue. She, like all the other elites, accepted Shin's commands. They left it to her to make the difficult decisions, and as she watched the demons rip through the ranks of the sentinels, Shin realized just how difficult it would be. She still didn't care for the prideful warriors, but the year spent training with them had tempered her hatred. It was easy to hate a concept, a nameless sect of people that identified under the same banner. Once you got to know the individuals within that group, however, it became harder to paint them all with the same brush.

Shin clenched her fists as she watched one of the Unnamed break through the sentinels' crisp formation. She almost ordered her elites forward then, but held off when she saw Sato meet the threat. The sentinels rallied around him, and for the moment, she maintained her patience.

"How's Beast faring?" Shin asked Lyla.

"The mugon aren't worth half of what the sentinels are, but Beast might be worth ten of Sato's honor guard by himself. Wherever the mugon are about to break, Beast appears and turns the tide." Lyla pointed.

Shin followed her finger and saw Beast whirling through the ranks of the Maramans and dealing death wherever he went. Shin had seen Beast fight before, but this was something else entirely. Whatever battle rage he'd tapped into was focused and efficient. The giant axe in his hands moved with the precision of a battlefield surgeon stitching a wound.

"How long can he last like that?" Shin asked.

"Hopefully, as long as it takes," Lyla replied.

"I think we can arrange that," Shin said with a smile.

What was the point of tapping into the entire potential of the realm if you didn't get creative?

Shin opened herself up to the realm. It felt the same as it always had as she crafted her sacrifice. She imagined a glowing ball of energy, speed, and strength. She suffused the ball with as much energy as she dared and then offered her proposal to the realm.

It felt... odd.

The realm accepted the offering, but nothing was taken from Shin. She was left with the feeling of owing a great debt to someone she feared more than anything. It felt unclean, but she pushed the feeling aside and accepted the terms. In front of her, a giant crimson orb floated. With her mind, she directed it across the battlefield until it was hovering over Beast.

She dropped it on him.

From where she was, she could just make out his wild hair, but once the orb enveloped him he pulsed with crimson light. She was too far to see his reaction, but it seemed to her that he continued the battle with renewed vigor.

Lyla smiled. "I bet that surprised him."

"He can thank me later. I think it's time." Shin pointed to the summoners lined up on the crest of the hill.

The summoners, bathed in crimson light, finally made their advance into the fray. Shin stopped counting at twenty and watched as they sprouted giant crimson weapons.

"It's time!" Shin called out.

"Let's go," Corin echoed the call to their mixed unit of sentinels and sin. It had taken some convincing, but Sato had eventually relented to her request to have her unit assigned to protect the elites.

She jogged towards the front lines with her elites

following behind. In her peripheral vision, she noticed the crimson glow as the elites weaved spells of their own. The closest summoner conjured a giant hammer and moved to bring it down into the fray. Lyla cast her arms forward and a giant falcon caught the hammer in its talons and flung it back at the summoner. The hammer winked out of existence before it could damage its creator, but it reappeared soon after. The action drew the summoners' attention toward the elites.

In her mind, Shin envisioned the battlefield parting so that the masters of the realm on either side could battle for the supremacy of Samas without distraction.

The reality was terrifyingly different.

The moment she crossed the battle lines held by the mugon the true nature of battle set in. Though Corin and the sentinels and sin arrayed before her bore the brunt of the action, Shin was still overwhelmed. The fights she'd been in at Dahl and against the demons hadn't prepared her for a full-scale military engagement.

Dust and smoke filled the air, making her lungs burn and her eyes water. She could barely hear the sounds of her own coughing over the clash of metal against metal and the screams of the dying and wounded. Blood, mud, or a mixture of both splattered across her face as she tried to navigate the chaos and bring her strength to bear.

A Maraman with arrows sticking out of his arms and chest stumbled through the sentinels ahead of her and swung awkwardly with his giant sword. More out of instinct than any conscious thought, she brought Harmony up to block the blow. A moment later, a crimson bear the size of a house bit the Maraman's head off.

Suddenly, Shin's focus was razor sharp.

"Hey!" Corin called over his shoulder. "You with us?"

Shin's resolve hardened. "I'm here."

"Good, because you don't really have a choice," Corin said with a small, reassuring smile.

As always, Corin's presence filled her with confidence.

Shin watched the elites fend off the attacks of the summoners. Lyla's falcon and bear patrolled the front lines of their unit, knocking away crimson spears, arrows and stones. Another elite created a shield of crimson light that absorbed blows until it shattered and was reformed.

All that power and creativity and they still weren't advancing the way they needed to.

"Take the fight to them!" Shin roared, using sacrifice to make her voice carry.

To punctuate her point, Shin created a giant fist ahead of her unit and pummeled the ground with it. Despite the fist being a construct of her will, she felt the sickeningly satisfying crunch of Maraman bones under each blow. Finally, two giant chains wrapped around the fist and pulled it until it ripped apart and disappeared.

Shin screamed in pain as her brain caught fire.

A moment later the pain dissipated, but Shin made note that even with their amendment to sacrifice, this was no free ride. Whatever spell they put out there, they would feel as if it was an extension of them. The faster they could end the summoners, the better.

Shin conjured up a cloud that spit lightning as it passed through the Maramans. It wreaked havoc until she was forced to throw up a wall to block a rain of very real spears heading towards her unit. Corin reacted quickly, leading his squad to deal with the spear throwing Maramans. Lyla grunted in pain as both her falcon and bear took blow after blow from the Maramans. But she never let the constructs fade.

Shin lost track of time as the battle raged. The elites sat in the pocket created by Corin and the sentinels and threw every weapon they could think of at their enemies. At first, Shin believed they were making progress. She felt every Maraman death the same way she would have had she cut them down with Harmony, but soon she started to feel their deaths less and the sting of her spells being destroyed more. She looked around at her elites and could tell they were feeling the same. Finally, Corin moved back to speak with her.

"You have to kill their summoners. We can't reach them," he said.

"I don't know how! We took them by surprise, but they're negating everything we do now."

Corin thought for a moment. "Can you make the sentinels stronger? As it is, the Maramans are containing our advance."

Shin couldn't help but flash a tired grin at Corin. She never would have imagined that the skinny, gap-toothed kid that she'd attacked in the fields below Dahl could have grown into the warrior before her. In response, she reached out to the realm and gestured towards Corin. He looked down in surprise as his twin swords were surrounded by a crimson glow that extended out well past their normal length. Corin gave them a few swings and smiled as he found the balance remained the same. The crimson glow surrounded his body and created a spiked armor that made him almost twice as tall and half again as wide. Corin tested his movement again and found that the glowing armor responded to his normal movements.

"I'm bigger than Beast." Corin grinned.

"Not quite, and definitely don't try fighting like him," Shin cautioned before turning to the elites. "Augment the sin and sentinels. We might not have the grasp on sacrifice the summoners do, but I'm dammed sure Maramans can't outfight Samasians!"

The elites began to focus their sacrifice in a new direction. Across the front lines, sentinels and sin alike looked around in surprise as the elites added to their already impressive fighting prowess. Weapons grew, armor was bolstered, and the fight was renewed.

"Lyla, can you keep your falcon on the attack?" Shin asked. "We need something to harass the summoners."

Lyla nodded grimly. "I've got something for them."

The falcon picked up the bear and flew it towards the summoners. A barrage of spears and spells assaulted the bird, but Lyla absorbed the pain of those that made contact. She screamed as a large crimson axe sliced into the falcon, but shook it off with only a flicker from her own sacrifice. Finally, she dropped the bear amongst the summoners.

Chaos ensured.

"Push forward!" Shin screamed, once more boosting her voice.

The Samasian forces surged forward and, for a moment, sliced through the Maramans in a shower of crimson sparks and screams. The summoners, entangled with the bear and falcon in their midst, were unable to react, and the Maraman forces protecting them were cut down. Despite the new weapons and armor, the Samasian losses were still heavy. The Maramans were like a force of nature on the battlefield, like a storm or an earthquake. It was impossible to face them down without losses.

And the losses were mounting. Their second wave would be landing soon, but they'd already lost more sentinels and sin than in the whole past year of conflict.

By the time Shin's unit reached and killed their first

summoners, Lyla let out a bone-chilling scream of agony that was so unexpected and frightening Shin almost dropped to her knees. The summoners had finally dispelled her animals, and Lyla had collapsed in a lifeless heap.

"Lyla!" Shin ran over to the elite, but any further words died on her lips.

Lyla's face was pale white and frozen in a tableau of such agony that tears pricked Shin's eyes. The physical toll of her spells being assaulted repeatedly was laid out in front of Shin.

And she'd ordered it.

Rage settled on Shin. Some was at herself. She'd ordered Lyla to a gruesome, painful death that the woman didn't deserve. But this was war, and she'd known this burden would be hers to carry. Her real rage was reserved for the Maramans that forced her into this position. All around her, sentinels and sin died to protect her. The surrounding elites were wincing in pain at the repeated blows to the spells protecting their protectors.

She'd had enough.

She unlimbered Harmony and spun it into her hands. The first Maraman that came within range of her blade died before he realized he was in danger. The next put up more of a fight, but Shin didn't mind. Every gash, every sliced tendon, and finally the severed artery in his neck was a little revenge for Lyla.

She strode forward in a haze. In the distance, she heard her name being called but she ignored it. There was only Harmony, humming with all the power their terrible sacrifice had gifted Shin.

And then she was surrounded.

Her violence had cut her off from her allies and put her in front of two summoners. She threw Harmony at one summoner and attacked the second with her fists. She landed a few blows dancing out of the way of two crimson swords. Harmony flew back into her hand in time for her to parry a blow from the giant glowing mace the second summoner wielded.

The summoners attacked her as though she'd insulted their emperor and spit in his face.

She dodged as she gave ground against her attackers. But the more she gave, the more likely she was to be impaled by a Maraman from behind. She wanted to reach out to the realm, but she dared not remove Corin's protections. She had no idea where he was and she would rather die herself than be the cause of his death, too. Then the summoners eased their attack for one moment as they prepared another assault. It gave her enough time to dip into a reserve of concentration and focus to summon a giant digging fork from the sky to impale one of the summoners.

He died confused. The digging fork disappeared, and then her world exploded into stars.

Bleary eyed, she could just make out the crimson mace held above the summoner's head. She willed her arms to lift Harmony and block the blow, but the best she could do was a small twitch. Shin watched her death descend towards her.

She blinked, and the summoner was gone. In his place was another Maraman, but uglier. Familiar though. The fog in her head cleared a little more and Shin grinned at Beast. His back was to her, and he blocked a blow from the summoner's mace that cracked his giant axe in half. Beast threw the weapon at his attacker and then wrapped his giant arms around him. The mace, pinned at the summoner's side, started to flicker in and out of existence as Beast's crushing embrace caused the Maraman to lose consciousness. When the limp body slumped to the ground, Beast casually crushed his skull with a swift stomp and bent down to help Shin to her feet.

"This is going poorly, Shin. I hope you have a contingency plan," Beast said.

Corin, his glowing armor and swords making short work of his own enemies, fought his way into the circle of calm that Beast and his mugon had created. Behind him, a glowing cadre of sin and sentinels protected the small knot of elites. When Shin had taken off in a rage, they had followed.

Shin felt the battle slipping away more than she could see it. Hers was not a tactical mind that could understand the ebb and flow of a battlefield, but she could sense the realm and sacrifice and there were far too many summoners on the field. They had lost too many elites and adepts to hope to stop the remaining summoners.

In the distance, Shin still sensed the emperor.

"We have to get to the emperor. That's the only way we end this," Shin said.

Corin relayed the orders. Soon, Shin was surrounded by sentinels and sin and she pointed them in the direction of the emperor. She looked at Beast, "Can you buy us time?"

Beast looked down at his skin, lightly glowing crimson, and grinned. "Feels like I could hold off this whole army by myself. I'll buy you your time. Just promise me you'll kill the emperor."

Shin nodded. They took off at a jog, fighting their way through the Maramans that stood between them and the emperor. Behind her, she felt the remaining elites struggle in the face of the summoners, but she had to press on.

They had one chance to win the day, and it rested on her shoulders.

# 44

Beast's heavy gaze lingered on the two young faces in front of him. He wanted to burn the moment into his memory, to remember the gravity of what this parting would mean. Instead, all he had time to do was glance behind him before he had to raise his axe to meet the Maramans charging their position.

"No one gets past us!" Beast roared. "Anyone who dies letting a Maraman through will have to deal with me in the afterlife, and I promise I won't be nearly as gentle as these Maraman pricks!"

His mugon pushed forward to slow the Maraman advance. From Beast's vantage point, their defense spoke more to their courage than to their wisdom. Each Maraman was twice as big as his motley collection of warriors, but he liked to think his mugon fought with twice the heart.

Beast had picked up the largest sword he could find, but it was a pale comparison for his great axe. Even with the smaller weapon, Beast shouldered the burden of keeping the battle on even ground. He pushed himself to force the Maramans back. His ferocity was one part necessity and one part planning. He needed them to forget that Shin had broken their lines and was chasing down their precious emperor.

Beast drew Benji's broken sword with his off hand and grinned. It wasn't quite as good as having Benji at his side, but it would do.

He thought of Benji, dying with his hand in Beast's, needing only the comfort of his friend to face down the final journey that so many feared their whole lives.

With a primal scream, he let his battle rage wash over him. All he saw was red. All he craved was violence.

He charged forward.

A slice of his sword opened a Maraman's neck. He ducked under the swing of a club and stepped forward, rolling the blow off his shoulder. He stabbed the broken blade of Benji's sword into the eye of his attacker. A huge arm wrapped around his face and tried to pull him down. He bit the flesh until the grip loosened and then spun around, stepping back so that he could hack the Maraman with the long sword over and over. Blood sprayed across Beast's face, and he licked his lips.

The line of mugon sagged wherever Beast wasn't. Every time he pushed a Maraman offensive back, he was forced to run to another part of the line so it would hold. He reached deep into his well of rage and drank deeply. His memories served as fuel for a fire that felt like it would never burn out.

He saw Jurian's grinning face offering him one of the snacks he always carried. He saw Shin, shouldering the burdens of a world that had rarely been anything but cruel to her. He thought of Vala, sacrificing her body to save others. And the fire burned with the intensity of the sun on a summer day.

Thoughts faded, and he found a strange peace in the

midst of the chaos. His battle-trained muscles attached directly to the well of rage within him and his mind was simply along for the ride. Block, punch, kill. Parry, dodge, stab, kill. Slash, slash, kill.

Kill.

Beast's vision cleared when he stepped backward and bumped into another mugon. He tried to adjust his footing, but the ground was strangely uneven. When he looked down, he saw there was no place left to plant his foot. He stood in the midst of a pile of dead or dying Maramans. He brought his boot down on the skull of one that was still twitching. The skull shattered under his foot.

It still wasn't enough. His anger was as hot as ever. And he'd accomplished nothing. For all his efforts, the Maramans still surrounded them and pushed the survivors into an ever-shrinking circle.

A familiar sound cut through the battle. Suddenly, the advancing Maramans were looking around desperately as thick, black smoke surrounded them. The battlefield grew oddly quiet then, but only for a moment. Soon, screams of pain and shouts of panic replaced the clashes of steel. Beast readied himself and almost swung on the giant figure emerging from the smoke.

For a moment, he saw a ghost, and he wondered if his thoughts of Jurian had summoned his old friend to aid him on the battlefield. He wasn't sure it would be the strangest thing he'd seen that day.

Then Keff appeared beside Hanz and the real world slammed into focus.

"I told you to stay away," Beast said.

"Yes, but isn't your favorite thing about me that I think for myself?" Keff asked.

"I prefer when you think for me."

"Someone has to," Hanz said, "but there's no time to discuss this. The battle is going poorly."

"Are we routed?" Beast asked, expecting the worst.

"No, but only because of the skill of the sentinels and the tactical prowess of Sato," Hanz said.

Beast grunted.

Hanz continued. "Come, we need to get behind the sentinel lines. When Shin broke ranks, she pushed through the Maramans, but it cracked the mugon lines in the process. Sato closed the breach with his sentinels, but it cost us half the beachhead we'd secured, and we might have lost it all were it not for you."

Beast looked around. They were east of the main battle. Hanz had taken a force of mostly islanders to come rescue what was left of the mugon he led. As they spoke, they hurried toward the sentinel lines. "It seems like the Maramans could have done more."

"They almost did, but you drew too much attention. They were like moths to a flame. Except you were a bonfire. They wanted you dead," Hanz said.

Beast looked back at the battlefield they left behind. There were mugon bodies all around, but just as many Maramans littered the killing floor. Beast thought he was protecting his forces by fighting like a demon, but all he'd done was draw more enemies to his mugon.

"Did our juggernaut survive?" Beast asked.

Keff answered. "Yes. Vala's legend might surpass even your own today. That monster she conjured had almost destroyed the first Maraman juggernaut when the second arrived to help. I don't understand how her sacrifice works, but with every hit that sea monster took, Vala suffered. Despite that, she wrapped both juggernauts up with the monster and caused an explosion that shook the whole ocean and sunk the Maraman juggernauts. We cleaned up what was left of the Maraman navy afterwards."

"Is she alive?" Beast asked.

"She's fine. Exhausted, but fine. Colas stayed with her. The rest of us came to help," Keff replied.

Beast and his rescuers made it behind friendly lines just in time for the Maraman forces to regroup and descend upon them. The sentinels met the advance with steel and discipline. Beast was glad for the brief respite, but wasn't sure how long the sentinel lines would hold. There were a lot of damned Maramans on this beach.

Hanz broke his string of thoughts. "Where was Shin going? If we just stand here and fight, we'll all be dead before the sun sets."

"To kill the emperor. She needed us to buy time. So that was what we did," Beast said. "I just hope that it's enough."

Hanz cuffed him upside the head, and he was lucky Beast didn't run him through with his sword.

"You fool! If she's behind the Maraman lines, your distraction is finished, and our forces are pinned down here, what chance does she have?" Hanz asked. "Especially against one as strong as the emperor. We need to find a way to help her."

"We won't make it in time," Keff observed, "but those riders might." He pointed to where Sato and his honor guard sat on their steeds.

"Sure, let's go ask Sato to send his cavalry away from the heart of a battle that he's losing. He's going to love that," Beast said. But it wasn't like they had a better option.

Together, they hurried towards Sato. The new Firstborn sat high on his horse, observing the battle and giving orders like he'd been born to it. The sentinel line held against the onslaught, but barely. The adepts, with their crimson tentacles ripping apart their attackers, mostly held the demons at bay. Sato used his cavalry rarely, but when they charged, they disrupted the Maraman advance before returning to relative safety.

"Sato!" Beast shouted.

Sato's honor guard turned to meet the potential threat, but a word from Sato put them at ease. "Beast. I see your mugon couldn't manage to maintain a simple defensive formation. I lost a lot of—"

"Get fucked."

Sato's face turned red, and for a moment, Beast thought he saw a vision of his death. But he charged forward. They didn't have time to bicker. "Good. We had our argument. Now, can we talk about how we win this battle?"

Sato's face flushed, but a whispered word from Crispin calmed Sato's anger. "And how do you propose we do that?"

"Shin went to kill the emperor. From the look of things, that might be the only way we win this fight."

"Perhaps if your mugon had held their ranks, we wouldn't need to put the fate of the battle in Shin's hands," Sato growled.

Beast grit his teeth but pressed on. "She's through the lines, but if we're going to win, we need to support her. We need to get forces there as fast as we can."

Sato snorted. "You can't expect me to give up my cavalry. It's the only force disrupting their advance. Our formations won't last long without their support."

Beast grinned. "I can be as disruptive as your damn horses. A sight better looking, too."

"Are you suggesting you alone can replace an entire regiment of mounted sentinels? That ego of yours has somehow managed to outgrow even you."

The two warriors glared at one another, and not even the war was going to stop their contest.

Finally, Crispin interrupted. “Sir, if I may?”

Sato nodded for Crispin to proceed, but he didn’t break away from staring at Beast.

"We can't win this fight, here. You know that. But if we can kill the emperor, we might still win the war," Crispin offered.

Sato thought for a moment. His eyes unfocused and he looked through Beast into the distance. Finally, he came back to himself. “Fine, we’ll go. But Beast, you make sure this line holds, or I’ll come back and deal with you myself.”

“Why don’t you come back and try that either way,” Beast snapped back. "We can settle this once and for all."

“I just might,” Sato said with an odd smile. “Crispin, remain with Helios and command the sentinel forces. Cooperate with Beast, if such a thing is even possible. Riders! To me!”

Sato wheeled his horse away from the battle lines and the remaining cavalry fell in behind him. When they had created some distance, they broke into a full gallop. A horn blew from the back of the charge and the sentinels' formation shifted. Sato's guard found the weak point in the Maraman line and turned. For a moment, the Maramans offered resistance, but the charge broke through.

Beast wished them well as the Maraman line reformed.

“Do you think they’ll make it?” Keff asked.

Beast shrugged. “They’ll catch up quickly, but if those Unnamed are waiting just beyond the rise, it may not be quickly enough. Not much we can do now, though.”

“We can kill some more Maramans,” Hanz suggested.

Beast grinned, but his heart wasn’t in it. The real battle would be happening somewhere else. He would fight, but it wouldn't matter. A renewed push from the Maramans drew his attention to the front.

"Keff, I need you to actually stay back this time," Beast said.

Keff nodded but still had his sling in hand. Beast turned and ran into the battle. Despite Shin's strengthening of his body, his muscles were weary. He bled from wounds he couldn't yet feel and there was a knot on the back of his head that made him dread the headache he'd have tomorrow morning.

If he was lucky enough to see another morning.

Beast put all of that out of his mind as he swung his sword. His cut was met by Maraman steel. Soon enough, the last of his thoughts drifted away and there was only battle.

# 45

Shin and Corin moved together in an almost seamless dance that ended Maraman lives in fluid motions. Many sentinels had disparaged Corin's twin sword technique, but he'd trained hard enough to develop a deadly competence.

Shin jumped back as a Maraman swung his sword at her. Corin stepped in and took the blow on his magically armored shoulder, causing the Maraman to stagger. Shin slammed Harmony's blade into the Maraman's stomach and sliced upward for good measure. The Maraman fell and suddenly the land between Shin and the emperor was empty.

Unless you counted the fifty ink-black Unnamed that surrounded him.

Shin swore. Her forces were exhausted, but even well rested, she wasn't sure they stood a chance against those Unnamed. Behind them, she sensed the emperor battling Rua. She couldn't guess how their fight would end, but she wasn't willing to squander this chance. It was the only one they'd ever have.

"Get everyone back," Shin told Corin.

She closed her eyes and was faintly aware of the sounds of her protectors backing up. She accessed the realm and began weaving a new expression of sacrifice. As she laid the foundation, she imagined clouds above roiling and spitting lighting. She imagined them coalescing and forming a deadly funnel. Before she was finished, she poured every ounce of her rage and sorrow into those clouds. She thought of those she'd lost, even those she couldn't remember any more, and put the pain of what was taken from her into every bolt of lightning that would strike her enemies.

When she opened her eyes, tears streamed down her cheeks, but a crimson tornado formed in front of the Unnamed. Thunder rumbled constantly and unnatural winds buffeted her, but she stared through stinging rain. This, she wanted to watch.

Shin grinned as the crimson tornado met the line of Unnamed. It would tear them limb from limb and strike them down with deadly power. Before her, they would scatter like sheep before a wolf.

The tornado struck the Unnamed, then winked out of existence.

Shin blinked. The last rolls of thunder still echoed in her ears, but there was no sign of the tornado. She focused and felt the last remnants of sacrifice, cast by the emperor. He was engaged in a pitched battle within the realm, but still flicked away her most destructive sacrifice on this plane like it was nothing. She was allowed one perfect moment of despair before the Unnamed charged them.

"Ready yourselves!" She heard Corin call out, and then he was grabbing her and pulling her back into the relative safety of their numbers.

Shin tried to clear her head. Now was not the time to

wallow. She was still alive and still had Harmony. If she couldn't stop the emperor with sacrifice, she'd have to cut his throat instead.

"For Samas!" Shin called.

Much to her relief, she heard a cry of support ring out from her remaining forces. There weren't many of them left, but they would fight to the last. Shin readied Harmony and felt blood rushing to her head. She still heard the thunder, but it was getting closer now.

"Forward!" Shin called out. They would meet their enemy head on.

The Unnamed were almost on top of Shin's warriors when they suddenly stopped their advance. They formed up, creating a defensive formation faster than Shin understood what was happening. Why would they stop?

Then the thunder she'd been hearing became a roar and a wave of horses, sentinels, and steel crashed into the Unnamed. Shin's forces continued their charge as the sentinel calvary tore through the Unnamed.

Somehow, through sheer strength and skill, the Unnamed stemmed the tide of the sentinel charge and pushed the mounted sentinels back. Shin's forces moved in before the Unnamed could beat the cavalry back. She fought her way into the battle, but a horse appeared beside her and she looked up to see Sato, sword drawn, looking down at her.

"We'll handle this. You stop the emperor," he shouted.

Shin hesitated for only a moment. Sato was right, even with the sentinels helping, the Unnamed were a deadly force. There was no guarantee they would win this fight. She had to stop the emperor now. Even though he'd just shown her how meaningless her strength was.

"Right," Shin said. First, she needed a way out of this battle.

She called the realm and created floating, crimson discs that hovered above the fray. She leapt from disc to disc, high above the fight below her. A few Maraman spears came for her heart, but they bounced harmlessly off the sacrificial platforms she created. The Unnamed tried to follow, but the platforms dissolved after she leaped off them. Thanks to Sato's sacrifice, it didn't take her long to descend and face the emperor.

"Hello, Shin," the emperor said without opening his eyes. "My name is Emperor Kordano."

The giant Maraman was sitting cross legged before her, but even then his head was almost level with her own. He wore a simple brown tunic that would be loose fitting on most, but showed his bulging muscles like a fitted shirt. Like all other Maramans, his head and face were shaved clean. Around his neck was a tattoo of twisted thorns.

"I have nothing to say to you." Shin readied Harmony.

The emperor seemed not to care. "I can understand that, but still hope we can talk. You believe killing me will end the threat to Samas, but the truth is, I am fighting the much larger threat as we speak."

Shin almost ignored him. Almost stepped forward and plunged Harmony's blade into his heart, but something in the emperor's tone stopped her. That and his complete lack of fear. She worried she had stepped right into a trap.

"You're fighting Rua," Shin said.

"Yes, and I'm losing."

"Good. Then all I have to do is wait."

"That would be unwise. I think you will find Rua to be a much more dangerous foe than I." Kordano's voice was deep and rumbling, with only a trace of an accent. She'd expected a hulking brute, and she wasn't disappointed in that regard, but she hadn't expected such composure and intelligence. In a way, his presence reminded her of Yuki's.

Then Shin remembered Yuki had died to destroy this man. "Rua was a sentinel. She and her sister founded the orders that protects Samas. I could ask for no better ally."

Kordano laughed. "Who do you think brought me here? Rua, whoever she was when she lived on Samas, is nothing more than a demon now. A unique one, to be sure, but a demon nonetheless. She fooled me. Offered me power and knowledge and brought me to this land of riches ripe for the taking, but it was all a manipulation. She needed to be here, close to the rifts into which she was banished, in order to return."

Shin raised an eyebrow. "Return?"

Kordano winced for a moment and sweat broke out on his brow before he answered. "Yes. She seeks to right an ancient wrong. She needed a body, and to be back here. After that, she waited until I was distracted before attempting to wrest control away from me. Now, you're here and I fear if I have to fight you as well, she will win."

"I'm still not sure why I should step in. You're here to conquer our land."

"And Rua may destroy it!" Kordano's veneer of calm cracked for a moment. "Whatever she was, Rua has gone quite mad within the realm. She's been there for centuries. If she takes my body, she will have power beyond imagining, and there will be no one to stop her or the realm."

"I'll be here," Shin said.

"If I can't stop her alone, then neither can you. Together, we have a chance. I am not expecting you to lie down and let me take your land once we defeat her. I'm no fool. I'm suggesting a temporary alliance to deal with a threat that could end us all."

Another voice spoke, adding to Shin's confusion. "I'm not your enemy, Shin."

Shin blinked and suddenly she was seeing two worlds at once. In one, the emperor was sitting calmly in front of her. In the other, she saw the emperor locked in a battle with a small woman that looked almost identical to Yuki. The two forms pushed away from each other and stood for a moment in a stalemate.

"You look just like her," was all Shin could manage to say.

Rua smiled. "Yes, my sister and I shared many traits. Chief among them was the desire to protect Samas. Please, don't let this brute fool you."

On the heels of her words, Rua tossed a ball of energy at Kordano that exploded on a shield he created. Kordano replied with a blast of lightning that Rua batted away.

"Are you trying to return to this land?" Shin asked.

"I don't even know if that's possible," Rua said. "I saw a chance to help stop the emperor, and I took it. I've been here, protecting Samas for years," Rua said.

"She's lying—" the emperor began.

Shin had heard enough. "No, you are. Rua founded the sentinels. Her sister was my mentor. I came here to kill you, so that's what I'm going to do."

The emperor shook his head and threw out his hands with a roar.

Shin put her own hands up defensively as a volley of lightning bolts flew her way, but she knew it was a futile gesture. She closed her eyes against the impact, but when she heard the sounds, she felt nothing. She opened her eyes to see that Rua had put up a crimson shield to protect her.

"Let's end this, for Yuki," Rua said.

"For Yuki." Shin opened her hands and a crimson version of Harmony appeared.

"I'll kill you both, then," Kordano said. He didn't seem disappointed by the result.

Shin threw Harmony, and Rua wrapped it in a sacrifice as it flew. When Kordano knocked Harmony away with a shield of his own, Rua's spell exploded out from the weapon and turned into a swarm of fist sized insects that harassed the emperor. He swatted at them with his hands for a moment, then grew furious and blew them away with a gesture.

Rua hadn't been idle in the moments Shin's attack gave her.

She charged forward with a lightning bolt in each fist. She threw one the moment Kordano dispelled the insects, and it hit him square in the chest. Shin heard his cry of pain.

For all his power, the emperor could be hurt.

Her conjured version of Harmony winked out of existence as Shin let go of her dependence on fighting the way she would in the real world. Here, she could do what she wanted. Kordano recovered from his blow and faced off with Rua once more. Shin conjured chains that wrapped around Kordano and held him tight. The moment before Rua could strike his face, he flexed his power, and the chains shattered, knocking them both backwards.

Shin summoned rocks to pummel the emperor, but they bounced harmlessly off his shield. She didn't give up hope, though. She could see he was distracted and kept up her assault so that Rua could land a killing blow.

Then, in her divided view, she saw the emperor stand up and draw a huge, curved sword in Samas. Reflexively, she focused on her physical body and brought Harmony up in time to block a powerful blow that made her hands go numb. She danced backwards from a flurry of swings and threw Harmony to buy herself time. All the while, in her strangely split view, she knew she was doing nothing to help Rua in the realm. She'd never trained in dividing her attention like this. So long as the emperor was attacking her here, she'd be no help to Rua within the realm.

"You're making the wrong choice, Shin," Emperor Kordano said, "I would have preferred to fight you with my full attention, but even with that magical weapon of yours it's easier for me to kill you here."

Shin charged forward. She would show him exactly how much of his attention she deserved.

She swung Harmony fast and hard.

Her forms were nearly perfect.

Kordano blocked every one, looking bored.

Finally, he parried a blow with such force that it knocked her off balance. He stepped in with his opposite fist and connected with the side of her head. It was like being hit with a brick, and Shin fell to the ground, her vision blurry.

"You fought bravely," Kordano said as he raised his sword. "For that, I'll grant you a warrior's death."

Before he could bring his sword down, his eyes darted to the side, and he had to bring his blade around to block a blow from a sentinel riding a horse.

Shin would have rolled her eyes if it hadn't hurt so much.

She was being saved by fucking Sato.

# 46

Sato's sword hand stung from the force with which the Maraman emperor had blocked his blow. Sato wheeled Nightmane around and was relieved to see Shin scramble up from the ground and shake her head to clear it. Sato had feared she wouldn't recover from the force of the emperor's fist.

"Ah, Sato. I wondered if you'd join us," the emperor said.

Sato kicked Nightmane into a charge.

As he had done a hundred times before, Sato bore down on his enemy with the full might of Nightmane underneath him. Reach, power and height were all to his advantage, and he put all three into a masterful stroke with his sword. Even the strictest of his instructors would have bowed in respect at the cut.

A cut that the emperor evaded, his massive bulk sliding away from Sato with casual indifference. Only whip-fast reflexes and a lifetime of skill as a horseman saved Nightmane from being hacked in the flank with the emperor's giant sword. Sato wheeled once more and considered his enemy. The normal advantages of being on horseback were almost completely negated by the size of the Maraman and his extraordinary strength. Sato's true advantages would be his skill with the blade and his agility.

He dismounted.

"You're going to need that horse when you want to run away," the emperor said.

Sato ignored him. Though he couldn't parse the specifics of the battle within the realm, this close, he could easily feel the struggle within. "Shin, help Rua. I can handle him here alone."

Shin, for once in her life, obeyed and ran away from the action. Sato grimaced. Of course the only order she'd listen to was the one where he gave her permission to flee. Kordano made to chase her, but Sato was faster, and his positioning was better. He put himself between the emperor and Shin and delivered a series of cuts that forced the emperor to defend. Sato feinted with a final high strike, and when the emperor shifted his sword up to block, Sato delivered a kick to his exposed knee.

The emperor dropped with a grunt of pain, but before Sato could deliver a killing blow, drew a long dagger. With the skill of a master, he deflected Sato's sword with the much smaller blade.

Sato grinned. Finally, a challenge worthy of his blade.

"I recognize that look. You think you're a match for me. Well—"

Sato didn't let the emperor finish. He attacked. His sword was everywhere at once, and the emperor was forced to react rather than dictate the pace of the fight himself.

Several small cuts opened across the emperor's body, but the combination of giant sword and wicked dagger served him almost as well as a shield. No matter how fast Sato attacked, the openings closed before he could reach them.

Kordano used one block to unbalance Sato, and the emperor seized the moment, forcing Sato back.

The emperor pushed his perceived advantage until Sato knocked the dagger from the emperor's off-hand.

Kordano shook his empty hand. "You're good. Maybe the best I've faced. If almost all my attention wasn't on the fight against Rua, however, I'd have killed you already."

Sato refused to rise to the bait. "We can only fight the battles as they appear before us."

"Sounds like a line from your precious Path of the Eternal Sun. Rua told me all about it. Sounds like drivel to me."

"It's that very drivel that will drive you from this land," Sato said.

"Honor and discipline and all of that? Try overwhelming force," the emperor suggested.

Sato sensed movement behind more than he heard it. At the last moment, he ducked out of the way of a giant ax, but the very edge of the blade caught him across the ear. He wasn't sure how much of it he lost, but he had no time to check as he brought his sword up to block the blows from the giant, ax-wielding Maraman.

"This is General Kordak," the emperor said, but his conversational tone was a distraction as he launched an attack.

Sato gave up ground desperately. He resisted the urge to block strikes, and instead used his footwork to put himself into positions where he could redirect the force of the giant weapons. The one advantage he had was that two large men wielding two large weapons needed a lot of space to operate, and Sato could use that to his advantage.

For a time.

He grew tired. One misstep, one poorly timed parry, and

this fight would result in his death. Instincts took over while his mind searched for solutions. He sensed a pulsing from the realm and followed it.

Suddenly, he was seeing two worlds. One was the desperate fight with Kordak and the emperor, the other was Shin and what looked like Yuki fighting a different version of the emperor.

*He has to pay attention to two places at once. When we draw his focus here, he's distracted there. Wait for my signal,* Rua said in his mind.

Sato forced himself to ignore the realm and focus on survival. A pulse from the realm signaled Sato and he noticed the hint of a distraction in the emperor. It wasn't much, but because Sato was looking for it, he noticed the emperor was a moment late in protecting the opening Kordak's giant swings created.

Sato darted into the opening and was rewarded with a deep cut across Kordak's thigh. He jumped back out of range in time to avoid Kordano's attack.

Distracted by Kordano, he didn't track Kordak closely enough. Kordak's ax hooked his ankle and sent him crashing to the ground. He rolled onto his back in time to see Kordak, bleeding from his outer thigh, raise his ax for another blow. Sato tried to scramble back, but the emperor was there, and Sato had to get his sword up to block. The emperor's heavier weapon pushed down on Sato's blade, leaving Kordak free to attack.

Then Kordak was flung to the ground like a child.

The emperor raised his sword to block an incoming strike.

Beast.

Sato was being saved by Beast. He'd never hear the end of it.

He and Kordak both raced to their feet, but Sato was faster. Kordak had been taken by surprise, and the cut on his leg slowed him down. Before he could defend himself with his ax, Sato drove his sword deep into the giant's chest.

The Maraman general struggled from a moment before his body finally gave out.

Sato didn't savor his victory. Instead, he turned to join Beast's attack on the emperor. When he turned, though, it wasn't proceeding as he'd expected. Beast and the emperor both stood on the edge of violence, but for now settled for glaring at one another.

"Where did you come from?" Sato asked Beast.

"I thought Shin could use some help."

"Yes, that's why I'm here."

"Some real help. So, this is the emperor?"

"I am Emperor Kordano. And you are a lost son of Maramas. It is time for you to return to us."

Beast looked the emperor up and down. "I thought you'd be bigger."

Sato shook his head. He would have been happier to see Roko or Alonzo show up to aid him, but he had to admit that Beast was likely the best suited warrior for the task at hand.

Beast wasted no time proving Sato right.

With a roar, he charged the emperor and Sato followed right behind him. Against two warriors of such skill, the emperor was forced to retreat. Sato and Beast both scored hits, but nothing was yet fatal.

Then both he and Beast were sent flying, though neither had been in danger from either a sword or a limb. He looked up and saw the shimmer of a crimson shield disappearing.

"Well, that seems unfair," Beast said.

Sato was about to agree when the emperor in this realm

dropped to his knees. Sato allowed his awareness to focus on the shadow realm, where he saw Rua and Shin pounding at the emperor with crimson spells.

"If he has to use sacrifice here, he's more distracted in the realm," Sato said.

"Where?"

"Just keep attacking him. It will give Shin a chance to defeat him!"

Beast nodded and stood up.

The emperor conjured a crimson horn and blew it. Sato turned to see a handful of the Unnamed engaged with the Samasian forces fight to break away from that battle. Sato cursed.

Before the Unnamed could break away, clouds of smoke exploded around them, and a group of people Sato recognized as Beast's island recruits joined the chaos.

"I brought help," Beast said. "I don't think they'll match the Maramans long, though, so we better hurry."

Sato renewed his attack on the emperor. He found something of a rhythm with Beast and the two forced the emperor into using sacrifice more often. Twice it was a shield to absorb an attack that would have otherwise killed him. Once he lashed out with a deadly crimson sword.

Each time he used sacrifice, though, he'd grunt in pain and recover a little more slowly. Sato risked a glance into the realm and saw Shin, standing behind the emperor and readying a thick crimson chain. Rua blasted him with a gout of crimson flame, but the emperor was completely encased in a shield that wasn't showing any signs of weakening.

Sato and Beast attacked the emperor again. Even though they had him on the defensive, they weren't landing any meaningful blows. In the realm, Sato saw the emperor turn the front of his shield into sharp spikes that he thrust forward. The unexpected switch from defense to offense caught Rua by surprise, and she was impaled by the spikes.

The world slowed.

Sato knew the emperor would turn his full attention to Shin next and that she would lose.

He knew that for all their skill, Beast and Sato couldn't match the power given to the emperor by the realm.

He raised a hand to his badly damaged ear and shrugged.

He accessed the realm. By instinct, more than anything, he crafted a simple spell. A throwing knife that would explode on contact. The realm offered the price and Sato agreed. A sharp pain and his ear was gone.

In his hand was a glowing knife.

He threw it at the emperor, who brought up a shield of crimson light so casually that Sato feared his plan had failed. Then, the emperor's eyes bulged in his head and his hands came up to claw at his neck. Sato focused on the realm where he saw Shin had wrapped the glowing chain around the emperor's neck and was squeezing with all her might.

Before the Emperor could react in either place, Sato moved forward, his blade ready.

His form was perfect.

His cause was pure.

His blade cleaved the head of the Maraman emperor from his shoulders.

A soundless thud pulsed across the battlefield. Sato and Beast were knocked to the ground and those farther away staggered. What demons remained among the Unnamed vanished and the Maraman forces faltered; their demon-supported ranks suddenly had gaping holes in them.

The sentinels, sin, and mugon who had been desperately fighting for their lives took advantage.

From where Sato kneeled, he saw his forces slowly gain the advantage. The Maramans still fought, but their hearts had already been ripped from them. Every Maraman on the field knew what the loss of the demons meant.

Shin walked over to check on Beast. The big man accepted her help and rose to his feet. They both looked over at Sato

"So, it's done," Sato said. He barely believed the words himself.

"It is," Shin replied.

There was a wary silence between the three disparate people. Sato realized he hadn't spent much time thinking about what came after. Victory had always seemed such a distant proposition.

The ghostly, crimson figure of Rua appearing before them broke the silence.

"Congratulations. Now, for what comes next," Rua said.

Sato forced himself to his feet. He was exhausted, but with the appearance of Rua, he had the distinct feeling that he was outnumbered. He glanced over his shoulder at the skirmish with the remaining Maramans, but his sentinels were still fully engaged.

"I sense your concern, Sato, but you need not fear. I am your one true ally here," Rua said.

Sato kept his guard up. "What does that mean?"

"I'm also curious," Beast growled.

Rua ignored Beast and Shin and walked towards Sato. "You have fulfilled your desire to become Firstborn. Now, is your first act going to be compromise? To allow this war criminal and a mere peasant girl to hold any kind of power in Samas? In *your* nation?"

Sato felt a slight nagging in the back of his mind. A familiar voice preaching understanding and tolerance. His old mentor imploring him to think about how far he'd come and how much he'd changed. To think about how the Path should be interpreted.

It reeked of compromise. It was what made his predecessor weak.

"What are you suggesting?" Sato asked Rua.

"You're a unique man, Sato. The only Firstborn who also has an aptitude for sacrifice. Let me join you. Allow me to show you how to wield true power," Rua said.

"Sato don't!" Shin yelled.

Never one for subtlety, Beast hurled the broken sword he carried at Rua. The weapon flew true, broken blade first, and passed right through the crimson ghost. Rua spared a smile for Beast's attempt to stop her and then returned her gaze to Sato.

"Well?" Rua asked.

Sato considered. He hadn't enjoyed sharing his mind with the old sentinel, but what was the point of being Firstborn if he still had to sully his order with the likes of the sin? If he had their power, the true power a Firstborn should wield, he would have no need for compromise.

He could guide Samas along the Path. Here, for the first time, was everything he'd ever wanted. A future of purity and truth.

"I will take your power," Sato said.

Beast charged him, sword raised.

Shin sat down and closed her eyes.

Rua disappeared, and then his body was filled with what seemed like limitless potential for power. He'd tasted the realm before, but he'd never imagined what it could actually do. He'd never imagined how much power he could possess.

Rua was right.

This was the way.

Sato smiled for a moment and then he raised his sword to block Beast's blow.

His body was weary no longer.

His body would never be weary again.

# 47

Shin left her physical form in Beast's hands. Having seen the way Kordano had mastered his abilities in both realms made her feel weak, but she didn't delude herself. If she split her attention between the planes, she would die in both. Better by far to fight in the realm, where she was strongest. She focused on the realm in time to watch Rua possess Sato.

The damned fool! Rua had offered him everything he'd ever wanted, and he never thought to question if it would be true. The temptation had been too great. Rua was far too strong. Kordano had held her at bay, but Sato didn't have the strength within the realm to fight, if the thought even occurred to him.

When the possession was complete, the resulting form was still Sato's. Rua's consciousness ruled the Firstborn's body.

Shin didn't know if she could fight Rua, even in Sato's weaker body. But perhaps she could still see reason. "Yuki wouldn't want the kind of Samas that an unchecked Sato will bring about."

"I've long stopped caring what my sister would want. She left me here, in this nightmare, for centuries. I've felt nothing but rage, knowing that every other emotion was right there, just out of reach. It almost drove me mad. I had to escape, any way I could."

Shin realized this wasn't the first time Rua had tried to escape the realm. "You were there when Yuki died," Shin said softly.

"You think I would miss my dear sister's passing?" Rua's tone mocked her sister's memory.

"You tried to steal her body. I felt something that night. I thought it was the realm trying to invade Yuki. To turn her into the monster she feared once she used up the last of her well of sacrifice. That wasn't the realm, though, was it? It was you. You were trying to use your own sister to return."

"It would have been so much simpler. She was dying and I could have taken her body for my own. She fought me though, stubborn as always. Then, as you saw, the emperor was less than amenable to sharing his body with me. Fortunately, Sato had enough sense to see the power I can offer."

Shin didn't know Rua, but she recognized the sound of an unstable mind. Hers had been the same, wandering the fields alone after her parents had died. Only Corin and the luan had brought her back. Rua had never had anyone like that for her. Whatever was left of the woman who had formed the sentinels was gone, stripped away by centuries within the realm. "Why did you wait so long to come back? Surely Yuki would have helped you if she'd known you were here."

Shin didn't really believe she could talk Rua down, but as long as they were talking, Shin was able to send out signals for help to the adepts and elites nearby.

"Geography works differently in this place," Rua said, gesturing around. "When the sacrifice that cost me my physical form was complete, I was cast through the rifts and didn't know where I was. It took decades for me to be anything other than one of those feral, formless beings casting out for any emotion they could find. Once I was able to claw back into my own consciousness, the first person I felt was the emperor. We developed a partnership, where I taught him about the realm and he promised to bring me to Samas. Now, here we are, and I finally have a physical form again. I like you, Shin, and I can see why Yuki did too, but I won't let you take that from me."

"I'm not sure it's me you have to worry about," Shin said as she watched the physical world through the split consciousness.

Rua's expression, shown through Sato's face, lost a little of its haughty confidence as it watched Beast charge forward and attack Sato. Any satisfaction Shin gleaned was short lived, however, as Rua's ghostly smile combined with Sato's smug face. "I think Sato is more than a match for your brutish friend. If not, well, once I'm done with you here, I'll be more than capable of helping Sato learn some new tricks with sacrifice."

Shin tried to gauge Beast's fight. She wasn't sure who the better warrior was, but Rua gave her no time to observe. Shin threw up a crimson barrier just in time to block a bloody ball of power that exploded and knocked her backwards. She kept her shield, but Rua lashed at her with whips of pure sacrifice. She felt the overwhelming well of power that Rua was drawing on and realized that whatever limitations Rua experienced through her lack of physical form in the real world were gone now that she was firmly anchored in Sato's body. She was stronger than before.

Shin summoned a crude wave of energy behind Rua, anything to slow the onslaught of power coming at her, but Rua dispelled the attempt as it formed.

"You're in my home, Shin, I know this place better than anyone alive. Where do you think the emperor leaned all that he knew?"

Shin couldn't focus enough to even speak. Every ounce of concentration was on holding her shield together, but it was starting to crack anyway.

Suddenly Rua cried out, and the onslaught lessened for a moment. On the physical plane, Beast had landed a glancing blow against Sato. The distraction lasted long enough for Shin to scramble back to her feet. She conjured a familiar weapon to impale Rua. The crimson version of Harmony almost struck true, but Rua deflected it at the last moment, suffering only a scratch.

Shin swore to herself. Strong as she was, even with the tremendous sacrifice of so many, she didn't think she could match this one woman, so determined to have a physical body.

That thought led to another. The beginning of a smile pulled on the corner of her lips. There was another way to end this.

The right way.

But everything depended on Beast defeating Sato. She couldn't do this alone. Looking back on her life, she'd never been able to do anything alone. She'd always had Yuki, Corin, and even Mateo. Before that, her parents had guided her.

She thought they'd be proud.

The moment of distraction passed. Rua conjured crimson warriors with a variety of intimidating weapons to surround her. Shin summoned the sacrificial version of

Harmony to her hands and readied herself. Beast had to kill Sato, but Shin had to survive, too.

The crimson warriors roared as they swarmed her.

# 48

Beast wasn't sure what had happened with the glowing ghost woman that had entered Sato, or why Shin had plopped down and closed her eyes. Seemed like a strange decision on the fiercest battlefield Samas had ever seen. But none of that mattered when he knew who his new enemy would be.

He *was* sure that beating the shit out of Sato was going to be the best day of his life.

For years, he'd listened to the stories about Sato being the best swordsman in Samas. For years, Beast had been forced to avoid direct conflict with the sentinels, for fear Sato would end up pursuing him.

Now, he finally got to see what that thrice-fucked, sun-worshipping sentinel was made of.

Their first exchange gave him a pretty good idea.

Sato was the best swordsman in Samas. No question about it.

Beast retreated as Sato delivered a flurry of strikes that Beast barely blocked. He had landed one shallow cut on Sato's arm in exchange, but since then the sentinel had been on the offensive. Beast didn't think he'd ever defended for so long. Normally, he determined the pace of the fight. Finally, Beast allowed a small cut across his ribs so he could knock Sato down with his shoulder.

The smaller man grunted from the impact, stumbled back a few feet, then landed on his back. Beast leaped forward, sword point down, to end the fight, but ended up slapping Sato's sword away as it came up to skewer him. The defense threw him off balance and he fell.

Beast let go of his sword so he could fight with both hands. This close, his fists were his most dangerous weapon anyway. His grabbed the hilt of Sato's sword and twisted. Strong as Sato was, he was nothing compared to Beast, and he was forced to let go. Beast tossed the sword away and brought his fist down.

Somehow, the little bastard's stiff fingers caught him in the throat first, and Beast crumpled. Sato hadn't hit him hard enough to kill him, but it had been a close thing. He gasped for air and swung a weak backfist at Sato's face.

Sato avoided the blow and recovered first. Though they were laying side by side, Sato threw a volley of punches that forced Beast to block. The position was awkward, but every time Beast tried to roll over and pin Sato, the sentinel would push him back with his legs. The blows Sato landed weren't that devastating, but each one was sure to leave a bruise, and Beast hadn't started this fight in the best condition. Sato, sensing an advantage, rolled on top of Beast and tried to control him by putting pressure on his hips.

Beast grinned.

Sato's technique was excellent, but if Beast could throw Hanz or Jurian off him, then the little sentinel never stood a chance. He heaved and was rewarded with a surprised grunt as Beast bucked Sato off.

Beast got to his feet instantly and had a choice to make. If he took the time to retrieve his sword, Sato would have time to reach his own weapon. They hadn't been fighting long, but Beast had seen enough to be convinced that the stories about Sato's swordsmanship weren't exaggerations. The man was a killer with steel in his hands.

Eager to see how Sato fared without a weapon, he charged.

Sato was on his knees and shaking his head to clear it when he saw Beast charging. Sato rose to his feet. Beast almost missed the whip-fast movement of Sato's arm and, more out of instinct that anything, was able to get his forearms up to block the small throwing knife. He felt the sharpened metal dig into his flesh, but he barely noticed. He was too close to Sato, and his time was now.

Sato retreated before Beast's assault. The Firstborn was fast, and his blocks felt like striking iron, but this close, Beast was an overwhelming force. Sato tried to keep space between them, to prevent Beast's sheer size from dominating him, but he was on his back foot. A small misstep allowed Beast to get in close. Beast grabbed Sato by the throat with one hand and lifted him in the air, prepared to deal a massive blow with his other fist.

Before he could, Sato grabbed the throwing knife that was still stuck out of the forearm grasping him by the throat. Beast was already in the motion of punching Sato, pulling the sentinel towards him and his fist, when Sato stabbed at this face with the knife. Beast moved his head back in time to avoid a fatal cut, but the vision disappeared from his right eye. A moment later, pain exploded in his head. With a roar of pain, he threw Sato as far as he could and put a hand to his ruined eye.

"You little fuck," Beast shouted, "I'm going to kill—"

Beast's head snapped back from the unseen kick Sato delivered. He recovered quickly, but Sato kept attacking, favoring Beast's right side. A rock-hard fist struck his cheek and Beast staggered back, blocking two more blows that followed.

If he didn't do something soon, he was going to lose a fistfight to this little prick. Sato continued to circle towards his ruined eye and pepper him with shots. Though Beast blocked many of them, enough got through that he was starting to regret picking a fight with Sato.

A burning slash across his stomach reminded him that Sato was fighting with a knife. He was going to carve Beast into little Maraman appetizers if Beast didn't find a way to regain the upper hand.

Beast ignored the pain and stepped into Sato's next attack. The knife glanced off Beast's ribs, but in return he landed a solid punch to Sato's kidneys. Sato stumbled backward.

The two men stared at each other, one bleeding from a nasty gash on his stomach and the other doubled over in pain. Beast wasn't sure how much blood he was losing, but his battle rage was fading. As was his consciousness. The cuts and bruises that he'd suffered over the course of the day's fighting were all starting to flare up. Normally when he got to this point everyone he was trying to kill was dead.

Sato was far from dead.

Beast summoned all the strength left to him and charged. His grin stretched from ear to ear.

If this was going to be his last fight, well, it was a damned good one.

# 49

Sato still reeled from the kidney shot that Beast had landed, but the gigantic criminal refused to die, and he didn't give Sato time to recover. Grudgingly, Sato had to respect Beast's toughness. Most enemies he fought would have surrendered against the punishment he'd served the Maraman.

No matter, Beast would die, broken or not.

The knife in his hand felt insignificant compared to the foe before him, but the weapon was far less important than the one who wielded it. He advanced on Beast, who brought his hands up to defend. As he did so, a fresh rush of blood seeped from the wound in his side. For another man, Sato may have felt pity, watching him struggle against an inevitable outcome. For Beast, he felt only respect.

He had to end this quickly. Too much fought for his attention, and he sensed the result of this battle would shape Samas for years to come. They needed to start on the Path with the right leadership.

He had allowed Rua to take control of his consciousness within the realm, but even with her experience, she was limited by his attention being taken here. Once he dealt with Beast he could finish Shin, and then the sin.

"Beast!" a voice called out.

Damn, Sato cursed to himself. Too late.

Corin approached, twin swords in hand. Somehow, he'd fought all the way through the last remaining Unnamed. Sato looked past him, hoping to see allies of his own, but it seemed the battle was still being fought.

"It's fine, Corin," Beast said, "I've got this."

"You don't even have both your eyes. And why are you fighting Sato?" Corin asked.

"I'm fuzzy on the details, but I think he's possessed by a demon," Beast said.

"I am possessed by no one. I am using Rua so that I may gain her power. We will return Samas to the Path," Sato said calmly.

Sato took a moment to retrieve his sword. Corin and his foolish twin swords might not be much of a threat, but he didn't like his odds against the sin with only a throwing knife. Beast was watching Sato warily and retrieved his own weapon. Sato couldn't believe the giant could still move.

"You and Rua are just going to what? Share your mind? You aren't even the kind of man who will share his uneaten food," Beast said.

Too late, Sato realized his mistake. While he talked with these two, more sin made their way toward this battlefield. Soon, he'd be hopelessly outnumbered, and Samas would be doomed. How did they know?

The answer came from the realm. He felt it through Rua. Shin was flaring her sacrifice, calling for help.

Sato dashed at the unprepared Corin. The boy, to his credit, reacted quickly. He got his swords up and defended well. But one of the weaknesses of the boy's style was that it was hard to match the power of a sword held in two hands. Sato knocked each sword away from Corin's body and exposed a wide opening.

Corin's panicked look brought Sato a powerful satisfaction. About time someone taught him one blade was superior to two. Too bad he wouldn't live long enough to learn.

Unfortunately, the thrust that would have ended the fool boy was blocked by Beast.

The giant man almost dropped his sword when it connected with Sato's blade. He'd lost too much blood to keep fighting. Sato could hardly believe he was still standing. "You can't protect the boy and yourself, not in the shape you're in."

"I don't need protecting," Corin said, and launched into an offensive of his own.

Sato blocked and casually gave up ground. Though he was never in any danger, Corin's pace kept him from attacking. And then more sin arrived. Just like the fucking plague they were. Hanz and Gorou were the first to arrive.

Sato stepped back warily. Even he knew he was no match for this many opponents, not in the shape he was in.

"Rua, I could use some help here," Sato said aloud.

*The girl is strong. I can't give you much time,* Rua replied.

"I won't need it. I'll stop them and kill the girl here," Sato said.

"The fuck you will," Corin said.

Before Corin could close the distance in a foolish heroic charge, Sato's power infused his limbs. His weariness faded as Rua tapped into the realm on his behalf. In a distant, rational recess of his mind, Sato was aware that something had been given up, but the question of what that was was too distant for him to focus on. Knowledge of the realm flooded into him, and his sword crackled to life with crimson fire. When he blocked Corin's double sword strike, both of the boy's blades broke on Sato's. His momentum carried him forward and Sato planted a firm kick in his side that sent the boy flying. Sato heard bones crack.

Sato hadn't known such strength existed. Even Beast couldn't match this.

His remaining enemies charged him, but the world moved in slow motion. Every strike he threw was perfect. Blocking three defenders at once was as simple as training a new recruit. All the while, in the back of his mind, he felt something being drained away.

But the power was too useful to refuse. This was the way. Today, he cleared Samas of all its enemies.

From the sin to the mugon, and everyone who thought they were superior to the sentinels.

*Faster! The girl is pressing her advantage!* Rua screamed in his mind.

Sato took a step away from his attackers and threw up his arm. A wave of crimson light knocked his assailants down.

He moved deliberately towards Shin.

Two forms stepped in front of Shin. It took him a moment to recognize Crispin. The sentinel was covered in blood and mud. The other was one of the strange islanders that Beast had brought to their shores. "Crispin, move."

"With all due respect, sir, I won't," Crispin said.

Sato raised his glowing sword. "Do you think I won't cut you down? Out of anyone here, you a should best know the strength of my conviction."

Crispin stood tall. "I do. That's why I won't ket you kill her. I don't know what's gotten into you, sir. But I know you, maybe better than you know yourself, and I know you don't want this," Crispin said. "Shin's not perfect, but you swore an oath to protect her, the same as you did me and all the sentinels under your command."

Sato scoffed. "You know nothing. All I've done is take the power that the sin kept hidden from the sentinels for so long. Finally, I am a true Firstborn, complete with the power to protect Samas without some sun-cursed sect working in the shadows."

"You sound like the emperor," the islander beside Crispin said.

Sato moved forward to strike down the insolent islander, but Crispin stepped in front of the boy. Sato stopped, but barely. Crispin was between him and the future of Samas.

Crispin showed no fear in the face of Sato's overwhelming strength. "When I first met you, I thought you were a self-righteous asshole that was so clueless about how his own nation worked that we'd all be better off if you were dead. I can't tell you how tempted I was, that day when I bested you in that duel. But I showed you mercy that day, and then your discipline showed me what I was capable of. It meant everything to me. But discipline means nothing without mercy."

That small part of his mind that nagged at him grew a little louder, but the flow of power through his body was a roar that drowned out the whispers. "I haven't lost anything, Crispin. I've only gained. Power. Strength. Conviction. Rua is a tool that I can use to my own ends."

Crispin smiled sadly. "That is dangerous thinking. First, it's something small. A petty infraction no one thinks much about. Then it's something a little worse. Pretty soon the ends always justify the means, and you look up one day to find yourself so far from the path that you can't even find the sun."

The power coursing through his Sato's veins screamed in anger at Crispin's insolence, but something about the words was familiar. The whispers from his sentinel mind became a little louder, and he realized Crispin was quoting his own words back to him. "You… remember me saying that to you?"

Sato's brain was buzzing and doing anything aside from cutting down everyone in front of him was a struggle, but he held on. His discipline held.

"Those words changed my life, Sato. Made me realize I could be the kind of man that can stand to look at himself in the mirror. That I could use my talents, the things I was best at, to serve Samas instead of hurt it."

Sato raised his sword for a moment and then shook his head. The whispers, they weren't just from him. They were from the Firstborn as well. His true mentor. His true friend. The man whose life he ended for the good of Samas. Was this for the good of Samas?

*That doesn't matter any more. Kill them and be done with it. You belong to me.* Rua's words were hateful in his head.

It would be so easy to give in. To take the power and lose control. To kill an unarmed girl sitting cross-legged on the ground, her eyes closed.

He shook his head. The world seemed more vivid than before. His vision was sharp.

His purpose clear.

By the sun, he was still a sentinel. He would walk the Path of the Eternal Sun in his final moments.

He would save Samas before he doomed it.

"Crispin, I can't hold her back for long," Sato said.

Tears prickled Crispin's eyes as he watched the crimson glow wink out from around Sato. "I know, sir." He stepped forward, the tears streaking down muddy cheeks. He bowed deeply to Sato, then stood right in front of him.

Cold steel penetrated his chest. He turned to see Alonzo standing like a ghost behind him, sword in hand, his lips quivering. Others were there, too. The battle must have ended. There was Roko, his steadfast companion. Helios, who he'd known since he was a child. Sato fell to his knees as Alonzo pulled his sword out. He slumped to the side, bracing himself with his right hand. The ethereal pinky he had earned while defending Samas flickered and disappeared.

"I'm sorry," he said to Crispin and Alonzo.

His two unlikely allies fell to their knees beside him. Alonzo laid a hand on his shoulder and Crispin took Sato's good hand in his own.

"There's nothing to apologize for. You defeated the Maramans and saved Samas," Crispin said. "You'll be remembered as one of the greatest Firstborns."

"But I—"

"But nothing," Crispin interrupted. "Your reign as Firstborn was short, but I promise you it will usher in a new era for Samas. One that your predecessor could never have brought about, but would be so proud to see. You owe Samas nothing, and it owes you everything. It's time for you to rest."

Sato nodded. He wanted to thank his friends for their service. Apologize for any times he'd been too harsh and tell them how proud he was of them both. As he looked into their eyes, however, he realized that those words weren't necessary. He felt his life fade away, and he didn't bother to fight it.

Sato nodded and closed his eyes. He could feel everyone that mattered close to him.

Crispin.

Alonzo.

Roko.

The Firstborn.

Even his father knelt in that bloody field beside him. Sato took his final breath and bid Samas farewell.

He'd taken his final steps on the Path.

# 50

Shin was a blur of movement. She blocked and parried crimson weapons and each time she connected with one of the conjured warriors, it flashed out of existence. Rua didn't seem concerned, but her attention was divided.

As Shin worked her way down to the last constructs, she spared a moment to turn her attention to the physical realm.

No wonder Rua was distracted. She'd been forced to help Sato. Help had come, in the shape of friends and new allies. Her magical cries for help had been heard.

Shin cut down the final construct and leaped to attack Rua. Her crimson blade almost met Rua's form, but Rua threw up a shield at the last moment. Distracted as she was, though, Rua wasn't able to do anything other than keep her shield up. Shin put all of her strength into her attack and slowly felt the shield buckle and crack. The blade moved an inch closer, and Shin dared to hope. Then she was forced back by a wave of unimaginable power.

Even as she flew through the air, Shin focused on the physical realm, and she saw Sato kneeling with a sword through his chest.

It was done. Only her part remained.

Rua stood before her, still stronger than anyone Shin had ever known. An army of one.

Rua snarled. "Do you think *you* can defeat me?" She spit on the ground. "Yuki's damn sacrifice might have sentenced me to this realm, but you know what else it did? It gave me eternal life. I'll never stop trying. I'll keep getting stronger. And you'll grow old and die."

"Not if I stop you here." Shin wished the words sounded more believable.

"I like your spirit, girl. I see why Yuki liked you." She paused. "Let me in."

Shin's heart leaped, but she forced out a bitter laugh. "In your dreams."

Rua stepped closer, completely unafraid of Shin. And why shouldn't she be? There was nothing Shin could do against her. For all of Shin's bold claims, she knew that. "If you fight me, I'll kill you. Everything you've sacrificed, everything you've done, and it will all be for nothing. I'll find my next willing host, and you'll have no say over the shape of Samas. But if you let me in, we can still work together. Establish a new Path where children never have to see their parents murdered instead of starving."

Shin considered Rua's offer. Really thought about what it would mean to have that power, to lead from strength and to get revenge for her parents. She thought about wiping the sentinels from Samas, like she'd always wanted to, and creating a free nation for people of any caste.

She held those ideas in the front of her mind. Then she let her shoulders slump. It wasn't hard to feel like she was surrendering.

"You're right. You'll listen to me? We'll make decisions together?"

She felt Rua probe her with sacrifice before she smiled. "Of course."

Shin took a deep breath, as though reaching a conclusion. "Then do it. I won't fight you."

At first, she felt nothing when Rua possessed her. Then her world went black for a moment. She feared she'd never see again, but then she opened her eyes, and she was in the field. In front of her, Corin, Beast, and several sentinels she recognized all crowded around Sato. She stood, and she felt Rua's power course through her. Her body was her own, but not hers alone anymore.

The feeling made her sick.

Corin was the first to notice her, and then everyone else turned around. They saw crimson power crackling all around her. Several backed away, and a few looked close to drawing swords. Only Corin and Beast stood firm.

"Shin! What did you do?" Beast asked.

"What I had to," Shin said.

*Kill anyone who stands against you! Start with the sentinels, then see if that brute will join your cause.* Rua was only making suggestions for the moment, but Shin knew that she could take control if she wanted to. There wasn't much time.

Shin accessed the realm.

*What are you—*

Shin heard Rua begin the question but once she had accessed the realm, it cut off. She made a proposal. An amendment to the spell she and the elites had created for this battle.

The realm agreed readily.

Shin opened her eyes and ended the spell.

All around the island she felt the few sin weavings still in use wink out and disappear. She felt the limits of her own power reduce, though Rua's were still formidable.

*What did you do?* Rua asked.

"Part of our agreement with the realm" Shin lied. Peace settled over her, and she felt lighter than she ever had. "In order for the realm to accept our sacrifice, we had to set a limit on how long we could use it. I just declared the end of the battle. The sacrifice is complete."

*A foolish idea,* Rua scoffed. *You could have held on to the power for longer. With it, I could have created incredible weavings.*

"Sorry," Shin said, not feeling even the slightest bit of regret. All of that was behind her now.

Rua ranted, but Shin ignored her.

She stepped toward Corin, but her step was unsteady, and she almost fell. The power around her faded.

She could already feel the realm begin to honor its end of the agreement. It was surprisingly gentle. Like falling into a deep sleep. She pitched forward and Corin caught her.

"What's wrong?" Corin asked. The concern in his voice made her smile. "Are you hurt?"

"No. I've never felt better. I amended the agreement with the realm. The sin won't have to give up half their lives. Only a quarter."

She saw the tears well in Corin's eyes. He knew, even if he couldn't admit it to himself. "In exchange for what?"

When Shin didn't answer, he asked again. "In exchange for what, Shin? The realm never gives anything for free."

"You know, Corin. Don't make me say it. You're free now. And Samas will be safe. Rua is within me, so it will all be over soon."

"No." Corin shook his head, his tears dropping on her face. "No."

Inside her, Rua raged, but her power weakened with

every heartbeat. She had leaped into a cage that would be the end of her.

Beast kneeled beside Corin. One of his eyes was a bloody ruin, but he still grinned down at her. "I knew you could do it, Shin. With my tutelage, I knew you could do anything."

Shin smiled weakly. "Do you even know what I did?"

Beast bent down and kissed her on the forehead, a gesture made even more gentle by the sheer size of the man delivering it. "I don't know exactly what happened, but I get the sense you ripped out their spines and shoved them up their asses. That about right?"

Shin nodded. "That's about right. Thanks Beast, for everything. Look after Corin."

Beast nodded but didn't say anything. Shin wasn't sure, but she thought she saw a tear in his good eye.

"It's time, Corin," Shin repeated to her friend.

"Please Shin, I—"

"You don't get a say, Corin. I'm sorry. Will you tell me about Mateo? About my father? I think I'll be gone soon, and I want to remember. Just a little."

Corin nodded through tears and then took a deep breath. Shin felt her life ebb away as her best friend, her only real family, whispered happy stories of her youth into her ear.

# 51

"You want me to do what?" Beast asked.

The wound in his stomach, packed with bandages soaked in some fluid that the sin insisted on and that stung like a thousand insect bites, ached as he moved but had stopped bleeding. His eye, on the other hand, kept weeping blood at the most inopportune times.

"To be the liaison for the sin, sentinels and the people of Samas," Crispin said again.

"Liaison? Sounds like a fancy way of saying I'll be bored out of my skull," Beast said.

"You would still be a general, and as such expected to act in your capacity as a soldier," Crispin offered. "Keff suggested you'd be best suited for the role."

"Did he now?" Beast raised an eyebrow at the islander.

"Face it, Beast, people trust you. If we want to rebuild the trust of the people of Samas in the sentinel and sin order, we need someone like you," Keff said.

"And what might you be doing?" Beast asked.

"Keff is going to be our first magistrate on the island of Parmos," Crispin said.

"Ah, so the sentinels find a new land and immediately decide it's theirs to claim?" Beast asked.

"Nothing like that," Helios said. "They will be the first in what I hope will be many allies for Samas."

Beast eyed the new Firstborn. He certainly looked the part and definitely had less of a stick up his ass than Sato. Beast still wasn't sure if he could follow orders, though, even if those orders were to question those giving the orders. He looked around the Firstborn's chambers in Bulas. He'd never been here, and while there was some damage from the Maramans, the majesty of the place was undamaged. Kordano had planned on making this the heart of his expanding empire. He had wanted it to inspire visitors, just as the Firstborn did.

"Would I get an estate here in Bulas?" Beast asked.

"You would," Crispin said.

"And what about paperwork and logistics? Can I have someone on staff to handle that?"

"Anyone you want," Helios said.

"And who might I be liaising with among the sin?"

"Hanz has taken the surviving sin back to their village for now. He's asked for a month of mourning for their losses. But he's promised to provide a contact after the time has passed."

Beast smiled. "Alright, fine. I'll be your general liaison in charge of making sure you all don't turn into assholes."

Helios tried unsuccessfully to hide his distaste at the title, but Crispin grinned. "Very good. I'll have someone show you to your new home, and we'll bring the paperwork up for you to sign. You can name your staff at that time. Any questions?"

"Yes," Beast said, "how come you aren't the Firstborn? You're the closest thing to a decent sentinel I've ever met."

"Sato named me Firstborn in the event of his death," Helios said, straining to remain patient.

"Right," Beast said with a wink to Crispin. "One day though, I'd bet."

"My job is to serve Samas in whatever capacity is required of me." Crispin's tone was perfectly neutral, but Beast had the sense he'd not shot too far from the mark. Someday, Crispin might be just the leader Samas needed. He knew the land better than almost anyone, and Sato had forged him into a fine sentinel. Beast didn't think he'd even want to be a rebel if Crispin sat on the throne.

Beast grinned and turned around. He had to admit, he liked Crispin a lot. Helios seemed fine, if perhaps a bit traditional, but so long as Crispin was advising him, Beast had some hope for this new regime. And if they failed, well, the local smith had just forged him a brand-new ax, bigger than any he'd ever held before. Perhaps he could use it on some uptight sentinel skulls.

Beast gave the slightest hint of a bow as he left.

"Making friends already?" Gorou asked as he exited the chambers.

"Always. Just so you know, I'm a general now. General Beast. I like the sound of that."

"I'm sure you do."

"And you're my captain."

"I know."

"How could you possibly know that? I just decided a moment ago."

"Because you could never do it without me."

Beast snorted. "You might be right, but I'll never admit that to anyone but you. Since you seem to know everything, has Colas left yet? I assumed she'd be on her way the moment the Maramans were dealt with, and her juggernaut was supplied."

"She's in Versun, being briefed on her next mission," Gorou said.

"Mission? So much for the freedom of the open seas."

"Actually, that's her mission. First, she'll be establishing supply lines between us and, what did Keff call the island?"

"Parmos."

"Yes, between Parmos and Samas, and then she's heading out to see if she can make contact with other nations. It seems the days of closed borders of Samas are at an end."

"What if we run into more people like the Maramans? What if they come back?"

"Then we'll be ready. Maybe more ready than we've ever been. With Helios as Firstborn, and Crispin advising him, we have a chance to make Samas a powerful nation. The Path of the Eternal Sun is gone. The Maramans may have broken it when they arrived, but the cracks had been forming for generations. Now, perhaps, we have a chance to reforge it into something better."

Beast stopped walking and looked at his friend. "That's a lot "we's" in there. Do you truly believe in this cause?"

Gorou smiled up at Beast. "I do. But only if you're a part of it. You stood up for the people the sentinels tried to squash under their rule. As long as you have your ax to their necks, I think they'll make the right choices."

They walked down the long halls. It seemed wrong, somehow, to be a general, when so many others had given so much for this future. He couldn't go half a day without seeing Corin, whispering in Shin's ear as she died.

Corin had gone back to the island with the sin, and Beast expected that when they met again, the young warrior would be leading his own squad. When Beast had asked him what he'd told Shin, he'd refused to say. Even when Beast threatened him.

Say one thing for his proteges; they were brave.

He wished Shin was here. He would have liked to share one more drink with her. Well, maybe he wanted more than one, but one would have been enough.

Dammit, he'd even be willing to drink tea with Sato. Asshole that he was, he'd done good at the end, there. And Beast had never fought a stronger sword. If Samas had a brighter future, the prick was a large part of the reason why.

Gorou interrupted his thoughts. "So, general. What are you going to do with your newfound authority?"

Beast considered his friend for a long time before he finally smiled.

"I think I'll get drunk," Beast said and clapped Gorou on the shoulder. His captain winced. "With the people, of course."

THE END

# THANKS FOR READING!

Thanks again for reading! In this era of unlimited entertainment choices, it means the world to us that you chose to spend your time in Samas, and we hope that you'll join us again soon.

If you'd like to learn more about Ryan or Taylor you can check them out here:

Taylor: www.taylorcrook.ca

Be the first to get your hands on Taylor's solo work, sign up for monthly newsletters or just check out some short stories.

Ryan: www.ryankirkauthor.com

You can purchase all of Ryan's extensive library as well as sign up for monthly newsletters to keep up with everything he is doing. Ryan has also created a membership program with all kinds of incredible benefits.

# AUTHOR'S NOTE

Well, we did it. Ryan and I embarked on this journey almost two years ago and, somewhere along the way, all of you joined us. Now that we've come to the end, all that's left is to say thank you.

So thank you for joining us on this little fantasy tour through Samas. I know all of you have completed a series before, and my writing partner Ryan is a veteran of the process of writing one, but this is a particularly special book for me as it marks the first time I've ever written a true ending.

So, an extra special thank you from me for sharing this moment with me.

See you for the next one...

Taylor Crook

January 2023

## ALSO BY RYAN KIRK

**Saga of the Broken Gods**

Band of Broken Gods

**Last Sword in the West**

Last Sword in the West

Eyes of the Hidden World

A Sword Named Vengeance

**Oblivion's Gate**

The Gate Beyond Oblivion

The Gates of Memory

The Gate to Redemption

**Relentless**

Relentless Souls

Heart of Defiance

Their Spirit Unbroken

**The Nightblade Series**

Nightblade

World's Edge

The Wind and the Void

**Blades of the Fallen**

Nightblade's Vengeance

Nightblade's Honor

Nightblade's End

**Standalone Novels**

Blades of Shadow

**The Primal Series**

Primal Dawn

Primal Darkness

Primal Destiny

## ABOUT TAYLOR

Taylor Crook is a fantasy author living in Hamilton, Ontario with his beautiful wife and two German Shepherds. Before taking on a writing career his life was shaped by nearly two decades in the restaurant industry. Long nights in bustling dining rooms have proven to be an invaluable and beloved step on a journey that led to finally achieving the dream of being a published author. When he's not writing, Taylor enjoys basketball, drumming, video games and, the hobby that started it all, reading. His favourite activity, though, is anything that he gets to do with his wife.

www.taylorcrook.ca

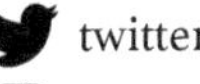 twitter.com/TaylorC68001927

 instagram.com/taylorcrookwrites

# ABOUT RYAN

Ryan Kirk is the bestselling author of the *Nightblade* series of books. When he isn't writing, you can probably find him playing disc golf or hiking through the woods.


www.ryankirkauthor.com
www.waterstonemedia.net
contact@waterstonemedia.net

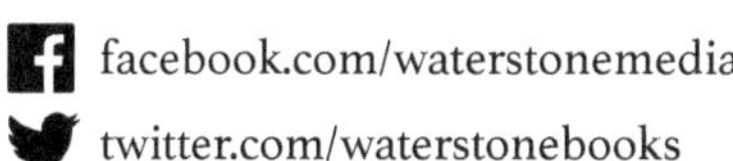

facebook.com/waterstonemedia
twitter.com/waterstonebooks
instagram.com/waterstonebooks

www.ingramcontent.com/pod-product-compliance
Lightning Source LLC
Chambersburg PA
CBHW060537310726
48982CB00009B/1286/J

* 9 7 8 1 7 7 8 2 8 4 0 5 2 *